# Praise for the Midnight Breed series by
## LARA ADRIAN

### BOUND TO DARKNESS

"While most series would have ended or run out of steam, the Midnight Breed series seems to have picked up steam. Lara Adrian has managed to keep the series fresh by adding new characters . . . without having to say goodbye to the original ones that made the series so popular to begin with. Bound to Darkness has all the passion, danger and unique appeal of the original ten books but also stands on its own as a turning point in the entire series with new pieces to a larger puzzle, new friends and old enemies."

*—Adria's Romance Reviews*

"Lara Adrian always manages to write great love stories, not only emotional but action packed. I love every aspect of (Bound to Darkness). I also enjoyed how we get a glimpse into the life of the other characters we have come to love. There is always something sexy and erotic in all of Adrian's books, making her one of my top 5 paranormal authors."

*—Reading Diva*

### CRAVE THE NIGHT

"Nothing beats good writing and that is what ultimately makes Lara Adrian stand out amongst her peers.... Crave the Night is stunning in its flawless execution. Lara Adrian has the rare ability to lure readers right into her books, taking them on a ride they will never forget."

*—Under the Covers*

"...Steamy and intense. This installment is sure to delight established fans and will also be accessible to new readers."

*—Publishers Weekly*

## EDGE OF DAWN

"Adrian's strikingly original Midnight Breed series delivers an abundance of nail-biting suspenseful chills, red-hot sexy thrills, an intricately built world, and realistically complicated and conflicted protagonists, whose happily-ever-after ending proves to be all the sweeter after what they endure to get there."

*—Booklist (starred review)*

## DARKER AFTER MIDNIGHT

"A riveting novel that will keep readers mesmerized... If you like romance combined with heart-stopping paranormal suspense, you're going to love this book."

*—Bookpage*

## DEEPER THAN MIDNIGHT

"One of the consistently best paranormal series out there.... Adrian writes compelling individual stories (with wonderful happily ever afters) within a larger story arc that is unfolding with a refreshing lack of predictability."

*—Romance Novel News*

## Praise for Lara Adrian

"With an Adrian novel, readers are assured of plenty of dangerous thrills and passionate chills."

*—RT Book Reviews*

"Ms. Adrian has a gift for drawing her readers deeper and deeper into the amazing world she creates."

*—Fresh Fiction*

Look for these titles in the *New York Times* and #1 international bestselling

## Midnight Breed series

# Other books by Lara Adrian

## Paranormal Romance

### Hunter Legacy Series
Born of Darkness
Hour of Darkness
Edge of Darkness

## Contemporary Romance

### 100 Series
For 100 Days
For 100 Nights
For 100 Reasons

### 100 Series Standalones
Run to You
Play My Game

## Historical Romance

### Dragon Chalice Series
Heart of the Hunter
Heart of the Flame
Heart of the Dove

### Warrior Trilogy
White Lion's Lady
Black Lion's Bride
Lady of Valor

Lord of Vengeance

# KING OF MIDNIGHT

## A Midnight Breed Novel

NEW YORK TIMES BESTSELLING AUTHOR

# LARA ADRIAN

ISBN: 9798831753103

KING OF MIDNIGHT
© 2022 by Lara Adrian, LLC
Cover design © 2022 by CrocoDesigns

**www.LaraAdrian.com**

Available in ebook and trade paperback. Unabridged
audiobook edition forthcoming.

# KING OF MIDNIGHT

# CHAPTER 1

Rogues.

The night was thick with them.

Through the stench of smoke and fire choking the ruined streets of Washington, D.C.'s Georgetown district, blood-addicted Breed males ran like packs of rabid dogs set loose on a terrified human public. Their feral howls rang out over the other disturbing sounds that filled the night. Wailing sirens. Explosions. Bone-grating screams from the random fools who hadn't heeded the mandatory sunset curfew of the past several nights and were now paying the price.

Fueled by Bloodlust, Rogues knew only their unending thirst and the need to quench it. They roamed, hunted, brutalized . . . slaughtered. No one, human or Breed, was safe in their path, and in their wake they left only mass destruction and rivers of spilled blood.

Darion Thorne's city wasn't the only one facing this recent outbreak of violence and death. Like a disease spreading on the wind, the Rogues that had been attacking major human populations all over the world of late showed no sign of slowing down.

No, it was only getting worse.

Each twilight seemed to multiply the Rogues' numbers by scores.

The attacks had become the Order's most immediate concern, not that the warriors lacked for problems. They had enemies closing in on all sides lately, each one nothing short of an existential threat—not only for the members of the Order, but for every living creature on the planet.

This explosion of Rogue violence across the globe was an annoyance they damned well didn't need.

Darion's lips curled away from his own fangs on a curse as he drove one of his large titanium blades into the chest of a Breed male he'd just chased down an alley.

The Rogue was on his back, dressed in what might have been an expensive suit at one point but now hung off him in shredded rags, his once-white shirt stained and foul with the evidence of his recent kills.

Darion held him down, pinned to the cracked pavement by the weight of his boot and the cold, razor-sharp metal that now impaled the Rogue through the chest. The male thrashed and snarled, out of his mind with Bloodlust. His eyes glowed fiery amber, radiating up at Darion like hot coals.

The murder in those transformed eyes turned to shock as the titanium of Darion's blade met the Rogue's diseased bloodstream and began to devour the male from the inside. His death would be quick, but not easy. The awful sound that erupted out of his foaming maw was nothing less than pure, primal agony.

Darion didn't take any satisfaction in this kill, or the others he'd already delivered tonight. There were still hours to go until daybreak. Before their patrol was over, he and his Order teammates would be crusted in spilled blood and gore.

Tomorrow night it would start all over again.

Bad enough that D.C. and other major cities were becoming infested with Rogues. What made it even worse was the fact that the secretive terror group behind the problem, Opus Nostrum, were likely laughing their craven asses off at the havoc they were creating.

Armed with a narcotic that could turn even the most docile member of the Breed into a blood-fevered monster, Opus had only been toying with Red Dragon for months. Amusing themselves with its power. Testing its capabilities as a potential weapon. Refining it, evidently.

Now, it seemed their gloves had come off.

Darion removed his blade from the dying male and stepped away. No reason to linger. Titanium meant a swift, certain end for a Rogue. Even one nick of a titanium blade spelled almost instant death.

Darion considered it a mercy to end the male. Far better than to be made to suffer the unquenchable, incurable thirst and insanity of Bloodlust.

As he strode back up the narrow alleyway, a deep, cool voice sounded in the earpiece of his comm unit. "Got a situation over on M Street. Anyone close?"

Darion's team captain, Nathan, spoke over the wail of sirens in the background of wherever he was fighting in the city. "Five human civilians are trapped inside a jewelry store. They've got Rogues swarming. Apparently, one of them is bleeding from a window he smashed."

A low scoff answered from another teammate. Darion knew the wry sound. It belonged to Rafe, his lifelong friend and comrade on patrol across town. "So much for the mandate that everyone stay off the street for the night."

"Fucking looters," snarled Jax, the fourth member of the unit. "Let the Rogues have them."

"They're kids," Nathan grimly pointed out. "Teens and younger, according to the hysterical girl who called it in a minute ago. Not that it should matter."

Jax only grunted in answer. With his cold stealth and penchant for throwing stars, he had never been the warmest male. But since his best friend and fellow warrior, Elijah, had been killed on duty by an Opus-instigated ambush several nights ago, Jax seemed almost glacial.

It was Eli's death that had left a vacancy on Nathan's team. Darion eagerly stepped in to fill it, despite hating the reason he was given the opportunity. He was determined not to let down his teammates—or his father, the Order's founder and leader, Lucan Thorne.

Darion had waited for a chance to serve as a warrior from the time he was a boy. He'd trained and prepared for it, even when it seemed he'd never be given the chance.

"I'm close to the area," he said, his long blade in hand and his feet already moving swiftly in the direction of the trouble. "I'm on my way now."

He didn't wait for confirmation. Summoning the full velocity of his Breed genetics, he flashed across the distance in a matter of seconds.

Just as Nathan described, the scene outside the jewelry store was going from bad to worse. The big window in front was smashed, jagged glass framing an opening that looked barely large enough to fit any of the five kids cowered and screaming inside, never mind the trio of hulking Rogues looking for a way to get in.

To the human youths' credit, they'd been quick-thinking enough to create a barricade between themselves and the broken window. The toppled jewelry display case they had lit on fire near the open glass was keeping a pack of three Rogues outside the shop. It was a small deterrent, though, one that wouldn't hold the Rogues back for long.

Not even another second, in fact.

One of the big males lowered his shoulder and slammed into the makeshift barricade. The display case exploded inward from the impact, splintered wood and twisted metal flying in all directions inside the small store.

The Rogue pushed forward, his two companions crowding behind him.

"Fuck." Darion rushed across the darkened street, his long blade gripped in one hand and ready for combat, his other hand moving for the pistol holstered on his weapons belt.

He wasted no time.

With the humans shrieking and stumbling over one another in their haste to get out of the first Rogue's swinging reach, Darion rammed his blade between the shoulders of the other one currently blocking a clear path inside. The male dropped to his knees on a howl. Darion stopped the third with a titanium hollowpoint up-close-and-personal to the side of the Rogue's skull.

Both large males went down, convulsing on the pavement as the titanium began its work.

Darion shoved inside the opening in the smashed window. The five humans were hysterical, scrambling in all directions. The Rogue grabbed for one of them, latching on to the loose jacket of a lanky preteen whose torn sleeve was sticky and dark with blood. The kid who'd injured himself breaking into the store.

The coppery tang of fresh human red cells made Darion's own gaze ignite with amber sparks. His fangs sliced out of his gums, an instinctual response he shook off with a low snarl.

The kid spotted him behind the attacking Rogue, Darion's face wild with combat rage and his bloodied blade gleaming. The human let out an even higher-pitched scream.

The Rogue paused, his big head swiveling toward his shoulder to see who might be coming after his prey.

Darion struck, shoving his blade under the Rogue's jaw. The fist holding on to the hollering human went lax. The kid just stood there, gaping as his attacker dropped to the floor in a heap of melting flesh and bone.

Darion scowled at the group of shell-shocked young humans. "I need to get you out of here. Now."

But it was already too late for that.

All of the ruckus—not to mention the pungent scent of the skinny kid's bleeding wound—was drawing more interest from other predators in the area.

Darion wheeled around, the group of humans behind him. Outside the wrecked storefront, low, animalistic grunts and growls drew closer. Several pairs of glowing eyes pierced the darkness as a new pack of Rogues seemed to materialize out of the darkness.

Five of them, fangs bared, gazes wild with the madness of Bloodlust.

In addition to the long blade Darion held in his right hand, he also had his semiautomatic full of titanium rounds in the other. He held his fire. A blast of gun shots would likely only bring reinforcements for the group of Rogues surrounding the open storefront. No doubt the single shot he'd fired a few moments ago had helped to alert these males to the area.

Stowing the pistol behind his back, he skewered the first Rogue that charged at him. The big male stopped short, but his four other companions surged forward as one.

Darion's blade was a blur of motion. Slicing and stabbing, he hacked down two of the Rogues but a third raked thick, jagged nails into his shoulder. Enormous fangs snapped in his face, blood and foul-smelling drool dripping off the Rogue's chin.

Darion avoided the bite and drove his blade deep, kicking the deadweight to the floor as still another Rogue tried to go through him to get to the defenseless human prey at his back.

He brought his blade up for another strike, only to see the remaining Rogue in front of him freeze in mid-lunge. The huge body tipped forward, blood oozing like acid from its nostrils and gaping mouth.

The dying Rogue fell away and there was Rafe, grinning as he cleaned off his curved dagger and sheathed it on his weapons belt. The handsome face that turned heads everywhere the warrior went was smudged with ash and grime and drying blood.

"I was in the neighborhood. Thought I'd stop by."

Darion smirked at his friend and comrade. "I had everything under control."

"Yeah, I can see that. Guess I shouldn't have wondered if you might need backup." Rafe glanced at the seven mounds of sizzling remains Darion had created before his wry gaze swung back. "Showoff."

Darion let the brotherly jab go unanswered. He was still in combat mode, all too aware that they likely had only moments before more Rogues came sniffing around. "We need to get the humans somewhere safe. The bleeder's going to need a ride to a hospital if the Rogues don't get him first."

The five youths had gone silent now, their faces ashen, eyes unblinking as they huddled together in the back of the sacked jewelry store.

Rafe nodded. "I've already called in for an evac."

As he spoke, an engine roared outside as a black SUV screeched to a hard stop on the pavement. The driver's side window slid down, revealing Rafe's beautiful mate, Devony.

The Breed female's long dark hair was scraped back into a sleek ponytail. Like Rafe and Darion, she wore black combat gear and her face bore evidence of the battles she'd fought tonight as an active member of the patrol team. As one of a handful of daywalkers in existence—and a skilled warrior in her own right—Devony had quickly proven to be a valuable asset to the Order.

She also had Rafe wrapped around her finger, something that amused Darion to no end.

"You two going to stand around shooting the shit all night?" Devony called from inside the vehicle. "Round up the civilians and let's get the fuck out of here."

Rafe grinned. "Damn, I love it when she's bossy. Gets me hot every time."

Darion grunted, shaking his head. "That's a mental picture I could've lived without."

"Says the one who's got a hard-on for nothing less than an actual fucking immortal queen," Rafe shot back, chuckling now. "Don't even try to say you haven't noticed how jaw-droppingly gorgeous Selene is—assuming you can look past her icy personality and homicidal leanings. Not to mention a ten-thousand-year age gap, give or take."

Darion felt his scowl darken. "The Atlantean queen is our enemy. She's made that clear on numerous occasions." In fact, in a contest between Selene, Opus Nostrum, and the newer threat that had exploded out of the Deadlands several nights ago, Darion wasn't sure which posed the greater risk to the entire planet and its inhabitants. To say nothing of himself and every member of the Order. "It doesn't matter how beautiful Selene is. If anything, that only makes her more dangerous."

"So, you *have* noticed, then."

As much as he may want to deny it, yeah, he'd noticed how attractive she was. Jaw-droppingly gorgeous and then some. He had only seen Selene once, and not even in person. Ever since she'd overridden the Order's command center technology to deliver an impromptu, drive-by threat to their existence, Darion had thought of little else.

He'd also spent an inappropriate amount of time wondering if the icy platinum blonde immortal had ever met a man she couldn't freeze out with that temper of hers.

Darion glowered at his friend. "Aren't you supposed to be helping to round up the humans? Or are you waiting for Devony to snap your slack ass to attention?"

"Looks like I've hit a nerve." Rafe winked, cuffing him on the shoulder. "Come on, let's evac these stupid kids before more Rogues start to swarm the place."

They hustled the young humans out to the SUV and situated them inside. Rafe held the open passenger door, ready to jump in beside Devony at the wheel.

"You coming, Dare?"

He shook his head. The mention of the Atlanteans and their beautiful, volatile queen, paired with the reminder of all the chaos and violence that Opus Nostrum had dealt the Order in recent years, lit a fire in Darion's already simmering veins. He wanted the madness to stop—no matter the price.

There was nothing he wouldn't do, nothing he wouldn't sacrifice, to make that happen.

All around him now, distant howls, screams, and sirens filled the night.

"I'm not finished here," Darion said. "I'll see you back at base after patrols."

Rafe stared at him for a moment, then gave a nod. He climbed into the vehicle. As soon as he'd closed the door, Devony hit the gas and the black SUV sped off with a roar.

Darion cocked his head, listening to the raw terror that still tore through his city. Pivoting on his boot heels, he drew his titanium blade from its sheath.

Then he disappeared into the night to deal more death.

# CHAPTER 2

A human scream carried from a remote chamber located beneath the Order's D.C. mansion headquarters. The sound was pathetic, full of terror and desperation, and hearing it gave Lucan Thorne an unhealthy amount of satisfaction.

"Sounds like Hunter's introduced himself to our guest," Gideon quipped, glancing over from his flotilla of monitors and keyboards in the tech lab.

Lucan frowned in response. "I should've called Hunter in immediately to deal with the situation. We don't have hours to waste on interrogations, let alone days."

The Order's human "guest" was a minor foot soldier of Opus Nostrum, one of many. This particular one had the misfortune of being captured by the Order after participating in a brutal attack on a theater full of Breed and human civilians a few nights ago.

After trapping everyone inside the building using semiautomatics and Opus's recent weapon of choice, firearms equipped with Breed-killing ultraviolet rounds, the gunmen demanded Lucan's surrender in exchange for releasing the hostages. Lucan had no designs on negotiating, never mind surrendering. He and his warriors had arrived ready for battle, something Opus had been prepared for, probably even intended.

Because Opus's plan had a second act.

The man currently wailing for mercy in the Order's holding tank and the rest of his comrades that night unleashed an even more horrific weapon on their innocent captives: Red Dragon.

The manufactured poison could turn even the most law-abiding Breed citizen into a lethal, bloodthirsty Rogue in mere seconds. And so it had. Dozens of them.

The scene inside the theater had been chaos, an out-of-control massacre, culminating with the Order being forced to put down the newly made Rogues or risk even more bloodshed.

To make the whole catastrophe worse, every hideous moment of it had been broadcast live around the world by the news crews Opus had summoned to the scene.

The fact that the strike on the civilians had come on the heels of another recent Opus attack that cost the Order one of their own, Elijah, made Lucan's blood boil in his veins.

And now all of the Order's patrol teams were busy combating a seemingly never-ending flood of new Rogues being made and turned loose on cities all over the world.

Lucan snarled just thinking about it. "If Hunter doesn't kill the human piece of shit in the process of blood-reading him, I fucking might."

Impatient for progress, he strode out of the tech lab. Gideon swiveled away from his computers and fell in behind him, walking briskly to keep up as Lucan headed for the room where Opus's man continued to holler and beg for his life.

The holding cell, like the rest of the headquarters' underground labyrinth, had been part of the historic mansion's original construction when the Order acquired it as their D.C. base of operations more than twenty years ago. Security enhancements and technological improvements had been implemented in the time since, all of them designed and overseen by Gideon. The Order's tech wizard was particularly proud of the cell's state-of-the-art, multi-functioning bars that encircled the cage. They were engineered to hold any manner of enemy captive, from garden-variety Rogues to hostile Atlantean immortals, or something even more dangerous than either of those combined.

All of Gideon's impressive engineering and technology was lost on the bony-assed human who'd been cooling his heels inside the eight-foot square prison cell since his capture.

His name was Elmer Gopnik, which made the Order's nickname for him of Scarface sound like an upgrade.

At the moment, Gopnik's sallow, pock-marked cheeks were streaked with sweat and tears, his unwashed hair matted against his head. The skinny arm hanging limply at his side sported twin puncture wounds still oozing a trickle of blood.

"Anything useful to report?" Lucan asked Hunter.

The former assassin wiped the back of his hand across his mouth, his golden eyes unreadable. "He knows nothing. All this human's told you so far are lies."

"As I suspected," Lucan growled. Even though the news came as little surprise, his fury spiked and his fangs lengthened. "I should kill him for that alone."

Hunter gave an emotionless nod of agreement. "He has no value to us."

With three Breed warriors looking at him as though he were nothing more than an insect, Gopnik sucked in a panicked breath and made a futile struggle against his restraints. "Let me go . . . please. Fuck! Please don't kill me. I'm beggin' you!"

Lucan stepped closer to the thick titanium bars. "You're begging me? You mean the way the Breed ambassador from Ireland begged you for mercy in that theater the other night—right before you and your comrades shot him full of UV light in front of his fucking family?"

Gopnik blanched. "I was only carrying out orders. I had no choice!"

"No choice?" Lucan practically spat the words. "You want us to play the video for you? Say yes, because if I have to see that goddamn massacre again, I will make you suffer a year for every second of torture that was inflicted on those innocent civilians."

Gopnik shook his head so hard it was like he was having a seizure. He shrank back on a shudder, and the acrid puddle of urine under the interrogation chair he was strapped to started to spread out farther as he sputtered and cowered.

Lucan stared at him, feeling nothing, not even pity. Gopnik had carried out his mission during the theater attack with sick enjoyment and bravado. It would be a fitting end if Lucan severed the human's head with his bare hands and stuck it on a pike outside the Order's headquarters. Or, better yet, send it back to Opus Nostrum with the promise that the cabal's inner circle would be next.

The only problem being the Order had yet to locate the members of that inner circle.

Gideon had been working on a possible solution, but the missing pieces were information and opportunity. Elmer Gopnik was a bust on the first item. As for the second, no matter how much Lucan might enjoy lethally venting his rage on one of Opus's foot soldiers, he could think of several ways they might yet be able to use the human.

Tearing off his head was still Lucan's top choice. If he had to look at Gopnik—or smell his stench—for another moment, Lucan might just give in to his murderous impulses.

Besides that, he had somewhere he needed to be.

"I'll deal with this scum later," he said. "If I don't decide to let him rot down here."

Indicating for Gideon and Hunter to follow him, he strode away from the barred cell.

"Wait!" Gopnik shouted after them. "I'm sorry for what I did. I'm telling you the truth now."

Lucan scoffed at the sudden attempt at remorse. "Keep talking. You're only pissing me off even more."

"Please!" Gopnik's voice climbed another octave. "You can't just walk away and leave me in this shithole!"

Gideon paused next to Lucan. "Hold up. Did he just insult my work?" Fangs bared, he swung around and stalked back in front of the gleaming bars. "Fuck you, calling this a shithole. This entire cell is a bloody technological work of art, you ignorant wanker."

Lucan cleared his throat, more amused than he should be, all things considered.

"Feel better now?" he asked as Gideon joined Hunter and him at the chamber's exit.

Gideon raked a hand over the spiky ends of his short blond hair, his gaze still burning amber with insult behind the pale blue lenses of his glasses. "Shame the asshole's only human. I'd love to give him a little taste of everything that cell is equipped to do."

Lucan smirked. "As much as I agree, we'll have to save the shock and awe show for another time. We've got work to do. Even more, now that we've hit a dead end here."

The three warriors stepped out to the corridor, Gideon activating the chamber's coded lock behind them. Once the door sealed shut, Lucan blew out a sharp curse.

"Goddamn Opus. They've got us by the balls, and they know it. That's not going to change so long as they're able to continue hiding away, wreaking wholesale terror around the globe. Red Dragon. UV weaponry. They're hitting us from all angles and until we can take out the nerve center of Opus's operation, all we can do is scramble to put out the fires as soon as they set them."

"Send me," Hunter said. "Stealth exterminations are what I was born for."

He meant it literally. There was none more proficient in the art of assassination than the huge Gen One Breed male who'd been bred, raised, and disciplined into an unfeeling, perfect killing machine in the labs of a madman who had once been the Order's chief adversary.

As diabolical as Dragos had been, Opus Nostrum was worse.

"You know I'll never doubt your skill, Hunter, but Opus is a fucking Hydra. Cut off one head and another rises up, then another. We've proven that ourselves. Each time we think we've won, a new leader assumes control. Faceless. Nameless. We have no idea how many sit at the top of Opus's chain of command, let alone who the sons of bitches might be."

"We have done some damage," Hunter reminded him. "Reginald Crowe and his treacherous daughter Iona Lynch, Fineas Riordan . . . along with several others, Breed and human, who'd still be serving Opus Nostrum had the Order not terminated them."

"True, but it's not enough," Lucan said. "We've only been making dents in the organization. We need to obliterate it from the top. Meanwhile, the entire cabal's identity is being shielded by layers of security and technology we've yet to penetrate."

"For the moment, that is," Gideon interjected. "The software worm I've written will burrow past any level of security. The trouble is, I need to know where to send it. We'd been hoping Scarface in there would have intel I could use, but obviously that's a bust."

Lucan despised the setback, something they damn well couldn't afford. "Then we'll keep sweeping up Opus foot soldiers until we get the intel we need."

Hunter gave him a grim nod. "Consider it done. I'll begin that directive as soon as we finish here. What will you do with the human we already have?"

"I'll tell you what I'd like to do. Haul the useless piece of shit into my Global Nations Council meeting tonight and make a public example of him. I could tear out his throat as the highlight of the ridiculous speech I'm being pressed to make when I should be on the street cutting down Rogues with the rest of our teams."

Gideon's brows shot up. "You mean, the speech that's set to be broadcast to every corner of the globe? Correct me if I'm wrong, but isn't the point of your address tonight meant to reassure the world that the Order is doing everything possible to restore and maintain peace?"

Lucan felt his scowl deepen. "What about it?"

"Well, perhaps the message might go over a bit better if you don't deliver it through bloodied fangs and with a human corpse at your feet. Just a suggestion."

Lucan grunted. "Says the one who was ready to light up Gopnik's ass inside that cell a minute ago."

Gideon conceded with a shrug and a cocky grin. "Anyway, as I was saying, all we need is a lead that gets me anywhere near Opus's connective tissue so I can inject my worm, then the real fun starts. We covertly unmask the inner circle, take out its members, and bring their whole operation crashing down."

Lucan appreciated Gideon's confidence. Hell, he shared it. But his nine centuries of living reminded him that few things ever went totally according to plan.

And there remained the ever-present threat of the Breed-killing arsenal at Opus Nostrum's disposal. Not even a male of Hunter's proven strength and skill would be able to withstand instantly lethal UV bullets or the mind-warping poison of Red Dragon.

The risks involved in going after Opus's leadership were some of the worst the Order had ever faced.

To say nothing of the other battles brewing for them. One in Atlantis against the immortals' spiteful queen.

And a second—the one that eclipsed them all—against an otherworldly danger that had recently escaped a godforsaken patch of Siberian wasteland armed with a pair of Atlantean crystals holding the power to annihilate the world.

Yet tonight, when most of D.C. and countless other cities were in flames, overrun with Rogues manufactured by Opus Nostrum, Lucan was expected to promise relief from the horror.

The entire world was looking to him to reassure them that one day soon the chaos and terror would be over, that peace would finally come again and last this time.

The hopeful words Gabrielle had helped him write and rehearse a few hours earlier would taste like lies when he delivered them tonight.

His human and Breed colleagues in the GNC were counting on him to soothe an anxious planet, but Lucan couldn't shake the feeling that things were only going to get darker.

# CHAPTER 3

It was too damned quiet, Jenna thought, working alone inside the Order's archives room.

She knew there were violent battles taking place all over the city outside, but within the secured walls of the mansion headquarters and the large library chamber that was her personal workspace, the silence was deafening.

The prolonged quiet inside her mind troubled her too.

It wasn't often that her mate, Brock, and nearly every last member of the Order's warrior teams were dispatched to patrols at the same time. Even the females who were trained in combat were on the streets tonight, fighting alongside their mates and comrades.

As a former cop, Jenna wished she could be out there with Brock and the others. She had never been one to sit on the sidelines during a crisis, but even she had to admit her time as an Alaska State Trooper felt as foreign to her now as the fact that she had also once been fully human.

Twenty years and counting. Some days, it seemed like yesterday. Other times, she could hardly remember what she used to look like . . . *before.*

Absently, she reached up to smooth her fingertips over the *dermaglyph* at the back of her neck. What started as a miniscule mark had grown exponentially over time. Now, her body was covered with the alien skin markings, a constant, visual reminder of the ordeal that had altered her existence in so many ways.

That ordeal had also brought Brock into her life, and that alone made everything else a little more bearable.

Her thoughts drifted back to a small cemetery plot in Alaska. The most painful thing she'd ever endured was the death of her ten-year-old daughter, Libby. Nothing could bring her back, but Jenna took the smallest measure of comfort in the fact that her child never had to know the terror the world was living through now.

"Knock, knock," a soothing female voice called hesitantly from the threshold of the open doorway.

Jenna looked up to find Gabrielle waiting to be invited in. Lucan's Breedmate was dressed in loose leggings and an oversized top, her long auburn hair gathered into a messy twist. In her hands was a loaded charcuterie tray that smelled delicious.

Standing beside her with an opened bottle of red wine in one hand and three long-stemmed wineglasses in the other was Gideon's beautiful mate. Savannah was dressed similarly, one smooth mocha-brown shoulder peeking out of the slouched neckline of her light-gray sweater.

"We brought provisions," she said, smiling at Jenna with soft understanding in her deep brown eyes. "I don't think you've eaten anything all day, have you?"

Jenna closed the dream journal she'd been writing in and shook her head. She wasn't a Breedmate like her friends, so taking nourishment from her mate's blood wasn't enough to sustain her. Brock fulfilled her needs in every other way and then some, but she had to admit the aromas of the smoked meats, creamy cheeses, and assorted savory snacks were a welcome diversion from her work. She wasn't going to complain about the wine, either.

Gabrielle set the tray down on the worktable while Savannah filled their glasses. Jenna chewed a small bite of cheese, then took a sip of the wine. She sighed with pleasure as the flavors mingled on her tongue.

"Thank you," she murmured, leaning back in her chair as the two women joined her at the table. "To be honest, I haven't had much of an appetite the past couple of weeks."

Savannah gave her a sympathetic nod. "You've been through a lot."

"We all have," Jenna pointed out, noting the shadows that rode beneath the gazes of her friends. "Has Lucan left for the emergency GNC meeting?"

"Yes," Gabrielle replied. "His speech is scheduled to broadcast within the hour. Needless to say, he wasn't looking forward to it. He'd prefer to be on patrol like everyone else. I barely convinced him to not wear his combat gear to the event."

Jenna smiled. "That sounds about right."

Gabrielle's mouth curved, but there was a weight to her gaze that didn't seem to lift. It had been there for a long time, no doubt a function of the blood bond she shared with Lucan. Like all bonded pairs, they felt each other's most intense emotions—both the good and the bad—as if they were their own.

Joy, affection, concern.

Fear, grief, pain.

All of it traveled through a mated couple's bond.

So Gabrielle's obviously deep and prolonged worry was Lucan's as well.

Not that they didn't have good reason for concern.

Everyone did, but especially the warriors of the Order. They stood on the front line of every perilous situation. They were the last fortified wall between the inhabitants of this fragile planet and the darkness currently threatening to consume it from multiple sides.

Jenna could recall just one other instance when the general feeling of alarm within Order headquarters and the larger world outside had come anywhere close to what it was now. She and the rest of the Order had thought that other hellish night two decades ago had been the darkest they'd ever seen.

Back then, they had been battling just one madman and his evil. Now, the Order faced no less than three powerful enemies, each one more dangerous than the last.

Selene.

Opus Nostrum.

And the Ancient otherworlder who'd nearly obliterated Jenna, Brock, and several other members of the Order and its extended family less than two weeks ago in the Deadlands.

Gabrielle studied Jenna for a moment, her gentle eyes drifting from the *dermaglyphs* that tracked along

Jenna's bare arms to the ones that marched all the way onto her scalp. "Still no sense of where the Ancient might be?"

"Nope. Nothing but silence on the alien psychic connection hotline." Jenna let out a harsh bark of laughter. "I never thought I'd wish to be mentally linked to one of those barbaric creatures, but now, when it would actually be useful, I've got nothing."

"Do you think the explosion he created could have broken the link somehow?" Savannah asked. "Detonating those two Atlantean crystals might have obliterated half of Siberia if Phaedra hadn't been there to shield all of you. Maybe all that power short-circuited something in that little piece of alien technology inside you."

"I don't know," Jenna admitted. "It's possible, I guess. Even after living with this chip in the back of my neck for twenty years, I'm still not an expert on how it works."

"Or maybe the connection is lost because the Ancient didn't make it out of the Deadlands that night after all?" Gabrielle suggested.

It was a slim hope. One that Jenna wished could be a reality as the hours and days and weeks passed by without any inkling that her subconscious mind was still tethered to the monster she'd come face-to-face with in the ruins of his wrecked craft.

Even her dreams had been wholly her own since returning home to D.C.

Still, the quiet was unnerving.

She didn't dare trust it, no matter how much she wanted to.

Savannah chewed an olive, then met her gaze. "Too bad there's not an owner's manual on alien biotechnology, right?"

Jenna couldn't help but laugh, despite the gravity of the situation. "We could use one for Atlantean crystals, too."

"At least we have a little help there," Gabrielle said. "I don't know where we'd be without Zael, Phaedra, and Jordana on our side."

"I'll drink to that." Jenna soberly raised her glass to the three immortals from Atlantis who were now part of the Order's extended family. Zael and his Gen One Breed female mate, Brynne, were currently on patrols in the city, along with Micah and Phaedra, the newest Atlantean to be welcomed into the fold as the mate of Tegan and Elise's warrior son.

As for Jordana, the ethereal platinum-blonde was full-blooded Atlantean, too, although she hadn't known it for the first twenty-five years of her life. She had discovered her true lineage around the same time she became mated to Nathan, one of the Order's best warriors.

"Now, all we need is to convince the Atlantean colony to ally with us against Selene," Savannah said.

"Easier said than done." Jenna set her wine down and reached for a small chunk of bread. "The Atlantean exiles on that hidden island need their crystal for protection. I can understand their reluctance to share its power with us. It's the only thing that's kept them protected from the outside world since they fled Atlantis and Selene all those centuries ago."

"Then I'll just have to find a way to convince them."

The statement drew the attention of all three women. They looked up as Jordana entered the room. She glided over to join the women, her easy, elegant style somehow managing to make loose-fitting denim and a simple top look as regal as a ballgown. Which was understandable, considering her grandmother was none other than Selene herself.

The Atlantean queen had enough animosity toward the Breed and their Ancient forebears without the added insult of her sole heir repudiating her lineage to share a blood bond with one of the Order's warriors.

Jordana approached the table. "It's too quiet in the mansion tonight. Mind if I join you all?"

"Please, do," Jenna said, indicating one of the empty chairs at the long worktable. "What do you mean, *you'll* have to find a way to convince the colony to work with us? I thought Zael and Brynne are working on those negotiations."

"They'll be returning to the colony in a few days to appeal to the council again. I've offered to go with them."

Jenna glanced at Gabrielle and Savannah, noting they looked as surprised by this news as she was. "Are you sure that's a good idea?"

Jordana nodded, pure resolve in her eyes. "I think it may be our best chance. Now that we know two of the five original crystals are in the Ancient's hands, wherever he is, we can't afford to wait any longer or to simply hope for the colony's cooperation when the time comes that we need it. I may be the only one they'll listen to. Phaedra and Zael agree. Brynne does, too."

Gabrielle's expression softened with concern. "How does Nathan feel about this?"

Jordana glanced down, her brow knitting. "He'll come around. He understands it's something I have to do, not only for my family here in the Order, but also for the people in the colony. They're my family, too, even if I've never met any of them yet."

Savannah reached over and squeezed her hand. "That male of yours is as unbreakable as they come, but not when it concerns you. He must know Selene would give anything to bring you back to Atlantis."

"Even if she has to bring you there kicking and screaming," Jenna said.

"I know," Jordana murmured. "My grandmother already tried to have me abducted once. But that was before I understood my Atlantean power and how to use it. I've only gotten stronger since my blood bond with Nathan. I'm not afraid. I know how to handle myself, and anyone else."

"That may be true, but none of us have personally gone up against Selene or her legion," Jenna reminded her.

Savannah nodded. "There's only one thing Selene wants more than the crystals or vengeance for the fact they were stolen from her. And that's you, Jordana."

"That's true," Jenna added. "We don't know what she might be capable of, or what she might be willing to do in order to get you back."

Until now, Gabrielle had been quiet, listening in pensive silence. When she spoke, her voice was quiet, her brown eyes haunted with an unspoken dread. "Let's hope none of us have to feel Selene's wrath for ourselves."

# CHAPTER 4

Blood and fire. Smoke and screams. A world gripped in darkness, choked with violence and ruin.

Selene had never witnessed such chaos, such sharp, nightmarish terror.

Then again, yes, she had. So long ago, it had faded into myth . . . but not for her.

*Never for her.*

She could still taste the bitterness of that other, older attack in the back of her throat, where even now she had to bite down on her tongue to keep her remembered fury from erupting through her gritted teeth.

But this time it was the mortal world in flames. Human and Breed lives being spilled in the streets. Not her realm. Not her people.

So why did the sight of all that carnage and suffering make her stomach seize? Her heart felt squeezed in a vise, a stranglehold that made her draw in a sharp breath.

"Your Grace?" The Atlantean seer who stood with Selene in the royal palace's salon glanced up anxiously from the scrying bowl. In the shallow basin she had conjured a window onto a horror-filled corner of the eastern United States at Selene's command. "If it please Your Grace, shall I illuminate a different location instead?"

"No." Selene's tone was as curt as her dismissing wave. "I've seen enough. Go, Nuranthia."

"Yes, Your Grace." Timid as a mouse desperate to avoid a cat's claws, the petite brunette skittered out of the chamber.

Selene stared at the large bowl of hammered gold seated atop its carved marble pedestal. Now that Nuranthia had left, the vision the seer had called up was gone too. Nothing but clear, pure water glistened in the shallow basin.

She didn't need Nuranthia's bowl to tell her the blood-soaked edges of the outside world were seeping ever closer to her shores. She had known it was coming for centuries. It had begun the moment the first of her people had lain down with a human and produced a female who could bond with the savage, blood-drinking progeny of the Atlanteans' most hated enemies.

For a while, she'd been content to let the Breed and humans prey on one another. Lately, however, things had escalated to a point she could no longer ignore.

Selene walked past the pedestal, her diaphanous skirts floating at her sides as she continued through the dome-ceilinged, open-air salon. A pair of pillar-flanked arches served as gateways to the beautiful garden courtyard outside. After glimpsing the darkness of the mortal world in its current state of chaos and destruction, she needed to breathe fresh air, needed to feel the cleansing heat of the Atlantean sun on her face.

The palace was a soaring fortress of smooth white stone and elegant, peaked turrets perched on a raised hill in the center of a lush, tranquil island. Selene's personal chambers occupied the topmost floor of the tower, high above where she stood now, in the garden off the grand throne room and salon on the main floor. Living quarters for her attendants, advisers, personal guards and palace staff took up the several stories between.

There were other towers and buildings within the palace grounds as well, and, beyond that, spread out in all directions was the gleaming citadel of the realm's general population. Or, what was left of it. The thousands living there now was a number vastly reduced from the original metropolis, and minus the handful of defectors and rebels who'd fled the rebuilt realm to make their own way on the outside.

Selene had yet to forgive those losses, too.

Surrounded by turquoise water and clear blue skies, this second Atlantean settlement was nearly as breathtaking as the one that had been stolen from her people.

To Selene, it was home. She would defend her realm to her last breath and heartbeat . . . and kill anyone who so much as imagined its ruin.

Pushing her dark thoughts aside, Selene walked farther into the garden. Bright sunlight canopied the whole of the island; above it were skies of purest blue. She drank it all in, the sun and sky, the surrounding turquoise waters that ringed the island, the air perfumed with the scents of the sea and citrus and countless flowers that bloomed throughout the garden.

There was a time when being among the calm here was enough, but not anymore. Not for a very long time.

Not as long as a part of her—Selene's sole heir—was trapped among the brutal offspring of Atlantis's destroyers.

Selene wanted to believe her granddaughter was being held against her will, but it seemed it was much worse. Jordana had chosen to live with the Breed, to bind herself to one of them.

*Chosen to,* even after her true lineage had been revealed to her.

Selene couldn't fathom the decision. She couldn't curb her outrage, her utter shock and abhorrence, to imagine one of her kin spending a moment among the warring brethren of the Order, never mind being shackled to a Breed male through blood and bond.

Selene frowned. Memories filled her mind of a recent verbal confrontation with Lucan Thorne and his son, Darion, a male who seemed even more aggressive and warlike than his father.

Although they hadn't said it outright, Selene had no doubt either one of those Breed males would see her dead—and possibly wipe out the rest of the Atlantean people too—before they ever willingly surrendered Jordana or the Atlantean crystal now in the Order's possession.

They were no better than the Ancients who fathered their bloodthirsty race. Those same otherworldly monsters had used treachery to steal two other crystals from her court millennia ago and then used them to destroy the paradise of harmony and light she had built for her people.

She would never be so foolish or blindly trusting again.

Selene stared out at the tranquil cerulean sea in the distance. The misty veil that shrouded the island from unwanted eyes glittered like stardust against the water. That veil had held for many long centuries. Heavens help her, she would not let it crumble now.

No matter how much it cost her.

"I thought I might find you out here."

The deep voice belonged to Sebathiel, a member of her court and long-time adviser. Selene pivoted toward the intrusion, still frowning from the weight of her thoughts.

The handsome blond official strode into the garden, his lean, muscled body garbed in the white-and-teal robes of his temple. When he saw her face, his brow knit.

"Is something wrong? I passed Nuranthia on my way in to see you. She didn't even lift her head as she skulked by me."

Selene waved her hand. "Nothing's wrong."

Sebathiel made a low sound of skepticism as he approached, concern still dimming his shrewd blue eyes. "I take it there was unpleasant news in the seer's scrying bowl today?"

"Just more of the same, Seb."

He nodded sagely. "If you're distressed, I could call for a healer from the temple to come and assuage you."

"I told you, I'm fine."

His chin rose at her crisp reply, but he didn't cower like the rest of her court and subjects. He was too proud for that, a fact she both admired and resented. Especially at times like now, when Seb's concerned gaze said he knew her better than anyone else in her court.

"If you'd rather tell me what's troubling you, my attention—and my advice, should you wish it—is fully yours." His voice took on a gentler tone. "'Uneasy lies the head that wears a crown,'" he quoted softly. "If you're weary, Selene, my shoulder is strong enough for you to rest against."

He lifted his hand toward her and Selene glared at the gesture. Wisely, Seb cleared his throat and let his arm fall back to his side.

"Do I look weak or weary to you, High Chancellor?"

Her question felt as sharp as a razor on her tongue. It sounded defensive, even to her own ears. Too much so.

If Sebathiel thought so, his face gave nothing away. His gaze lingered on hers before he slowly lowered his head and stayed there. "No, My Queen. Never that. I beg your pardon."

She scowled at the top of his golden hair in hot silence, her molars clenched. As loyal as he had proven to be over the years, she had half a mind to cut him loose from her court. With enemies just waiting for the opportunity to pounce, she couldn't afford to let anyone question her strength or authority.

Selene could allow no one to doubt her power. Not even Sebathiel.

Against her will, her thoughts returned to her conversation with Darion Thorne and what the brash Breed warrior had said to her the day she had infiltrated the Order's technology to warn them who they were dealing with.

*The biggest fool is the one who thinks that he—or she—has no weaknesses.*

She had been seething over that conversation ever since. He had more nerve than most, daring to challenge her the way he had. She could still see his fearless, dark eyes and his stubborn jaw that seemed carved of granite. He spoke as if he had never met an opponent he couldn't best—either by brute force, or his sharp, reckless tongue.

She almost welcomed the chance to meet the arrogant Breed male in person. He wouldn't be so quick to challenge or denigrate her if she gave him a taste of her Atlantean light.

"Stand up, Seb," she told her adviser irritably. "Why were you looking for me?"

He straightened, looking every bit the diplomat she knew him to be. "Taebris came to see me at the temple this morning."

"My legion general?" She scoffed lightly. "Was he lost? He's hardly the type to seek out soft things like prayers or absolution."

Seb gave her an acknowledging look. "Perhaps not, but today he leads the search party into the Deadlands to look for the crystals. Taebris and the soldiers currently en route with him all came to the temple requesting blessings before they departed for their mission."

"Did they?" The news took Selene aback. "Does Taebris have reservations about the mission? If so, he didn't voice them to me."

"Nor would he voice them, Your Grace. The general is committed to his duty, to the realm, and to you."

This wasn't the first expedition she'd sent into that forbidden swath of mortal land, but it was the most important one by far. Every Atlantean had felt the disturbance that had originated in the Siberian taiga a few nights ago. What had merely been suspicion for some long centuries, that the Ancients who used the stolen pair of crystals to destroy Atlantis had secured them somewhere in that frozen, uninhabited region was no longer in question.

Only the crystals could have created the kind of power recently unleashed in that remote area. What had yet to be answered was *who* had wielded them?

Had the Order somehow uncovered the crystals? Selene shuddered to consider it.

If the Order had managed to sway Zael and Jordana to their side, how many other Atlantean defectors might be persuaded to join their ranks in a quest to bolster their defenses against her—or worse, to join forces and go on the offense?

The Order already had one crystal in their possession. Two would be deadly enough, but the combined power of three?

If that were the case, it was a miracle they hadn't already made their strike against her.

Seb held her in an intense stare. "We need those crystals, Selene. What's more, we need them before they're allowed to fall into the hands of anyone who might turn them against us."

"Do you think I don't know that? Do you imagine for even one second of my waking hours that I'm not wholly aware of what those crystals mean to my people—to our very existence?"

He gave her a sober nod. "Of course not, Your Grace."

"If I want your opinions, Seb, I'll ask for them," she bit off sharply. "Last I checked, the crown you seem so concerned about sits on my head, not yours."

"Yes, Your Grace," he murmured.

Her fury was uncalled for, but Selene couldn't stop it. Nor could she curb the dread that lurked in her heart when she thought of how vulnerable the Atlantean realm remained for as long as they only had a single crystal to protect them.

How long would she be able to bear the racking guilt she felt in knowing she alone was to blame for that loss?

Her foolishness and naivety had cost so much.

Never again.

Whether the stolen crystals were in the Order's possession or not, Selene would not go down without a fight.

She had promised war against the Order for defying her demands for their crystal and Jordana's return. It was time she started making good on that vow.

Stepping past Sebathiel, she headed for the palace at a brisk march.

# CHAPTER 5

Lucan stalked out of the GNC meeting following his televised speech, tugging at the collar of his buttoned black shirt. The damn collar felt like a shackle around his neck.

He was more accustomed to wearing his patrol gear and combat boots. Unfortunately, Gabrielle had been adamant that he couldn't deliver his public address garbed like he had walked into the meeting straight from battle. She had also insisted that he leave the bulk of his weapons stowed in his vehicle for the duration of the gathering. No baring of his fangs on camera, either.

Lucan had conceded to her better judgment on all counts, if only barely.

He didn't want to add to the escalating panic among the human public by showing up looking like the battle-hardened Gen One Breed warrior he was, no more than he could go on air and pretend everything was going to return to normal for the civilian populations anytime soon.

The situation in the streets of nearly every major city around the world was getting worse. Opus Nostrum was coming at the Order hard, and with every weapon in their seemingly unlimited arsenal.

There would be more bloodshed. More death and destruction.

The truth of it was, everything was going to shit on a nightly basis, not getting better.

He didn't need to say the words aloud for everyone with eyes and ears in their heads to understand. Each time the sun set came the start of another battle to be fought, another fresh round of Rogues being loosed on otherwise peaceful communities in nearly every corner of the globe. The Order was holding the line so far, but how long could they maintain it?

Add in the threat of ultraviolet weaponry and the Atlantean crystals currently in enemy hands and Lucan wasn't sure how he and his comrades might eventually win their multiple wars.

All he did know was that they had to find a way.

Lucan kept to his scripted remarks for his wary global audience, well aware that his enemies would be listening too. He couldn't give Opus—or anyone else— the slightest indication that the Order might bend even a little under the strain of everything they had been called to do.

Lucan had ended his speech with a personal message to all who were listening, renewing the promise he had made to a terrified, uncertain human public some twenty years ago.

The Order was committed to true, lasting peace. He and every last warrior under his command would give up their final breaths to see that vow come to fruition.

Lucan just hoped for fuck's sake it wouldn't come to that.

Exiting from a back door into the corridor outside the secured meeting room, he growled under his breath to see a small gaggle of press gathered like vultures at the far end of the hallway. One of the female reporters spotted him and hurried in his direction.

"Lucan Thorne! A moment of your time, please?"

The woman's shout drew everyone else's attention and the pack started toward him en masse.

"Not a fucking chance," he muttered, pivoting away.

Using his Breed genetics, he ducked into the nearby stairwell as a blur of motion and sped to the underground garage level.

Unfortunately, another handful of reporters had already found their way down there as well. Across the concrete parking area, half a dozen people swarmed his black SUV, nattering among themselves while they waited to pounce on him with their cameras and microphones. Two of the humans appeared to be protesters, if their T-shirts printed with his face sporting fireball eyes, devil's horns, and huge, blood-dripping fangs were any indication.

Lucan was not in the fucking mood.

He had half a mind to let his critics see the monster they apparently thought he was. His lip began to curl away from his teeth and emerging fangs as he took the first steps toward the crowd.

He had hardly gone three paces before a fast-approaching sedan roared up erratically beside him from another area of the garage. The tires shrieked to a halt and the driver peered up at him from the opened window with a look of horror in his panicked eyes.

"Chairman Thorne! Oh, thank God you're still here!" It was Owen Keener, one of the GNC members who'd attended tonight's emergency meeting. The timid human diplomat was pallid under normal circumstances, but now his face was ghostly white with fear. His fingers were clamped on the steering wheel in a death grip. "I don't know what to do!"

All of Lucan's annoyance with reporters and protesters silenced by the obvious distress of his GNC colleague. "What's wrong?"

"Rogues. At my house." Keener dropped his chin and sobbed. "My wife just called . . . she's trapped inside." He swallowed hard, lifting an imploring, desperate stare at Lucan. "They're going to kill her. You have to help me save her, I beg you!"

*Shit.* Lucan scowled in the direction of his SUV and the reporters who were still surrounding it, but suddenly getting curious about what was happening across the garage from them.

It would take precious seconds to reach his vehicle and chase everyone out of his way.

Fuck that. He had a semiauto full of titanium hollowpoints tucked down the back waistband of his dress slacks. He could take out a dozen Rogues singlehandedly if it came down to it.

Right now, the most important thing was making sure Oliver Keener's society darling wife didn't end up getting slaughtered, let alone have it happen on the evening news.

"Move over." Lucan pointed to the passenger seat. "I'll drive."

Keener scrambled from behind the wheel as Lucan climbed in. Across the garage, the crowd was beginning to realize they were about to be ditched. They started scrambling over.

Lucan punched the accelerator and the sedan squealed into action.

He sent a mental command to the electronic gate and it swung open just as he reached it. Keener's sedan exploded onto the darkened street.

Keener attempted to stutter directions to his estate, but Lucan ignored them. He already knew the way. He'd been patrolling every corner of the District with his brethren for the past two decades and counting. It was as much home to him as the Order's former Boston location had been. He hated like hell seeing either city under attack, and he was more than ready to make it all end.

The city-wide curfew kept most of D.C.'s residents inside, so it only took minutes to navigate the wrecked streets and areas littered with burnt-out debris left behind from the night's earlier battles.

Keener sat slumped in the passenger seat, his thousand-yard stare fixed on the road ahead. Lucan hoped he didn't notice the handful of bodies they passed in the dark, all hapless victims of the Rogues prowling the streets and neighborhoods, slaves to the unquenchable thirst of their Bloodlust.

Keener's big house stood on a prime lot of semi-secluded real estate, surrounded by old-growth trees, cultivated lawns and gardens. Lucan killed the headlights and turned onto the long driveway. A black delivery van was parked on the pavement. Inside the Federal-style home, warm lights burned with a welcoming glow.

No sign of trouble whatsoever.

Lucan swung a look at Keener. "What the fuck?"

Keener swallowed, looking guilty as hell. "I-I'm sorry—"

At that same instant, a blinding spotlight fired up in front of the sedan. Lucan brought his arm up to shield his eyes, just enough to see that the light was coming from the back of the delivery van.

Behind Keener's sedan now, a huge, armored SUV barreled into them. The delivery van roared in reverse, sandwiching Lucan and his duplicitous passenger between the heavier vehicles.

Teams of soldiers in tactical gear and armed with assault rifles closed in from both sides. Not just ordinary rifles. Lucan spotted the unmistakable iridescent blue glow of UV rounds in the men's weapons.

Lucan's fury was like gasoline in his veins.

"I'm gonna fucking kill you," he seethed at Keener through his teeth and fangs.

But first, he needed to deal with the dozen-plus Opus soldiers surrounding the vehicle. He was only one hair-trigger finger away from getting ashed right where he sat.

From the looks of it, Opus had sent enough ultraviolet firepower to this ambush to blast him into the next century.

He'd never been one to give in to fear, but damn if the threat of all that liquid UV didn't make him dial back his urge to smash out of the car in the hopes of taking out a few Opus men before they lit him up.

And then there was Gabrielle.

*Fuck.*

Any pain he felt here tonight—including his death—would travel down their blood bond as if his agony were her own.

His sweet Breedmate.

The only woman he'd ever loved.

The extraordinary soul who'd saved him, made him feel, who gave him the precious gift of their son. Gabrielle made him desperate to live for another nine-hundred years, but only he could do it with her by his side.

Regret rolled up on him like a dark wave.

He couldn't die here. Not like this, burned alive behind the wheel of Keener's fucking useless vehicle before he could even draw his own weapon to defend himself.

He had to live.

For Gabrielle, if for no other reason. He couldn't put her through the pain of his death.

He was prepared to surrender if that's what Opus demanded of him. He'd find a way out of it later. All he had to do right now was not get his ass smoked before he had the chance to fight.

He slowly raised his hands.

As he did, his gaze locked with that of the guy whose gun was aimed at Lucan's head. A slight, satisfied smile lifted the edge of the human's mouth. As if this had all been just a fucking game. As if somehow it still was.

"Let me out of here!" Keener wailed. "You promised I'd be protected if I brought him to you. You said you'd protect me and my wife! You said we'd be safe!"

The men outside chuckled at Keener's complaints.

"Don't worry," one of them taunted. "Your bitch doesn't need anyone's protection anymore."

"In a few seconds, he won't either," added another.

Then the soldier in front gave a nod and someone opened fire on the vehicle. Only a single round, shot through the window into the crumpled backseat.

Another bullet pierced the window on the other side of the car.

For a fleeting instant, Lucan wondered if the soldiers were only trying to torment him before they filled him full of UV.

But then, he began to understand the true purpose of Opus's game here tonight.

Red Dragon fumes billowed up from the spent rounds inside the car.

The rifles loaded with ultraviolet bullets were only meant to hold him captive while the real fun began.

As the realization settled on him, more rounds pierced the sedan. More choking vapor poured in, filling the entire cabin in a matter of seconds.

Keener's screams grew more high-pitched as he banged his palms against the window glass and begged for the men to let him out.

No one moved. Those UV rifles remained locked on Lucan from outside, daring him to give someone a reason to make him fry.

He should have done it.

The Red Dragon was a strangling wreath around his head. He tried not to breathe it in, but there was too much. He could already taste the bitter scarlet gas in the back of his throat.

A roar exploded out of him and more Red Dragon was dragged into his mouth.

The pain of it shredded his lungs. His transformed eyes glowed bright amber in the darkened vehicle, barely penetrating the thick fog that kept multiplying all around him.

Lucan rammed his shoulder against the door from inside, taking a small measure of satisfaction in the way the human soldiers all took a step back, not quite certain they wanted to face the beast they'd been sent to create.

It didn't matter, anyway.

Some of his fight was leaking out of him. He couldn't even lift his hand to reach for his gun, not that his titanium hollowpoints would give him any advantage over a dozen rifles loaded with UV. Slumping in the seat, he fumbled to locate his comm unit. He struggled to retrieve it, his fingers heavy and uncooperative, his grasp too weak to pull the device from his pants pocket let alone make a call to headquarters for help.

Not that there was anything to be done for him now.

The fumes completely filled the vehicle. In the seat beside him, Keener had gone hysterical, screaming and wailing for mercy he wasn't going to get from the Opus soldiers watching from outside.

There was no mercy coming for Lucan, either.

As his vision swirled and a searing chemical madness began to erupt deep inside him, only one thought penetrated his agony.

*Gabrielle.*

"I'm sorry," he murmured, his tongue thick against his fangs. "My love . . . I'm sorry."

# CHAPTER 6

Gabrielle stepped into the spacious suite she and Lucan shared in the Order's mansion headquarters, her heart full of pride for her formidable mate.

She had just left Savannah, Jenna, and Jordana, where the women, along with Gideon, had watched Lucan's televised speech in the mansion's large living room. Lucan's speech had been one of the most important he'd ever delivered, and he had done it with both compassion and candor. In particular, the personal remarks he'd added toward the end of the pre-written portion of the address.

It was rare to hear Lucan speak with such raw feeling; all the more so in a public setting. But Gabrielle knew he had meant every word—right down to his vow to protect the fragile peace between mankind and the Breed with every breath in his body. He had been committed to true and lasting peace for most of his long life.

That dedication had been galvanized during the time Gabrielle had known him. Not even Lucan's brother, Marek, had been allowed to stand in the way of that goal.

Dragos had risen in the wake of Marek's defeat, bringing even more evil plans and destruction. He had also ultimately fallen to Lucan and the warriors of the Order. Now, there was Opus Nostrum to contend with, and Selene of Atlantis. As well as the Ancient.

Gabrielle shuddered to think what any of those three adversaries might do in an effort to further their own plans for the world they all seemed determined to control. But Lucan didn't shudder under any of those threats. He never faltered or hesitated to do what was right, what was necessary. Nothing seemed capable of breaking her formidable mate.

Gabrielle couldn't wait for him to return home so she could show him how proud she felt to be his blood-bonded mate. If not for the war raging outside the headquarters' gates, she'd demand to have all night with Lucan to demonstrate her pride and affection for him.

A smile curved her lips at the thought . . . until a shocking jolt of pain racked her body.

Gabrielle cried out, staggering forward to catch the edge of the dresser for support.

Her lungs felt on fire. She inhaled a sharp breath, but instead of oxygen it seemed as though she were breathing in ashes. Searing, suffocating agony sliced through her.

It choked her. She coughed and wheezed, struggling for air.

What was happening?

Confusion flooded her consciousness as her knees quaked beneath her. Even the smallest breath was torture. Her head spun as her vision began to cloud over in a blinding, red haze. Every cell in her body screamed at the sudden, relentless assault on her senses.

She sank to the floor on a jagged sob.

The excruciating pain was more than she could bear. And it wasn't entirely hers.

"Lucan," she gasped.

*Oh, God.*

Her agony was his. Her inability to breathe. The choking gas that seemed to fill her lungs and make her feel as if she were drowning in poisonous fumes.

It was Lucan's suffering, sent through their bond to her.

It was his regret she felt, too, as pain and a hideous kind of madness swamped him.

"No," she groaned. "Oh, no. Lucan!"

An urgent knock sounded on the closed door to her suite but it sounded muffled and distant. Gabrielle hardly heard the panicked voices calling her name from the corridor outside. She couldn't respond, anyway. Her skull was splitting in anguish and she could barely draw a breath as she writhed on the floor.

A rush of cool air poured into the room as the door flew open. Savannah and Gideon hurried to Gabrielle's side.

"Oh, my God," Savannah gasped. Her fingers lit on Gabrielle's cheek, gentle and warm. "Gabby, can you hear me?"

Gabrielle gave a weak nod and a pitiful-sounding groan. "I-I can't . . . it's Lucan."

"Ah, fuck." Gideon's deep voice held a sobering tone. "I just got a ping from his comm unit, but I'm unable to reach him. He's not responding."

"No," Gabrielle moaned, terrified to hear her fears confirmed.

The fact that Gideon wasn't already reassuring her that everything was going to be okay only made the agony cut even deeper. If the violent pain she felt was only her own, she would bear it. This was Lucan's suffering, though. Her indomitable mate, laid low by something she hardly dared to imagine.

Fighting off the waves of red-hot agony, she levered herself up off the floor with Savannah's tender assistance. "Have to . . . help him."

Gideon gave a grim nod. His eyes were too serious behind his pale blue shades. "I've sent word to all the teams. We've tracked his comm unit to the vicinity of one of the GNC members' estates. It hasn't moved since the signal came through."

"He's hurt, Gideon." Gabrielle inhaled gingerly, forcing herself to speak through the pain. "Something's very wrong. Oh, God . . . I think he might be . . ."

*Dying.*

That's what it felt like to her, but she refused to let the word fall from her lips.

She refused to think it, no matter what the blood bond was telling her.

"We have to find him," she whispered, desperation in every syllable. "Gideon, we have to find him now."

# CHAPTER 7

Darion tore through the city as if his heels were on fire.

Gideon's broadcast to all of the Order teams in the D.C. vicinity a moment ago still rang in Darion's ears.

One of their own had signaled for assistance, and was currently unresponsive.

Not just any warrior. Lucan. Darion's father.

*Fuck.*

He sped toward the site where Lucan's comm unit signal had originated. Darion knew practically every square block of the city, including the affluent area where GNC member Oliver Keener's estate was located. Wooded acreage surrounded the mansion, a luxury in a metropolis full of concrete and asphalt.

Darion moved swiftly, stealthily, across the grounds at the back of the house, his gun full of titanium rounds locked and loaded at his side. Up ahead, lights were on inside the two-story estate. No overt signs of trouble from within or without.

The quiet of the place bothered him.

If Lucan needed backup, where the hell was the fight?

There was no sign of his father anywhere. No sign of anyone at all.

Still, his instincts stayed on high alert as he crept farther onto the property.

As he neared the side of the big house, those instincts began to scream like sirens.

The unmistakable smell of blood and death reached his nostrils. Whoever was inside the mansion was human, and long dead.

Darion stepped onto the darkened driveway. An abandoned delivery van was parked halfway down, its back doors wide open. Directly behind it on the pavement, its hood smashed in from a collision with the van, was a black sedan with diplomat plates. The sedan had been rammed from behind as well, but whatever beast of a vehicle had plowed into its rear end was gone now.

As he drew closer to the sedan, he spotted single bullet holes in the side windows. Had it been an assassination attempt on Keener? Or something even worse?

Like the mansion behind him, the sedan reeked of blood and death, too.

*And something else . . .*

A trace of bitter, noxious fumes immediately made Darion's eyes water and burn, even from fifteen feet away. He brought his arm up in front of his nose to keep from inhaling any of the fumes as he approached.

Thick red fog coated the inside of the windshield and windows, making it impossible to see into the car.

Holy shit.

It could only be one thing: Red Dragon.

Understanding—and a marrow-deep dread—dawned on him as he took in the evidence of the poisonous narcotic that had been deployed into the vehicle.

Now that he was drawing up next to the diplomat's car, he realized someone was alive inside. Not that Darion took much comfort in the fact.

Sounds of feeding and low, animalistic grunts made his skin prickle with sick anticipation as he reached for the driver's side door handle with one hand, his other gripped around the pistol full of Rogue-killing titanium hollowpoints.

Darion yanked the door open. Red Dragon mist clouded into the night air, and he held his breath as he aimed the gun at the back of the big Rogue's skull as it feasted on the shredded throat of Oliver Keener.

There was no saving the human. No saving the Rogue who had killed him, either. Death would be a mercy compared to an existence ruled by an insatiable hunger for blood.

Yet something held Darion's finger on the trigger of his firearm.

His senses staggered as his brain acknowledged what his heart refused to admit he was actually seeing.

It wasn't just any Rogue who'd attacked and slaughtered the GNC diplomat.

It was Lucan.

Ah, Christ. His father was mindless in his Bloodlust, savage with a fury Darion had never witnessed in him before.

And no wonder.

There had been enough Red Dragon pumped inside the vehicle to turn a dozen Breed males into Rogues.

At that same moment, Lucan swiveled his head at the interruption of his kill. His transformed eyes were molten, pupils barely slits of darkness amid all that amber. His fangs were enormous, dripping with Keener's blood.

Darion stared in horror. "Jesus. How did this . . . *who* did this to you?"

But he knew the answer.

Opus Nostrum.

Somehow, they had gotten close enough to his father to poison him. And it would have taken something of a miracle for Lucan Thorne to fall into an Opus trap. A miracle, or an act of unforgivable duplicity.

Darion's gaze flicked to the dead human slumped in the passenger seat. The damage to the sedan, the stench of a human corpse inside the house . . . it all pointed to an ambush on the Order's leader. Almost certainly aided by Oliver Keener in some way.

Lucan had gotten his vengeance on the traitor, but at what cost?

Darion cursed. "Those sons of bitches. I'm going to kill every last one of those Opus bastards if it's the last thing I—"

On a roar, Lucan lunged at him. He took Darion down beneath him onto the pavement of the driveway in a blur of snapping jaws and feral, mad Rogue eyes.

Darion fended off the assault with his free arm, blocking his father's strikes and dodging those razor-sharp fangs by fractions of an inch. The titanium-loaded gun in his other hand felt like a lead weight, but he refused to lift it in defense.

Lucan could kill him before Darion would so much as consider using his weapon on his father.

"Stop," he uttered tightly, struggling with the big Gen One Breed male. "I don't want to hurt you."

Father and son were nearly a match in size and strength, but Lucan was fueled by the disease coursing through his veins.

Darion bellowed, summoning all his might and power to throw Lucan off.

He scrambled to his feet, breath heaving, heart cracking open inside his chest as he stared at the feral stranger crouched in front of him, ready to pounce again.

Darion met and held those murderous, searing eyes. "Father, it's me, Darion. You have to see me. I know you can."

Lucan panted, his chin and chest painted with Keener's lifeblood. His hands were held out at his sides, fingers splayed like claws. Darion had never feared his father even once in all his life. He had always respected him for his ability to shoulder any responsibility or burden, no matter its weight.

No Breed male—not even his indomitable father—could carry this weight.

Opus had struck true this time, straight to the heart of the Order.

"You need help," Darion told him. "We'll figure this out. I promise, we will."

Lucan snarled, curling his lip away from the long daggers of his fangs. His transformed gaze slid for an instant to the weapon Darion still clutched in his grasp. Even though Red Dragon had a hold on his mind, there was still a part of Lucan that seemed to recognize the threat of titanium rounds.

Darion swallowed, giving an understanding nod. Slowly, he stooped to place the pistol on the ground beside him. He held up his hands in a show of trust.

"Let me help you, Father," Darion said. "Let me take you back to headquarters so we can try to find a way to get you through this."

Lucan grunted, madness and regret swirling in his transformed gaze.

"If you won't do it for me, then do it for Mom. I can't go back to her tonight without you."

Lucan's attention snapped away. Tilting his head, he listened to their surroundings.

"The rest of the teams are on the way," Darion told him. "Gideon got the ping from your comm unit earlier. We're all searching to find you and bring you home."

Movement in the air alerted Darion that his comrades were closing in on the estate now. They were likely already in the wooded areas, moments away from the standoff taking place in the driveway.

"He's here," Darion called out to them. "I found him. He's alive, but he's—"

Darion didn't get the chance to say another word.

One moment his father was standing in front of him, the next he had bolted away, vanishing into the darkness.

# CHAPTER 8

They searched for hours, Darion and the rest of the patrol teams looking for Lucan in every corner of the city. He was nowhere to be found.

Darion couldn't shake the shocking image of his father staring back at him with the feral gaze and mad fury of a Rogue. He would never be able to purge the horror he felt at seeing the Breed male he respected and admired above all others turned into a snarling animal by the poison that Opus Nostrum had unleashed on him.

"I'm going to search the Metro stations again," he said to his teammates who'd regrouped a few minutes ago near the nightclub, Slake. The popular place was dark and vacant tonight, as was the rest of the city, still under curfew as the Rogue violence continued.

Nathan put a hand on Darion's shoulder. "It'll be daybreak in less than half an hour. We can start again tomorrow night."

Darion shrugged off his captain's concern. "There's still time for another look. I'm not leaving until I find him."

"You won't find Lucan if he doesn't want to be found."

This time it was Hunter who spoke. He was one of several warrior elders who had assisted in the search. The Gen One assassin's normally cool stare held an edge of sympathy that did less to comfort Darion than drive home the hopelessness of the situation.

Hunter slowly shook his head. "He's gone to ground for now, somewhere we won't find him."

Brock nodded in agreement. "No doubt. That's what I would do."

Darion couldn't argue with them, even if he wanted to. The only people who knew Lucan half as well as Darion's mother were the warriors who'd been through hell and back with him over the past two decades and longer. Some of them much, much longer than that. They had all grown as close as any brothers could be, and it was clear they shared Darion's concern for his father's condition.

"We need to put some daywalkers on him. The longer he's left out there on his own, the worse things could get for him."

Brock's dark eyes locked on Darion with sympathy and something else. "As bad as things are for Lucan right now, he's not the only one suffering. Your mother—"

"Ah, Christ." Understanding hit Darion like a physical blow. *The blood bond.*

He'd been so focused on his father, he hadn't paused to consider the other harm Opus was inflicting tonight. Those fucking bastards.

He didn't want to imagine what his poor mother must be feeling through her Breedmate connection to his father. Without a mate of his own, he truly couldn't imagine it, but he could guess well enough. The bond that was the deepest gift between a mated couple could also be the sharpest weapon. And now his gentle, loving mother would be feeling his father's agony and madness as if it were her own.

The thought of her enduring even a fraction of the suffering he saw in his father earlier tonight was more than Darion could stand.

Reluctantly, and with a low growl of renewed rage for Opus Nostrum, he gave his comrades a curt nod.

"Let's go, then."

With Darion in the lead, they rounded up the rest of the patrol teams in other parts of the city and headed back to Order headquarters.

Gideon greeted the teams as they rushed inside. His gaze scanned Darion's face, then the others. "Shit. He's not with you."

Darion gave a tight shake of his head. "Where's my mother?"

"In your parents' quarters. I tranced her so she could rest, but she's not—"

Darion didn't wait to hear any more. His booted feet chewed up the distance as he raced from the command center to the residence.

The door was partially open, so he stepped inside without knocking and walked through the spacious living area to the equally expansive bedroom. There, he froze.

His mother lay on the bed in loose-fitting pajama pants and a sleep tank, restless despite the trance Gideon had administered. Savannah sat beside her on the edge of the big mattress, holding a damp washcloth in her hand. She pressed it to Gabrielle's brow, but it seemed to do little to soothe her. Her long auburn hair was a matted tangle that clung to her pale, sweat-sheened face.

Jenna stood on the opposite side of the bed, along with Jordana and two of the elder warriors' Breedmates, Elise and Corinne. As Darion approached, the women all glanced at him with worry in their eyes. And fear.

"How is she?"

Savannah offered a gentle half-smile. "She might be better now that you're here. Come and sit with her."

His stride felt stiff, his throat ash-dry. He'd never seen either of his parents as anything less than indefatigable, individually and as a couple. They were an enduring force of strength and unshakable support that had formed the bedrock of his own existence. Now, in the space of a few hours, he was witnessing both laid low by the same offensive strike.

Possibly never to recover.

*No.* He refused to think it. He refused to let Opus take so much from him. *From them.*

Savannah moved so he could take her place on the edge of the bed. With the cold compress in his hand, he brushed it tenderly along his mother's cheek. She stirred, groaning with the pain that coursed through her, bringing her limbs in tighter, her body clenched into a ball.

Darion frowned, stricken to see her like that. Gideon's trance had a hold on her, but the blood bond was stronger. She moaned and whimpered, tears leaking from the corners of her closed eyes.

That she was still in agony meant Darion's father was still alive somewhere. A cold comfort to be sure. Still, so long as Lucan was breathing meant there was a chance of finding him.

Finding a way to reverse his Bloodlust before it completely consumed him was an impossibility Darion refused to consider. Right now, all his attention was on offering what comfort he could to his cherished mother.

"I'm sorry," he murmured, pressing the cloth to her brow as beads of perspiration formed there. His deep voice rasped thickly as he stared down at her suffering. "I'm so sorry I can't take this pain away for you."

Another pained groan racked her, but her eyelids cracked open just a bit. Her dry lips moved, barely able to form words. The question that came out of her was more breath than sound.

"Lucan?"

Darion frowned. "No, Mom. He's not here."

She moaned, and the anguish in it seemed less about any of her physical discomfort than a bone-deep heartache. The sigh she released was jagged, a shudder that shook her frail-looking body. The trance pulled her under, mercifully, and she slipped into a motionless doze.

Darion swiveled a look at Savannah. "Has she been like this the whole time?"

A sober nod. She motioned for him to follow her out of the bedroom. Elise walked over to take the cold compress from Darion, offering his arm a tender squeeze before she sat down to tend Gabrielle.

Darion stepped out to the living area with Savannah.

"We've sent for Tess," she told him. "She and Dante should be arriving from Boston any minute now. I don't know if Tess's healing ability can do anything for your mom, but we're going to try everything we can to make her comfortable."

"Thank you."

Savannah offered a tentative smile. "Tess and Rafe were able to work a miracle once when they combined their healing touches. Maybe they can help Gabrielle and Lucan too."

Darion had his doubts, but he wasn't about to rule out anything. "First, we have to find my father and bring him home. That's assuming he comes without a fight. What I saw in his eyes tonight, Savannah . . . it was almost worse than seeing him dead."

Her brow knit over sympathetic brown eyes. "Don't give up hope. Right now, that's all any of us are clinging to."

"Not all," he said. "Rage. Hatred. Vengeance. I want Opus heads to roll for this. Every last one of them."

As he spoke, Gideon appeared in the open doorway to the apartment. From the animated look on his face, at least it didn't appear to be more bad news. "We've got something."

Darion's attention snapped to full alert. "Tell me," he said, crossing the room to meet Gideon in the corridor. "What's going on? Is there word about my father?"

Gideon grimly shook his head. "It's something else. Remember that photo Devony brought back to us from her family's house in London?"

Darion nodded. Rafe's mate was the daughter of the late Roland Winters, a JUSTIS director who was killed along with Devony's daywalker mother when Opus Nostrum blew up JUSTIS's London office a few weeks ago. Before he died, Director Winters had been gathering intel on a personal investigation he was conducting—one that got a little too close to Opus for their liking.

As it turned out in the end, it was Devony's own brother, Harrison Winters, who had become a traitor to both his family and his oath when he helped Opus orchestrate their murderous attack.

"You're talking about the photo Devony's father had tucked away for safekeeping—the one she's certain he wanted her to find if anything happened to him?"

"That's the one," Gideon said. "If you recall, there were three men in the picture. Harrison Winters, Reginald Crowe, and another man—one whose face was turned away from the camera as the photo had been taken."

Given his evident rapport with Crowe and Devony's brother, both members of Opus Nostrum, the Order had been working to ID the third man ever since.

"I just got a lock on him," Gideon said. "His name is Ahmed Touati. He's Breed, working as attaché to the ambassador of the Breed nation in Algeria for the past four months. Touati's got an apartment here in D.C. Turns out, he was at the theater the night of the Opus attack, but managed to escape unharmed."

"That's some kind of luck," Darion all but growled, full of suspicion.

"Yeah," Gideon said. "Want to guess where he was the day before the JUSTIS bombing in London?"

"Son of a bitch." Darion's vision flashed amber with rage. "Where is Touati now?"

"From what I could gather so far, it appears he's still here in town. He's due to fly back to Algeria tomorrow."

"Then let's go get him. Let's drag his ass down here for questioning right fucking now. I'll handle the interrogation personally."

With his father missing and his mother suffering in equal measure, Darion had little patience for anything. He wanted to inflict maximum pain on Opus and its members, and he wanted it to start yesterday.

"I understand where you're coming from," Gideon said, "but we need to tread carefully. Ahmed Touati's our best lead on Opus at the moment. He's also our only lead. We need to ID them all before we strike. If word gets out that we're bringing Touati in by force, don't think the others won't scatter like rats off a sinking ship."

Darion knew Gideon was right. That didn't mean he had to like it.

"What about Scarface down in our holding cell? You think he and Touati might know each other?"

Gideon considered for less than a second. "Decent chance they do, yeah. That theater attack didn't execute on its own. Someone had to let Gopnik and the other Opus gunmen inside that night without raising any alarms."

Darion's blood seethed at the thought.

That Touati would be willing to stand by while other members of the Breed nation—innocent civilians, at that—came under attack by Opus was unconscionable enough. To think he'd likely been complicit in the attack made him the worst sort of scum.

The human offal sitting in the Order's holding tank wasn't any better.

Gopnik was nothing more than a grunt foot soldier, albeit a sadistic one, but in terms of intel on Opus he'd proven to be a dead end.

At least, so far.

That was about to change.

With contempt—and a deadly craving for some payback—boiling in his veins, Darion stepped past Gideon to set a hard pace toward the opposite end of the corridor.

"If you're planning on talking to Gopnik, you won't get very far," Gideon said, falling in alongside Darion. "If he had anything useful to tell us, Lucan and Hunter would've pulled it out of him by now."

"I'm not interested in anything Gopnik has to say anymore."

Gideon gave him an uncertain look. "Then what exactly to you have in mind?"

Darion didn't answer, mostly because he knew Gideon wouldn't approve.

None of the other warriors would, his father included, if he were there.

At the moment, Darion didn't care. He knew what needed to be done, and he wasn't looking for anyone's permission. Things had gone too far and it was time to take the fight to Opus with every tool at their disposal.

Stalking through the winding corridors with Gideon at his heels, Darion headed for the chamber where the Order's captured enemy was being held. Gopnik vaulted to his feet inside the locked cell the instant he spotted the two Breed males stalking toward him.

For one brief second, there had been a spark of hope in the human's eyes. It vanished as soon as his gaze lit on Darion's glower.

"Does the name Ahmed Touati mean anything to you?" Darion demanded as he approached.

Gopnik swallowed hard, taking a step away from the bars caging him. "I-I don't know."

Darion scoffed. "No? Not sure?"

Gopnik vigorously shook his head. He screamed a second later, because that's all the time it took for Darion to open the cell door and flash inside to grab the lying bastard under his jaw with one hand. Darion lifted Gopnik in his grasp, higher and higher, until the human's feet danced an inch off the floor of the cell.

"How about now?" Darion glared into the Opus soldier's terrified eyes, his lip curling away from his emerged fangs. "Touati knew about the assault on the theater, didn't he? He's the one who made sure you and your crew were able to get in past any security."

Gopnik sputtered what sounded like an affirmative. His face was turning from red to a sick-looking purple under Darion's vise-grip around his throat. "P-please," he gasped. "Please! I can't . . . can't . . . breathe . . ."

It took every bit of self-control to keep from snuffing the life out of the piece of shit right then and there. Gopnik didn't deserve to live after the scores of deaths that stained his and his comrades' hands. Didn't deserve any mercy after what had happened to Lucan tonight. Because of this human and his associates, Darion's mother was suffering in unspeakable agony just a few hundred feet above their heads.

Darion dropped the man unceremoniously to the cell floor. While Gopnik coughed and wheezed, Darion sank into a crouch in front of him.

"As of tonight, breathing is the last of your concerns."

"Ah, shit. Dare, what are you—"

Gideon's alarmed voice barely reached Darion's ears before he had yanked Gopnik forward and sank his fangs into the human's neck.

Blood gushed into his mouth while Gopnik screamed and struggled. All futile efforts. Darion drank hard and fast, without an ounce of hesitation.

But his goal wasn't to kill the human.

He was going to drain him—just to the brink of death, where Gopnik's humanity would ebb away, leaving a pliable shell in its place. A Minion. Unquestioningly obedient, and bound to serve the Breed vampire who made him.

Gideon obviously realized what was happening and uttered a curse under his breath. "For fuck's sake, Darion. This isn't how we do things . . . there are lines we don't cross."

Darion let go of Gopnik and swiveled his head toward Gideon. The warrior wasn't alone behind him anymore. Several Order members had arrived and now stood in the chamber with him. Rafe and Devony. Hunter, Brock, Nathan and Jax.

They all stared in stunned silence. Even a bit of horror.

Darion rose, wiping his bloody mouth on the back of his hand. "New rules," he announced tersely. "After what Opus did tonight, there are no lines we can't cross."

He glanced down at his Minion, who was already recovering from the draining bite. Gopnik blinked dully at the audience gathered outside the cell, then his gaze lifted to find Darion.

"Master," he murmured, getting up from the floor as if awaiting instructions.

Darion looked at his fellow warriors again. "No more waiting or searching for a way in to Opus's inner circle. We've got everything we need right here. Let's get to work."

He strode out of the chamber and headed for the Order's war room, his comrades silently following his lead.

# CHAPTER 9

Nathan stepped out of the Order's war room several hours later with Rafe, Devony and Jax. None of them said a word as the sound of their combat boots echoed crisply on the marble floor of the corridor.

What was there to say after the night they'd just been through?

Lucan Thorne was as good as a walking dead man after Opus Nostrum's attack.

His Breedmate was in so much shared agony, not even a heavy trance had eased her suffering.

As for their son, the fact that he had made a Minion of the captured Opus soldier had shocked everyone. Not only because that kind of act was considered a violation of honor among the Order, a tactic used by their enemies but never by them, but also because the warrior who had chosen to cross that line had been one of the steadiest, most calmly logical and strategic voices in all of the Order.

Tonight, even Darion Thorne had been pushed beyond his limits.

Nathan could hardly blame him.

Vengeance boiled in the veins of every Order member, himself included. No Breed male wanted to consider the hellish madness of Bloodlust. Nor the horrific suffering it would inflict on their blood-bonded mates.

None of the warriors who'd been in the room with Darion tonight or reporting in virtually from other locations was ready to give up on Lucan. Yet few of them dared hope the Gen One leader of the Order would, by some miracle, be able to recover from the massive dose of Red Dragon he'd ingested.

Nevertheless, the Order agreed as a whole that the search for Lucan would continue and he would be brought home—no matter his condition. Joining the effort, commanders from all major districts, along with their mates, would be en route to D.C. as soon as possible. They were family as much as comrades, and there was nothing more important than coming to the aid of one of their own.

That vow was shared tenfold when it came to Lucan.

Darion hadn't formally declared his intention to assume the Order's leadership during his father's absence—however permanent it may be—but tonight he had stepped easily, if reluctantly, into that role. Nathan and all the rest of the warriors, including the eldest among them, had deferred to Darion for decisions about how they would proceed when it came to Opus. After all, it was his parents who'd both been laid low by this latest strike.

"This is so fucked up," Jax murmured under his breath as the group headed up the corridor. "But I'll tell you what, I bet it was damn satisfying for Dare to drain that son of a bitch tonight."

Rafe let out a short breath. "There won't be any satisfaction for him or the rest of us until there's nothing left of Opus but blood and ashes."

Jax smiled coldly. "Damn straight. What I wouldn't give to be a daywalker, man. Stroll right through their UV bullets and gut every one of the bastards with my bare hands."

Nathan saw the flicker of apprehension in Rafe's eyes at the mention of daywalkers. There were few of them in existence, fewer still who were combat-ready members of the Order. Rafe's mate, Devony, being among that exception.

She had been the first at the war room table tonight to suggest using daywalker warriors to go after suspected Opus leaders, but Nathan was certain everyone had been thinking the same thing.

Everyone, perhaps, except Rafe.

Wrapping a protective arm around Devony's shoulders, Rafe pressed a kiss to her temple. "I've heard enough about Opus and war for one night."

She gave him a weary smile, leaning into his embrace. "Me too. All I want right now is to be in bed and to think about nothing for a while."

Rafe stroked her cheek. "I can help with that."

Jax rolled his eyes as the couple walked away hand-in-hand. "How about you, Captain? It's still early. Want to spar a few rounds with me?"

Nathan shook his head. "Another time, Jax. Jordana will be waiting for me."

The warrior shrugged, then sketched a salute. As Jax headed off toward the weapons room at the other end of the command center, Nathan went up to the residential quarters in the mansion.

He opened the door to the quarters he shared with Jordana and found her pacing the length of the living room rug in a thick bathrobe. Her feet were bare, her long platinum hair still wet from her bath. She froze as he entered the room, then went to him in silence and burrowed deep into his embrace.

For a long while, neither of them spoke.

Nathan rested his face against the top of her head, inhaling the sweet scent of her silken hair and warm skin. He brought her closer, encircling her slender body in his arms and wishing he never had to let go.

"I didn't realize how much I needed to feel you like this until now," he murmured.

Her shallow nod felt more like a tremble. "I know. I can't believe that Lucan is . . ."

She moved in his embrace, tilting her face up to his. Fear and worry shone in her oceanic blue eyes, a deep anxiety he could feel vibrating through the bond they shared.

"Do you think he'll . . . is there any way Lucan can recover?"

Nathan swallowed, gave a slow shake of his head. "I don't know, but it doesn't seem likely."

She drew back some more, her pale brows furrowed. "But didn't you tell me Sterling Chase had nearly gone Rogue once? And what about Tavia? Didn't she come back after months of Bloodlust after Dragos poisoned her with Crimson?"

"Yes, but this is different. Chase beat his blood addiction before it owned him. Tavia had a unique medical history that was reverse engineered in order to help treat her. And as bad as Crimson was, Red Dragon is worse. It's stronger, corrupts faster. I don't know how much of that shit was fired into the vehicle Lucan was trapped inside, but based on what it looked like when we arrived at the Keener place, it had been enough Red Dragon to turn ten Breed males Rogue."

"Oh, God." Jordana's voice reduced to barely a whisper. "And poor Gabrielle."

Nathan gritted his teeth, contempt for Opus's double-edged attack running like acid in his veins. He couldn't help but imagine how easily any one of the warriors could have found themselves in Lucan's position. Even him.

Nathan had never concerned himself with his own welfare—not as one of Dragos's ruthless Hunters, not during the years following his rescue from that hideous program and his subsequent enlistment with the Order. It wasn't until Jordana had entered his life that thoughts about his own life—and death—gave him a bit of pause.

He would rather be dead than bring a moment's pain to his beloved mate. He knew Lucan felt the same about Gabrielle. Every mated Breed male carried that resolve in his heart.

Yet the thought of being separated from Jordana forever, even by death, was an unbearable ache Nathan hoped he never had to face.

"We're going to make Opus pay for what they've done. We're not going to stop searching for Lucan until we find him, either."

"And then what?" Jordana searched his face with an optimism he wished he could feel.

Nathan frowned, lifting the edge of his fingers to stroke Jordana's cheek. He didn't have that answer. No one did. And the odds of having even a slim chance of saving Lucan dwindled with every minute that passed without his return.

"We won't give up on him," Nathan said, gathering Jordana close again. "I don't want to talk anymore about what happened tonight, all right? I just want to feel you. I need to be inside you."

"Nathan, I—"

She moaned as he took her mouth in a heated kiss. Her body was soft against him, fragrant with the mingled scents of soap, shampoo and the creamy, citrus-sweetness that was Jordana. He slid his hand around to the front of her bathrobe and groaned at the soft feel of her bare skin.

She gasped when he picked her up, scooping her into his arms. He walked into their bedroom and his booted feet abruptly stilled.

A pair of Jordana's slacks lay draped over the edge of the big bed along with a pretty silk blouse. On the floor nearby was a pair of low-heeled sandals. The outfit was one of Nathan's favorites on her, something she often chose to wear to the museum on days when she was meeting someone important or presenting a significant exhibit.

"What's this about?"

She flattened her lips as she gazed up at him. "That's what I was going to tell you."

Something about her uncertain expression made his heart begin to thud heavily in his chest. He slowly set her feet down on the floor, but couldn't seem to uncage her from his embrace. "Tell me now."

"The meeting with the colony."

He scowled at the reminder, even though he already knew there would be no persuading Jordana not to accompany Zael and Brynne to the Atlantean conclave. They were planning to fly to Rome in a couple of days, then sail on to the hidden island for the meeting with the colony's council of elders. Nathan couldn't make her stay—nor would he ever stoop to forcing her to his will—but damn if the idea didn't tempt him just a little.

Especially when it appeared she was preparing to go sooner than expected.

She rested her hand lightly on his chest. "After what happened tonight, everything just became more urgent. That includes our alliance with the colony. We can't afford to let any more time slip before we try to solidify their willingness to ally with us if and when the time comes."

"What time is your flight?"

Her long lashes shuttered her eyes for a moment. "We're not flying to Rome anymore. Brynne has decided to stay here in D.C. to help with the search for Lucan, and to strategize with the other daywalkers as needed. So, it'll just be Zael and me going to meet with the colony. He'll use his crystal amulet to teleport us directly to the island."

The amulet that could only transport Atlanteans across time and distance.

"When?" Nathan's voice sounded hollow, even to his own ears.

"We'll be leaving in a couple hours."

He couldn't curb the low growl that curled up from his throat. Ever since she'd informed him of her intention to go to the Atlantean colony in hopes of persuading their trust regarding the Order's proposed alliance, Nathan had been harboring a dread he couldn't express. He knew Jordana was a strong, smart, capable woman who could hold her own intellectually or physically with anyone. She was pure-blooded Atlantean, immortal and powerful, her innate gifts bolstered even further by the blood bond she and Nathan shared.

But he couldn't shake the niggle of apprehension he felt that something—anything—could possibly go wrong on this trip while he would be thousands of miles away, helpless to protect her.

"You're brooding," she gently pointed out. "I wish you wouldn't worry about me."

He scoffed. "You might as well ask me to stop breathing too. You're my mate, Jordana. You're my heart, my reason for living." He stared into her mesmerizing, tropical blue eyes and felt a surge of intense emotion rise inside him. "You're my everything," he whispered thickly. "If anything were to happen to you . . ."

She rose on her toes and pressed her lips to his, chasing away some of his fear with her tender kiss. "I love you, too, Nathan. With every fiber of my being."

"Then don't go." The plea slipped out of his mouth before he could bite it back. It shamed him to hear it, to feel the desperation that sent the words to his tongue. "I don't like this, Jordana. The thought of you so far away, with people I don't know and damn well don't trust, considering it wasn't very long ago that one of the colony inhabitants was exposed as a loyalist to Selene."

Jordana reached up, cradling Nathan's taut jaw in her palm. "I'll be fine. I can handle myself well enough. Besides, Zael will be there with me. Do you think he'd let anything happen to me?"

Nathan shook his head. He didn't doubt his mate or their Atlantean friend. It was everyone else with possible designs on the sole heir to the Atlantean throne who concerned him. To say nothing of Selene herself.

The colony was hidden by a veil that concealed their island from outsiders, thanks to the crystal they had in their possession. There were also lethal Atlantean sentries on guard around the clock, protecting the colony from breaches. But once Jordana was in their domain, who was to say if any of those purportedly peaceful Atlantean exiles might pose the greater threat to her wellbeing?

Nathan's body tensed at the notion. "I'd be more comfortable if I went with you."

Jordana gave a soft laugh. "Even if it were possible for you to teleport along with us, bringing a snarly, scowling Breed warrior to the colony isn't going to make the council more comfortable."

"I'm not always snarly and scowling."

Her contrary-sounding hum vibrated against him. "It wasn't a complaint on my part. I love your snarly, scowling side."

"Careful," he warned, "or that's not the only side of me you'll be stirring."

"That sounds like a challenge I'd like to test."

"Is that right?" A smile tugged at the corner of his mouth despite the fact that he wasn't feeling particularly playful. Then again, Jordana had a way of pulling him out of all his dark moods.

He drew her closer, loosening the tie on her robe at the same time. The front of it fell open and he shoved it off her completely, sucking in a hiss as the heat of her naked body seared him through his clothing. She felt so good, so soft and warm. A spike of need ripped through his veins, making his fangs punch out of his gums while the rest of him went hard as steel against her.

Nathan brought his hands up her sides, spearing his fingers into her hair as he took her mouth in a hungry kiss. The sound she made nearly undid him. When he pulled back from her mouth she was smiling.

"Challenge accepted, then?" she asked, grinding her nudity against his arousal.

Nathan chuckled darkly. "I'm filthy from patrols and you're fresh from a bath. Wouldn't you prefer I clean up for you first?"

Her gaze held his with smoky desire as she shook her head, making her unbound hair dance around her bare shoulders and arms. "All I want right now is you, Nathan."

"I was hoping you'd say that," he growled against her lips as he kissed her.

He took her down with him onto their bed, his love and need for her eclipsing all the ugliness of the past hours . . . and the dread he knew he'd be feeling once it was time to watch her leave for the colony without him.

# CHAPTER 10

As soon as the sun went down that following night, Darion and the rest of the Order hit the streets.

Rogue violence was still rampant all over, but Lucan's longtime comrades had each committed to joining the effort to search for him while their warrior teams held down the forts in their various districts. Chase and Tavia, Tegan and Elise, Rio and Dylan had been among the first to arrive.

Dante had also come with his Breedmate, Tess, whose background in medicine had been immediately put to use in treating Gabrielle. When Darion checked in on his mother before leaving for patrols, she'd been sleeping almost peacefully under a strong sedative Tess had administered.

As for Darion himself, there could be no peace until he'd located his father. So far, he and the team accompanying him on the search had covered more than twenty square miles of D.C. with little to show for it.

Each time they encountered a Rogue on the street or hunkered down in some murky shithole feeding on fresh human prey, Darion held his breath, torn between hoping it was Lucan and praying to hell it wasn't.

Each time he fired one of the Rogue-smoking titanium rounds from his pistol, he wondered how long his father could be expected to survive in the grip of Bloodlust before one of those bullets might seem like a mercy.

Fuck.

The not knowing was a torture of its own. Seeing his fellow warriors—his father's closest friends and brethren—look to him for direction and leadership was nothing he'd ever aspired to, either.

He thought back on all the conversations he'd had with his father about wanting to be in the thick of the action, not simply studying strategy and diplomacy in books and theory. How many times had he pressed for the chance to prove himself in combat as one of the warriors?

He had trained hard for it, been ready for a long time.

He'd never meant for the responsibility to come to him like this, though.

As he and his patrol unit combed a residential area lined with a mixture of suburban houses, Darion's instincts began to prickle with warning. There was nothing overtly suspicious about the modest brick Tudor-style home that sat quietly at the end of the cul-de-sac. Like most of its neighbors, its interior lights were darkened and shades pulled closed according to curfew, yet something about the place gave him pause.

He'd been born with his mother's ability to sense the presence of Breed activity from a healthy distance, and right now those senses were clanging like church bells.

Silently, he motioned to his comrades to split up and surround the house.

Nathan led Rafe and Jax around to the back, while Tegan and Brock joined Darion as he prowled toward the front of the home. There was no need for extrasensory abilities to signal the place was currently occupied by Rogues. Darion could smell spilled blood and death before he got within shouting distance of the house.

The other warriors registered the stench too.

They closed in as one, invading the Rogue nest from both directions in a chaos of smashed doors and broken windows. Every warrior was armed with an ample supply of titanium rounds, yet none of them were quick to pull their triggers as they swept inside.

Not until they were certain Lucan wasn't among the startled pack of nearly a dozen Rogues who'd been sleeping off their recent gorging in the house they had evidently commandeered.

The place reeked of death. Several human bodies, pale from total blood loss, lay motionless on the floor of what had once been a pleasantly appointed living room. Family photos in blood-splattered frames sat on the mantel. A child's sketchbook and brightly colored pencils had been crushed under boots caked with gore.

Based on the neighborhood, Darion guessed they were standing in a Darkhaven, although whoever the Breed family was who'd once occupied it was either slain or turned into blood-addicted monsters like the ones now crouching and hissing as the warriors invaded their den.

None of the twisted, feral faces belonged to Darion's father.

A big male leaped toward Nathan, only to drop to the floor an instant later as the warrior shot him between the eyes. The Rogue contorted violently, howling like a banshee as the titanium did its thing.

The rest of the Rogues flew at the team now. All but one.

As Darion and his comrades ashed one after another, he caught sight of a Rogue attempting to escape down a basement stairwell in the kitchen.

Darion broke away from the others to follow the runner.

He landed at the bottom of the stairs on silent feet, pistol locked and loaded.

The Rogue was cornered, too slow to break the small window and scramble out before Darion caught up to him. Panting heavily, body rocking with the effort, the Rogue started to pivot around slowly.

Darion didn't realize he was holding his breath until he stared at the feral, filthy face and confirmed he'd never seen the male before. Blazing amber eyes threw heat like a furnace. Behind cracked, blood-caked lips, the Rogue's fangs were enormous, dripping thick saliva.

Darion knew he needed to shoot the poor bastard.

If not to protect more innocents from the fate of what happened to the humans upstairs, then to relieve this Breed male of his insatiable hunger and madness.

The Rogue cocked his big head, still panting hard and staring at the weapon aimed at him. Even though there was no discernible sanity in the male's eyes, it wasn't difficult to imagine how normal his life might have been before Red Dragon had him in its grasp.

He hadn't asked for this torment. He didn't deserve it. No one did.

*Pull the damn trigger.*

Darion hesitated another second. The indecision cost him.

The Rogue lunged, springing off his heels at him like a great cat.

From behind Darion's shoulder, a sudden gunshot exploded. The Rogue went down, landing no more than an inch from Darion's boot. Death took hold quickly, but not painlessly.

Darion swung around and met Tegan's cold green gaze in the dark. "Sympathy can get you killed."

Darion nodded once, a grim acknowledgment. In the next moment, Brock and the rest of the team came down the stairs.

"All clear up there," Nathan said.

"Here too," Tegan replied.

And then, a quiet rustle on the other side of the basement drew everyone's attention.

The sound was muffled, but unmistakable. It seemed to be coming from within the wall.

Five warriors prepared to open fire, but Darion held up his hand.

He crept silently toward the area the noise had come from. Household clutter and an old art easel had been carelessly rummaged through and left where it had fallen. It blocked the access to what appeared to be a small cupboard door built into the basement wall.

With his weapon in one hand, Darion cleared the way. He reached for the metal latch and yanked open the door.

A small, pale face peered out.

"Holy hell," Brock cursed from the other side of the room. "It's a little kid."

Darion frowned at the terrified-looking boy. He was Breed, probably around five or six years old. His strawberry-blond hair drooped into his face, matted and tangled. His cheeks were sallow, his big brown eyes ringed with dark circles.

"Come on out of there," Darion said, holstering his pistol. "We're not going to hurt you."

The boy crawled out of the cubbyhole, his movements stiff and weak. His thin shoulders hunched forward, accentuating his emaciated appearance. He wobbled unsteadily on his feet, licking parched, cracked lips.

Brock approached and dropped into a crouch in front of the boy. "What's your name, son?"

"Caleb."

"Do you know where your parents are?"

He lifted his gaze to Brock's and tears started to well. "My dad got really sick. He hurt my mom real bad with his fangs. She wouldn't wake up. He ran away then. I ran down here and hid because I was afraid he was gonna come back and hurt me too."

Darion felt a tendon pulse in his jaw as he listened to the child explain his father's descent into Bloodlust. "How long ago was that, Caleb?"

A weak shrug. "I'm not sure."

Brock's concerned gaze swung to Darion. "From his condition, I'd say he's been in there for close to a week. He's practically starving."

"Shit." Darion glanced at Tegan and his other comrades. "We can't leave him here."

Nathan shook his head, a response echoed by the rest of the warriors.

"First thing he needs is nourishment," Brock said.

Darion nodded. "There's a place in Georgetown."

"I know the one," Jax said. Most unmated Breed vampires were familiar with the parlors that employed willing human blood Hosts. Since the Rogue trouble started and curfews were put in place, few of the reputable parlors remained open now. "The owner's a friend. She'll make an exception for this."

Darion could see that despite Caleb's fear, he trusted Brock. The kid had no place with the Order, but it didn't appear he had anywhere else to go.

"Brock, take the boy and go with Jax. After he's fed, bring him to headquarters. Find somewhere there for him to stay until we can figure out what to do with him."

The big warrior carefully steered the child away from the worst of the carnage in the Darkhaven as the group exited the house.

Darion's gaze snagged on the fireplace photos as he passed, noting that the smiling face of Caleb's father looked undeniably familiar. It was the same face that belonged to the Rogue who'd been ashed in the basement only moments before they found the boy.

With a low curse, he stepped around one of the dead humans and headed for the bracing chill of the night air outside.

# CHAPTER 11

The kid had barely uttered a word between the time Brock and Jax had driven him to the blood Host parlor in Georgetown and the ride back to the Order's headquarters afterward.

As Jax paused at the compound's gate, Brock pivoted to look at Caleb in the backseat of the Order's SUV. "You doin' okay?"

A shallow nod. The boy didn't look at him. He stared out the dark-tinted windows at the spacious grounds and the large mansion that practically glowed under the moonlight overhead.

"What is this place?" he finally murmured.

"This is the Order's compound. It's where we all live and work together."

Caleb glanced at him. "You mean it's your family's Darkhaven?"

Brock nodded. "Yeah, I guess it is."

It seemed a little strange to call the command center with its weapons room and tech lab by the name typically applied to civilian Breed homes. Then again, Brock knew of few families who were closer-knit than he and his warrior brethren and their mates.

"You'll be safe here, Caleb. I promise."

The boy gave him another nod, still a bit uncertain. And no wonder. The hell he'd lived through—the terror of what happened to his parents—it wasn't going to leave him anytime soon. Possibly never.

Brock wished his Breed ability for taking away pain extended beyond basic humans. God knew Caleb could use help purging some of the shock and grief that still radiated from his small frame.

The best anyone could do for the orphaned kid right now was make him comfortable until they could find a relative or someone else to come claim him.

Although leaving him in the city to fend for himself had been out of the question, the last thing Brock or anyone else at headquarters needed right now was a foundling in need of a home and family.

Jax drove into the underground garage and parked the vehicle.

Brock glanced at him. "Give me a few minutes to drop Caleb with Jenna, then we can head back out to rejoin the patrols."

Jax nodded. "No problem."

Brock helped Caleb out of the vehicle and led him into the command center. He probably should have called ahead to warn Jenna he was bringing the kid, but she wasn't the type to balk at helping someone in need. Especially a child. After losing her six-year-old daughter, Libby, long before she and Brock met, Jenna had an extra-soft spot for children.

"Who's Jenna?" Caleb asked as he walked the corridor at Brock's side.

"She's my mate."

The boy nodded, then peered up at him in question. "Do you have any kids?"

"No, but not for lack of practice."

Caleb's face scrunched. "What do you mean?"

Brock smiled. "Never mind."

They paused in the hallway outside the archives room, Jenna's natural habitat. The door was open, but when Brock peered inside she was nowhere to be seen.

"She must be in our quarters up at the residence." Brock put his hand around Caleb's thin shoulders. "Come on, it's this way."

Brock attempted casual conversation with the boy as they took the elevator up to the mansion at street level. Caleb's answers were short and somewhat shy, but at least some color had come back into his cheeks since his feeding. After a bath and fresh clothes, he'd smell a hell of a lot better too.

"Hang on for a second," Brock told the kid once they had reached the door to the quarters he and Jenna shared. "I just want to give her a heads-up before I make the introductions, okay?"

"Okay," Caleb said.

Brock opened the door and stepped inside. "Hey, Jen?"

No reply.

"Babe, you in here?" He walked through the living area, his steps quickening as a prickle of unease skated over his senses. "Jenna?"

He found her on their bed, sound asleep.

Except, something about the stillness of her body— and her lack of response when he called out to her— turned that gnawing unease into full-blown alarm.

*"Jenna."*

He was at her side in a flash of movement. She was breathing shallowly, yet steadily.

Alive, but unconscious.

Brock lifted her hand to his lips, the warmth of her a small relief when she was lying there as motionless and silent as a corpse.

"Wake up, Jenna." He shook her gently, then with more force. And still no response. "Come on, angel. Please, wake up."

He had known a lifetime's worth of concern for his extraordinary mate over the years, but seeing her like this raked him wide open.

The strangled cry that tore from his throat brought Caleb running to him. Panic filled the boy's face. He stared at Brock with a thousand-yard gaze, perhaps because of Jenna's unusual appearance, or because of the emotion in Brock's eyes that he was powerless to hide.

Caleb swallowed. "Is she—"

"No." The answer burst out of Brock like a curse. "Go get help, Caleb. Find anyone you can in the mansion. Tell them where I am. Hurry."

The boy nodded vigorously, then took off in a blur of motion.

# CHAPTER 12

Seated on the elaborate throne in the hall of the grand palace, it was an effort for Selene to listen and smile approvingly as a group of Atlantean musicians played the piece they had composed in her honor.

The music itself was lovely. The angelic voices of the three females and two males filled the palace as if it were a cathedral, while soaring strings and playful horns parried and danced with the ethereal notes of an elegant harp.

Music and art were revered among the Atlantean people. Selene normally enjoyed both, but today her mind was restless. She shifted on the velvet cushion of the fussy throne made of carved white marble with inlaid jewels, pearls, and abalone shells. Personally, she'd have preferred something less ostentatious, however, the piece had been crafted for her as a gift from the realm's best sculptors as part of the new palace's construction.

Her fidgeting drew the attention of one of the musicians, who apparently mistook her distractedness for displeasure and nervously plucked a discordant note on her harp.

The mistake drew gasps from a few of the courtiers and royal attendants who had gathered in the palace to enjoy the entertainment at Selene's invitation. As the song ended, total silence filled the chamber.

Gazes lifted to the throne on the platform at the top of the marble steps, everyone waiting for their queen's response to the imperfection.

Did they truly think her such a tyrant?

Selene didn't want to know. She shouldn't need to fret over what her people thought of her. Her sole comfort came from the knowledge that every citizen under her rule was kept safe and protected because of her. Because of the sacrifices she had made in order to preserve the Atlantean way of life.

Whether they feared her or despised her was of little consequence so long as each man, woman, and child was able to thrive in peace and harmony. At least, that's what she told herself at times like this, when several hundred faces were looking toward her as if she might erupt with lightning shooting out of her fingertips and her hair on fire.

"Delightful," she declared coolly, giving a mild nod of approval to the group of musicians.

Applause broke out at once, an almost palpable wave of relief sweeping over the cavernous room.

The troupe bowed and curtsied, happy smiles beaming. As they collected their instruments and departed the chamber along with the rest of the audience, Selene's attention drifted to her seer, who stood over her scrying bowl in the salon just off the main chamber. Nuranthia's dark brows were knit as she swept her hand across the surface of the water in the golden basin.

Selene tried not to stare, but her every instinct was pricked with warning. The hubbub of the departing citizens faded to background noise as Nuranthia glanced up and her troubled eyes met Selene's gaze.

Something was wrong.

As soon as the hall had emptied, Selene descended the steps from the throne and crossed the gleaming floors to where Nuranthia waited. The woman was nervous as Selene approached, restlessly folding and unfolding her arms across the front of her.

"What is it?" Selene asked, her own anxiety making the question sound like a demand. "What do you see?"

"Your Grace, I—" Nuranthia flattened her lips, her eyes darting from the bowl to Selene and back again as Selene approached. "I'm not sure why this vision has appeared. I don't know who this is, but doesn't she look a bit like . . ."

Selene peered into the bowl. Her breath rushed inward and stayed there, frozen in her lungs as the name Nuranthia was hesitant to speak rang like a clarion in every fiber of Selene's being.

Soraya.

Except the beautiful blonde woman strolling through the sunlit garden bursting with ripe lemon trees and bushes laden with enormous roses wasn't Selene's deceased daughter. It was Jordana.

She smiled as she paused and brought one of the velvety red blooms to her nose. The pureness of her joy brought a lump of raw emotion to Selene's throat.

Her granddaughter looked close enough to touch.

Of its own accord, Selene's hand reached toward the water in the basin, hovering above the liquid image of the one person who meant everything to her.

As Selene stared at the vision in the seer's bowl, someone else stepped close to Jordana, drawing her attention away from the rose. Selene's outstretched hand closed into a fist as the face of Jordana's companion came into clearer focus.

Zael.

And the traitor wasn't alone.

They were among other Atlanteans. Faces Selene hadn't seen for thousands of years but would never forget.

Exiles who'd chosen to desert her in favor of creating their own community.

Jordana was at the colony this very moment.

Nuranthia quietly cleared her throat. "Your Grace, those people . . . aren't they—"

Selene dropped her hand into the water with a splash. The vision dissolved, nothing but small, rippling waves in the bottom of the bowl. "Say nothing of this to anyone, Nuranthia."

The seer nodded and bowed. "Yes, Your Grace. As you wish."

Once she was gone, Selene let go of a furious curse. She could think of only one reason that Zael and Jordana would be at the colony: They wanted the crystal.

So, the Order was not opposed to using her own granddaughter against her? Using Jordana against her own people?

It was no surprise that a faithless defector like Zael might attempt to charm his way into the colony's good graces, but had Jordana's time among the Breed corrupted her so thoroughly too?

Selene fumed at the very notion.

As for the colony and its council of elders, Selene harbored more than a little bitterness for them as well. Many of them she had considered friends once. Perhaps that was why she had permitted their insult to stand when they broke away from the realm to form their colony.

They had thought themselves so clever, stealing away to their private haven with one of Atlantis's crystals. Selene had known of its location within the colony all along, yet resisted the temptation to reclaim it.

Ripping it away from them would be tantamount to sealing their doom, because like her own realm the colony was only hidden and protected as long as they had a crystal in their possession.

If the Order had sent Zael and Jordana to recruit an alliance with the colony in hopes of winning the crystal for Lucan Thorne, they were in for disappointment. The colony could never give it up willingly and hope to survive.

Unless the Order intended something more underhanded.

Would they stoop to stealing the crystal?

There was nothing more heinous to her mind than duplicity. Yet as she thought about the thinly veiled threats flung at her by Lucan's arrogant son not so long ago, a sick kind of worry built in her gut that the Breed warriors might, indeed, stop at nothing to obtain enough crystal power to rule everything in their sight.

She could not let that happen.

But even more piercing than that fear was the ache in her heart that lingered after glimpsing Jordana in the seer's bowl. How she longed to hold her only kin again. It was a right she'd been deprived of for more than twenty-five years, first by Jordana's father Cassianus when he abducted the precious infant from the realm and hid her away among the Breed and mortals, and now by the Order.

To think her grandchild was practically under her nose at the colony.

The urge to summon her royal legion and storm the island en masse beat like a war drum in Selene's ears. But the same veil that sealed off the colony to outsiders would also shield it from her army.

Only another crystal could breach the veil's protection.

Or something nearly as powerful.

*Her.*

# CHAPTER 13

Gabrielle was burning up and freezing at the same time.

On a groan, sleep still weighing her down with unnatural heaviness, she pushed the coverlet away from her shivering, yet feverish, body. Darkness surrounded her in the quiet bedroom. No sound at all but the wet patter of rain sluicing down the shaded windows and the pair of French doors on the other side of the room.

Tess had pulled the curtains away from the glass doors the last time she'd come in to check on Gabrielle and to administer another dose of the strong tranquilizers that were barely managing to keep the worst of her pain at bay.

Gabrielle hadn't wanted the sedatives. As excruciating as her agony was, feeling it meant Lucan was still alive. She could hardly bear the havoc being wreaked on her body and mind, but the only thing worse was the fear of waking up and discovering she no longer felt him at all.

Another wave of pain lanced through her, making her jackknife up off the mattress on a sharp hiss.

Swinging her heavy legs over the side of the bed, she sat there for a moment, her body heaving with every breath, her heart banging inside her rib cage like a drum.

But beneath the terrible discomfort, a low vibration seemed to pulse deep in her marrow.

Beneath the racking hunger she felt through the blood bond, and thick fog of Tess's medicines, she felt something else. A sense of yearning. The quiet echo of a bleak sorrow and jagged regret that seemed to have no end.

"Lucan?" Her voice was airless, her throat too parched to make any sound.

She stood up, pushing through the nausea that swamped her and blurred her vision. Her legs trembled beneath her as she slowly staggered across the floor of the bedroom, guided only by her senses and the thin light from a crescent moon that filtered in through the rain-soaked French doors.

As she drew nearer, she saw a large, dark shape slumped against the glass.

She blinked away the narcotic haze that clung to her senses. The outline of broad, muscular shoulders and a lowered head covered in wet black hair came into clearer focus with each halting step she took.

She didn't need to see Lucan's face to know it was him. Her heart would recognize him anywhere, and there was no drug strong enough to dim her blood connection to him.

"Lucan!" The hoarse cry tore from her lips as her legs gave out and she sank down on the floor in front of the glass doors.

Her sob drew his head up slowly. Rain soaked him, droplets streaking down his hollowed cheeks and off his chin. His glowing amber eyes scorched her, the pain in them carving right into her soul.

"My love," she gasped, and reached up to unlock the door.

Lucan's feral growl shook the glass. The warning in that terrible sound was unmistakable. He moved away from her, snarling through his enormous fangs.

He was a terrifying sight, yet she had never wanted anything more than to open the door and run into his arms. His growl only deepened, and she feared if she pushed him now he might disappear—possibly never to return.

Instead, she flattened her palm against the cold glass. She held his feral gaze, mouthing his name as hot tears spilled down her cheeks.

It took him a moment, but then he slowly moved forward again and pressed his big hand against hers. His fevered skin seemed heated enough to melt the glass that separated them. His face was dirty with soot and grime beneath the wet hanks of hair that drooped over his brow. Dried blood stained the strong, squared chin that was now shadowed with dark whiskers.

And his eyes . . . the fiery irises swallowed up his elliptical pupils, staring back at Gabrielle with torment and the wild madness of Bloodlust.

She started to cry.

She didn't want to be weak in front of him, especially when it was he who bore the worst suffering. But she couldn't help herself. Sorrow sliced her wide open.

"I'm sorry," she murmured, understanding she was only making his pain worse by giving in to her own.

She could feel his hunger and longing as he stared at her. He was starving, even though it appeared he had recently hunted and fed. His blazing eyes slid away from her gaze, down to the column of her throat.

"Lucan, please, let me help you," she pleaded with him through the glass. "You can beat this, I know it. We'll do it together."

Sweeping her hair around to one shoulder, she bared the side of her neck. He growled again, but his amber eyes remained fixed on her carotid.

Hope flared inside her.

"That's right," she said. "Let me be strong for you this time."

Slowly, she reached up for the lock on the door. When it clicked free, the sound echoed like a gunshot in the quiet of the bedroom. A small red light blinked to life above the door frame, signaling the headquarters' silent security system had been activated.

Gabrielle hardly noticed it, all her attention rooted on Lucan's hungered expression.

Not even a moment later, the suite's primary entrance burst open from the corridor. "Mom, are you all right?"

Gabrielle was getting to her feet to open the French doors when Darion rushed into the bedroom. He halted, one strong hand moving to the pistol holstered around his weapons belt as he stared at the Rogue crouched outside.

"Holy hell. Mother, move away from the glass."

She couldn't obey the command, even if she couldn't deny the small note of fear she felt in the face of Lucan's advanced condition.

Outside, Lucan got to his feet as he stared at his son. Then he started to pivot away.

"Don't go," Gabrielle cried.

She was about to open the door but Darion moved faster. One instant he was several paces behind her, the next he had thrown open the French doors and was on Lucan's heels as his father attempted to run.

Darion tackled him to the ground. Lucan's roar split the night, as deep as the thunder that rolled overhead. Gabrielle's heart lunged into her throat to see the two men she loved more than anything else in the world locked in a violent struggle on the ground.

"Stop, both of you!"

They were both too strong-willed to surrender. Too similar in so many ways.

And too evenly matched in terms of power and strength.

Several other warriors stormed into the room now. Tegan. Dante. Rio. Nikolai. They flashed past her and out to the yard where Lucan was beginning to gain some advantage.

It took all five of them to slow him down, but his rage was animalistic, his madness making him brutal and unhinged.

Dante's Breedmate, Tess, came running into the room now too. She carried her medical bag in hand, pausing only long enough to dump the contents onto the bed and hastily prepare a handful of syringes.

Gabrielle swung a panicked glance at her friend. "Please, don't hurt him."

"I promise, I won't."

Out on the wet grass, Darion and the others finally had Lucan subdued, though he continued to struggle and roar his rage. Gabrielle watched with her heart in her throat as Tess ran out to assist the warriors. Lucan's confusion and fury as they tackled him and forcibly held him down was almost as unbearable as his other pain.

Tess's hands moved like quicksilver as she administered one dose of medication after another to Lucan. Gabrielle felt some of his fight leach out of him as the tranquilizers raced into his corrupted bloodstream.

She felt the worst of his agony and hunger begin to ebb as the sedatives took hold. Then she watched in a tangled mixture of relief and unspeakable worry as his son and brethren carried his listless body into the house.

# CHAPTER 14

The meeting with the colony's council of elders was not proving as productive as Jordana and Zael had hoped.

While the four Atlanteans who currently governed the island settlement had been more than welcoming since she and Zael had arrived, talks surrounding their crystal had reached a standstill.

"I trust you understand the colony's position," said Baramael, a large male with short, spiky jet-black hair and dual-colored eyes, one blue, the other as gold as a coin. "We'll do whatever we can to assist you and the Order if and when the need for our help is required—against Selene or equally dangerous threats—short of giving up our crystal, that is."

"I do understand, of course," Zael replied, but the glance he sent Jordana's way was one of grim disappointment.

The group had decided to conclude their meeting away from the confines of the council chamber to stroll casually through one of the fragrant, beautiful gardens that bloomed outside.

Although the purpose of their visit to the colony had been a sober one, Jordana found it next to impossible to resist stopping here and there to enjoy the colorful flowers, ripe fruits, and lush greenery.

One of the females on the council, Anaphiel, slowed beside her to point out a trellis that burst with a riot of unusual, rainbow-hued blossoms.

"This one you'll only find in Atlantean gardens," she told Jordana, her sapphire-blue eyes sparkling with pride against the buttery, mocha-soft glow of her lovely face. A coil of delicate black braids sat atop her head like a crown. "Come and smell its perfume."

Jordana leaned forward to inhale the sweet, multi-layered fragrance that reminded her of nothing else she had ever known. "It's . . . heavenly."

"That is exactly what it's called, but in the Atlantean native tongue," Anaphiel said.

Then she spoke the unfamiliar word, and the melodic sound of the foreign syllables stirred a sense of wonder and innate belonging inside Jordana.

"You remind me so much of your mother, the princess," said the other female, Nathiri. The gentle blonde had been quietly studying Jordana ever since she and Zael had arrived on the island. She smiled now, her silvery-gray eyes tender with remembrance. "Soraya was a dear friend of mine a long time ago."

Jordana's heart squeezed. "I don't recall anything about her."

Nathiri soberly shook her head. "You were an infant when . . . when your father took you away to live in the outside world."

"You were going to say when my mother died." Jordana tried not to think about the awful way her mother had chosen to end her life. Zael had told her enough when she first met him, but many of the details of her mother's life in Selene's court remained questions Jordana didn't know how to ask.

Nathiri exchanged a sympathetic look with the other colony members before meeting Jordana's gaze once more. "Your mother was beloved by everyone in the realm, including those of us here in the colony. News of that horrible tragedy hit us all very hard. We mourned the news of Cassianus's death more recently too."

"My father was a good man," Jordana murmured, earning a confirming nod from Zael. "I only wish he'd trusted me with the truth of my origins from the beginning. He cheated me out of knowing either one of them."

Anaphiel rested a tender hand on Jordana's arm. "Sometimes, people do things out of love without weighing all of the ramifications."

"What about my mother's father?" Jordana asked, curious now. "Who is he?"

"Only Selene knows that answer," Nathiri said. "The queen has never taken a mate or acknowledged a consort."

Harroth scoffed under his breath. "There was one man who found his way into Selene's bed. Endymion." He spoke the name like a curse.

Baramael's expression was filled with contempt as well. "He's the traitor who played Selene for a fool and cost the realm everything when he gave two of our crystals to the Ancients. But Endymion is not your grandfather, Jordana. That man was fully human, and you are pure-blooded Atlantean."

"Selene and Endymion." As Jordana said the names, her thoughts whisked back to the sculpture that had been in her exhibit at the Museum of Fine Art in Boston. That piece had been an elaborate fake, a clever ruse her father had used to hide the crystal he'd taken from the realm the same night he'd stolen her away.

"What happened to Endymion?" she asked.

Zael was the one who answered. "After the theft was discovered, Selene summoned her legion and hunted him down personally. She took her time killing him with Atlantean light, not satisfied until there was nothing left of him but ashes."

"Not that it mattered," Harroth said. "The damage had already been done. Because of her, the crystals were lost to our enemies. Within days, the entire settlement of Atlantis was swallowed up by the great wave they unleashed on us."

Jordana pressed her hand to her stomach, sick with the thought of both Endymion's betrayal and the massacre of the Atlantean people that followed. There was even a small part of her that felt a little sympathy toward Selene for having placed her trust in the wrong person and then been forced to live with the devastating consequences of her mistake every day since.

"For obvious reasons," Anaphiel interjected, "we all have cause to be wary when it comes to Selene, but I can't help but wonder if perhaps she is the lesser existential threat than others. Rumors are swirling even among our people about the power of this terror group in the mortal world that calls itself Opus Nostrum."

Zael nodded at the female. "Opus is a problem, yes. But the Order is handling it even as we speak."

Harroth made a low, skeptical noise in the back of his throat. "Another thing you have yet to bring up since you arrived is the recent disturbance that occurred on the Asian continent. Every Atlantean around the globe felt the explosion that occurred in the region of Siberia. It could have only been created by an Atlantean crystal."

Baramael's bi-colored gaze was deadly sober. "More than one crystal, based on the sheer force of the detonation it caused."

Zael glanced at Jordana and cleared his throat. "I can assure you, we are also aware of the event in the Deadlands. That, and the escalating trouble with Opus Nostrum are both of utmost concern to the Order."

"As they should be," Baramael replied. "In the meantime, we've sent a group of colony sentries to the region to investigate the disturbance."

Jordana drew in a breath. "You sent people into the Deadlands? Do you think that's wise?"

All four Atlantean council members looked at her in confusion—and no small amount of suspicion.

A scowl furrowed on Harroth's dark brow. "Why do you ask? What is it you and Zael haven't told us about—"

He didn't get a chance to finish speaking.

A hot breeze kicked up out of nowhere, followed by a burst of white light.

In the next moment, a female shape appeared inside the center of the large, blinding orb that hovered barely an inch off the ground.

"Fuck." Zael's curse exploded off his tongue as he reached for Jordana, thrusting her behind him. *"Selene."*

He didn't have to say the Atlantean queen's name aloud for Jordana to understand the threat that had just become very, very real.

Her sandaled feet touched down on the soft earth of the garden, all of her surrounded by the halo of pure white light. She wore a pale peach gown that looked as fine as gossamer, with figure-skimming long skirts and a similarly diaphanous cape that flowed off the back of her shoulders. A braided circlet of gold rested around her slender waist.

She was, in a word, breathtaking.

Her long hair was a similar platinum shade as Jordana's, but infused with an otherworldly pearlescence that seemed to make it glow from within. Her face was beyond beautiful, heart-shaped and delicate, with high cheekbones and perfectly bowed lips.

She might have been mistaken for an angel if not for the dangerous glint in her shrewd, glacier-blue eyes. Those arresting eyes looked past Zael's broad shoulders, zeroing in with laser focus on Jordana.

"What a lovely day for a stroll in the gardens."

Zael and the other Atlanteans stood as if poised for combat, their palms illuminated with powerful energy. Harroth slanted a dark glare in Zael's direction.

"Did your carelessness lead her here? She's never been able to find the colony and breach our veil before now."

"No," Zael answered with force. "I would never do that. I swear it."

Selene smiled with chilling amusement. "Do you forget your queen's might so quickly? I am the oldest and purest of our kind in existence on this Earth. Few barriers can stand against me if I will it."

Baramael lowered his head like a bull about to charge. "If you've come for the crystal, you'll have to get through me and the rest of the colony first."

"Careful, Baramael." She sliced a furious look at him. "You do not want to tempt me. Do you think you'd still have the crystal if I had decided to take it back?"

Her attention returned to Jordana. Zael swore a curse and edged her farther behind him.

"She's come for something else."

Jordana drew in a breath, seeing the dark intent in her grandmother's beautiful face. All of Nathan's warnings and worries began to replay in her mind. So did the promises she'd made him—her reassurances that she would be safe, that she could handle herself if anything went wrong at the colony.

Now that she stood in front of this astonishing being in the flesh, it was all Jordana could do not to tremble.

Instead, she balled her fists, summoning the power that lived inside her.

Zael edged away from Selene and the orb that surrounded her. He shook his head. "You can't have her, Selene."

"No? We'll see about that."

A jerk of her wrist sent a huge bolt of light flying at him. Zael released his own light to block it, but the power shooting from his glowing palms wasn't enough. Selene's assault drove him to one knee. As formidable as Zael was, the blow took everything out of him, leaving him coughing and heaving for breath.

At the same time, the other Atlanteans, including Jordana, released their power at Selene. The jagged streams of light bounced off her shielding orb, but they didn't let up. Jordana gritted her teeth with the effort, letting loose a roar of fury and determination.

To the Atlantean queen, it must have all seemed like a joke.

With barely a flick of her finger, she sent fiery spheres of light hurtling at each of the Atlanteans. They went down to their knees one by one, panting, utterly drained.

And then, only Jordana remained standing.

She unleashed everything she had on the woman calmly staring at her from within her cocoon of light. To no avail. All she accomplished was her own exhaustion.

"I haven't come to cause harm to you, Jordana." Selene's voice sounded so sincere, it would be easy to believe her. Easier, if not for the five depleted immortals groaning and struggling to catch their breath on the ground at her feet.

"You are my own blood, child. I could no more harm you than harm myself."

Jordana bit off a sharp, humorless laugh. "Is that what you told my mother before you locked her away and drove her to set herself on fire rather than live under your tyranny?"

Selene's head snapped back slightly, a shocked, wounded look on her face. It was there and gone in an instant, replaced by icy resolve.

"I'm bringing you home, Jordana."

"My home isn't with you," she shot back. "It never was."

She sent another blast of power forward, but it was no use.

Selene's shield glowed brighter and brighter . . . until its light was all Jordana could see.

She heard Zael call her name. It was a distant-sounding shout, muffled and fading fast.

The soft earth of the garden path beneath her feet fell away, then the world around her sped into a dizzying blur of light and motion.

# CHAPTER 15

It was sometime past dawn following what felt like one of the longest nights of Darion's life.

His father was home at last, though not out of the woods by a longshot when it came to his physical and mental states. After wrangling him inside with the help of several Order warriors, Lucan was currently sleeping off several gorilla-sized doses of Ketamine in the command center's holding tank.

The irony wasn't lost on Darion that the titanium-reinforced, ultraviolet-light-enhanced bars that Gideon had engineered to hold a raging Ancient, if they ever needed to, were now the only thing keeping the Order's leader from escaping. Although, even that was up for debate if they ran low on Tess's supply of sedatives.

Even laid low with pain through the blood bond, Gabrielle was a forced to be reckoned with herself. She had protested the plan to hold Lucan in the prisoner's cell, but Tess, Savannah, Elise, and the other Breedmates who'd arrived in D.C. overnight with their mates had managed to convince her that it was the safest place for him to be for the time being. However, there had been no dissuading her from demanding a cot be set up for her to sleep in the chamber adjacent to Lucan's cell.

And the hits kept coming.

Jenna remained unconscious without explanation. Her vital signs were strong, but Tess and Gideon had determined she'd slipped into some kind of coma. Brock was practically out of his mind with concern, hardly willing to leave her bedside. Darion had made Brock personally responsible for the Darkhaven boy, hoping that looking after Caleb might help the big warrior cope with the uncertainty of his mate's condition until they could figure out what had happened to her.

The only good news to arrive in the past few hours was the report from Darion's Minion that he had met with Ahmed Touati at his office as directed. Unbeknownst to the Opus covert operative, Gopnik had hand-delivered a nasty little surprise package which Gideon had prepared especially for the occasion.

"You're sure this is going to work?" Darion asked, looking at Gideon across the war room conference table from him and several other Order warriors.

"I'm sure." He winced slightly behind his glasses. "I'm about ninety-nine-point-nine percent sure."

Darion wasn't used to hearing even that much doubt in the tech genius's estimates. No one else gathered around the table looked comfortable with the thought, either.

"What might go wrong?"

Gideon scrubbed a hand over his disheveled blond hair. "Probably nothing, but there are a lot of moving parts to this plan."

"That's situation normal for us," Sterling Chase interjected. The Boston-based commander leaned forward, resting his elbows on the edge of the table. "I thought you said your software worm was airtight."

"Yes, I did. And it is."

"So, where's the problem, Gid?" Dante pressed from his seat next to Chase.

"I had a bit of a scramble adjusting to our new delivery method."

"Delivery method," Kade echoed, his smile almost wolfish. "You mean, AKA Scarface, our Minion courier?"

Nikolai grunted at the reminder of Darion's overstep. "More specifically, Gid's talking about the nanobot technology Gopnik carried into our unsuspecting Mr. Touati's office. Nice work on that, by the way."

Gideon grinned. "Thanks. The technology is impressive, if I do say so myself, but it's delicate."

"How so?" Tegan piped in from the far end of the table.

"Well, for one thing, it requires skin-to-skin contact in order to transfer from the carrier to the host."

"We're covered there," Darion said. "I gave Gopnik specific instructions that he had to find a way to put his hands on Touati. Handshake, fist bump, face punch. Whatever worked. He's assured me he completed the task."

Gideon nodded. "That's step one. Now, we have to wait and hope that Touati touches his phone or computer so he can transfer the nanobots to one of the devices and deploy the worm to infiltrate his secured network. Once that happens, we can pinpoint where each of his Opus comrades are located and go after them. So far, Touati hasn't made the transfer. My console will light up like a Christmas tree the second we're in."

Dante smirked. "Anyone got Touati's private number? I'll call and tell him his refrigerator's running."

A few of the warriors chuckled. Even Darion's mouth quirked in spite of the gravity of the conversation.

Gideon cleared his throat. "And, of course, there is a further wrinkle. If this attempt ultimately fails and we're unable to hack into Opus's secured network from either of Touati's devices, we're right back where we started."

"Then we start over." This time it was Hunter who spoke. His golden eyes shone with flat logic and cold determination. "We keep going until our mission's goal is met."

"Ah, right," Gideon hedged. "Unfortunately, it's not quite as simple as that."

Darion didn't like the sound of that. He folded his arms across his chest. "Explain."

"The software worm is the easy part. I've been ready with that for weeks. I can recreate the nanobot tech too. The problem is delivery. The bots can live for approximately twenty-four hours before they begin to degrade." He let out a sigh. "When the nanobots break up and die, they also kill both their carrier and host."

Darion scowled. "You're saying by this time tomorrow, both Gopnik and Touati will be dead?"

"Yeah, give or take a few minutes."

*"Madre de Dios,"* Rio muttered, slapping his palms on the table and pushing out of his chair to pace. "It took this long to get a bead on Touati. How long will it take us to ID another member of Opus's inner circle?"

"Not to mention the fact that we can't go around making Minions out of every Opus foot soldier we find," Chase remarked with a pointed look at Darion. He may have left his Enforcement Agency past far behind in the decades he'd been part of the Order, but there was still a rigid by-the-book sense of propriety about the male.

"I'm not making any apologies when it comes to Opus," Darion growled. "Nor when it comes to anyone else who thinks the Order's going to sit back and watch the world burn on our watch. Opus. The Ancient. The Atlanteans and their queen. Far as I'm concerned, they're all on notice. We didn't start this war, but we're sure as fuck going to finish it."

Assenting nods circled the room as he spoke. Even Chase finally gave in, inclining his head in agreement over the tops of his steepled hands.

"You honor him well," the commander said. "Lucan would be damned proud to be in this room and see you now."

Darion mentally shook off the praise, feeling undeserving. "I'd rather see him back at the head of this table again. Until that's possible, we're all going to do whatever it takes to win this fight. Agreed?"

"Agreed," they all answered as one.

Just then, a roar went up from somewhere in the command center.

Everyone jolted out of their seats. Anxious gazes swung from one warrior to another at the enraged howl that echoed all around them.

"Sounds like Lucan's gonna need another hit of Ketamine," Kade said, his tone more grave than humorous.

Darion shook his head. "That's not my father."

At the same time, Nathan burst into the war room. His face was ashen, his eyes stark with fury . . . and fear.

"Jordana." His voice shook with dark emotions. "Something's happened to her. She's scared as hell and I—"

A sudden charge crackled in the air of the war room then Zael dropped to the floor, materializing out of nowhere. The Atlantean soldier looked bone-weary, beaten. He lifted his head and his regret-filled gaze searched out Nathan.

"She's gone," he gasped. "I'm sorry. Selene has taken Jordana."

# CHAPTER 16

It hadn't gone the way Selene had hoped at all.

She teleported back to the realm with Jordana, touching down in a luxuriously appointed chamber on the same floor of the palace as the royal living quarters. As soon as their feet touched the rug-covered marble floors, Jordana lunged at her with a furious scream.

Selene blocked her granddaughter's clawing hands with a wave of her wrist, constructing a thin wall of light between them.

"Please, don't fight me, Jordana."

"Fight you?" she snarled. "I'll kill you if you don't let me go!"

Selene frowned, rubbing at the heaviness in the center of her chest as she stared into Jordana's tear-filled, desperate eyes. Selene had actually thought Jordana would be relieved—even if just a little bit—to be returned to her true home. Grateful to be reunited with her sole remaining family and her own kind.

Instead, she was enraged.

Terrified, even.

Jordana's beautiful face was filled with fear and loathing as she summoned fireballs to her palms and tried to let them fly at Selene. Tried, but failed.

Even at her young age of twenty-five, Jordana was surprisingly powerful. Being of the royal Atlantean line, it came as no surprise. But Selene had not been boasting when she reminded Zael and the others at the colony of her matchless strength as one of the eldest of their kind and their queen.

Still, leaving the realm and combatting the group at the colony had taken its toll.

This struggle with Jordana was costing precious energy as well.

Selene deflected yet another attempted blast from the young woman's glowing palms. She couldn't let it continue. Not only for her own wellbeing, but Jordana's as well.

Using the power of her mind and the energy that lived inside her, Selene wrapped Jordana's wrists in manacles of soft white light, immobilizing them.

"I'm sorry, Jordana. This is the only way."

Jordana vigorously fought their hold, but she would not get free. Tears streaked her face. "What kind of a monster are you? Dammit, let me go!"

The words cut deeper than expected. It wasn't the first time Selene had heard them flung at her by someone who meant the world to her. She could hardly look at Jordana and not see Soraya.

Was she making a similar mistake again?

She didn't think she could bear it if her impulsive actions today ended up hurting Jordana any more than they already had.

"I am sorry," she repeated, then turned and quietly departed the room.

When she stepped outside and closed the door behind her, she found Sebathiel standing there. His blue eyes narrowed on her, stern with disapproval.

"Tell me that's not who I think it is inside that room."

She stepped past him. "I don't have to explain myself to anyone. That includes you, High Chancellor."

"Selene." He reached for her arm, halting her. His face softened, though not by much. "What have you done?"

"What I would've done years ago, if I'd had the chance."

Seb shook his head and let out a low curse. "Where was she? Who brought her to you?"

Selene pulled out of his grasp, lifting her chin. "Does it matter?"

"It does to me. You, of all people, should understand why."

She bristled at the intimacy of the statement, despite the fact that there was no one else around to hear it. "And you, of all people, should understand the only one with any say over my heirs is me. In case you need a reminder, I suggest you take another look at the rich temple you named as the price of your discretion."

His reply was cool. "Yes, Your Grace, I do recall the terms of our transaction. But that has never prevented me from caring. About Soraya . . . or about you." He glanced down at the arm she drew tight against her body and his golden brows rankled. "What's wrong with your hand?"

Alarm shot through her. "Nothing."

Using her skirts to better conceal it from his view, she stepped away from him without any excuse.

He bowed as she passed, wisely saying nothing and remaining in place behind her as she continued toward her royal apartments.

She couldn't get inside fast enough.

Her legs felt unsteady as she hurried through the spacious quarters to the chamber no one but her was permitted inside. The locks on the heavy stone door to this other room responded only to her light. It swung open on silent hinges, revealing the otherworldly treasure that rested within the chamber.

The glowing, egg-sized crystal hovered atop a slender pedestal of snowy-white marble and gold.

Selene approached, realizing she'd likely only had minutes left before her legs would have sagged beneath her had she not been able to reach the crystal in time.

The hand she'd kept tucked against her looked almost withered. The skin on her arm was turning pale gray and translucent, revealing spidery blue veins that started at her fingers and spread up to her elbow. Her heart rate slogged, making her breath labor and her vision spin.

She had known leaving the realm was a risk. All the more so when she'd used even more of her life force to wield her light against Zael and the others. Including Jordana.

Selene gingerly reached for the crystal, cradling it in both her palms.

Light bloomed within it, sending warmth and power into her hands, her arms, her entire being.

Selene was as much a prisoner of the realm as she'd tried to make her daughter. Or, now, Jordana.

Because without a crystal to restore her, Selene—and the realm she would sacrifice anything to protect—would cease to exist.

Maybe she was a fool to allow the colony to have their crystal.

But they were her people too. She would never leave them vulnerable, even to aid herself.

As she drew more strength from the crystal in her hands, she realized there was another way to ensure the longevity of the Atlantean people.

One that might also take away some of the guilt that scored her heart as she listened to the distant sound of Jordana's weeping reverberating through the stones of the palace tower.

# CHAPTER 17

Nathan leapt on Zael. "You were supposed to protect her. You gave me your fucking word you'd keep her safe!"

The two large males crashed to the floor. With eyes gone volcanic with rage, the normally stoic Nathan unleashed bloody-minded fury on the Atlantean. Zael dodged his lightning-fast blows, his palms glowing despite that he refused to deliver even a single strike in return.

"Fuck," Darion growled, lunging into the fray.

The other warriors moved swiftly to help him peel Nathan off Zael. Restraining him wasn't easy. Nathan was a wall of muscle and born to be a killing machine. What made him even deadlier now was his concern for Jordana. His big body vibrated with lethal menace, all of it trained on their friend and ally.

"I told you she shouldn't go with you," Nathan hissed. "You swore to me nothing would happen to her."

Zael's expression was more miserable than Darion had ever seen it before. "I tried to protect her, Nathan.

All of us did, but not even four of my strongest friends and I combined were enough to hold off Selene. Neither was Jordana. I'm sorry."

*"Sorry?"* Nathan spat the word, making another lunge for him. "She's gone and you're telling me you're sorry?"

Darion and the other warriors holding him tightened their grasp, likely the only thing keeping Zael from being torn to pieces if Nathan were to get his hands on him.

Not the only thing. Zael's mate, Brynne, entered the war room on a rush of Breed motion. "Zael!" She was at his side instantly, glowering at Nathan as she assisted Zael to his feet. "What happened to you? What the hell is going on?"

"Jordana," Darion said soberly. "Selene has taken her."

"Taken her? How?" Brynne put her shoulder under Zael's arm, giving him support as his big body leaned against her. "What happened?"

"Selene teleported to the colony by herself. I don't know how she knew Jordana was there, but it was obvious she came with an agenda."

Brynne's face blanched. "The crystal, too?"

He shook his head. "She only came for Jordana."

Darion exchanged a look with his brethren. It felt cold to know a bit of relief that the colony's crystal hadn't also fallen into the Atlantean's queen's hands, but if it had, the odds of ever seeing Jordana again would have dwindled to nil.

As it stood, the chances were far from hopeful.

"Let go of me," Nathan snarled, gnashing his fangs at Darion and his fellow warriors. "I have to go after her. Nothing else matters without Jordana."

"You can't go after her," Zael told him soberly. "Even if you knew where the realm's island is, you're an outsider. The veil would bar you from entering uninvited."

Nathan's chest heaved with the breaths that rolled between his teeth and fangs. "Then you fucking go. Why are you here when you should've chased after Selene and taken her head for even touching Jordana?"

"I was banished from the realm a long time ago," Zael replied tonelessly. "With the crystal protecting the island, I can't breach the veil, either."

"Goddamn it, we have to do something," Nathan roared. "No matter what it—"

Without warning, the war room plunged into sudden darkness. Lights and equipment blinked off momentarily, then came back online in a manner that seemed eerily familiar to Darion.

Everyone went still, including Nathan, who shrugged out of his brethren's hold. "What's going on?"

He had no sooner asked the question than the large screen monitor on the wall lit up with the face of the Atlantean queen.

Christ, she was gorgeous.

Darion had been haunted by her stunning face and brilliant blue eyes since the first time she overrode the headquarters' technology network to make demands on the Order. His memories of her celestial beauty felt like crude sketches now that he was looking at her again.

Beautiful and dangerous, he reminded himself.

Behind that breathtaking face lurked an unpredictably ruthless immortal being. Her abduction of Jordana was evidence enough of that.

"You bitch," Nathan growled, stalking toward the screen. "Where is she? Let me see Jordana. What the fuck have you done with my mate?"

Selene's expression didn't so much as flicker in acknowledgment. She stared straight ahead at Darion, her glacial gaze locked on him alone. A small, cold smile curved her pretty mouth.

"It seems I have come into the possession of something of value to the Order."

Darion held the queen's unflinching stare. "I'd heard your treachery had no bounds, Selene, but what you've done today sets a new low."

"My treachery?" She scoffed. "That is rich, coming from one of your kind, Darion Thorne."

Even though she spoke his name with sharp disdain, the sound of it on her lips stoked an unwanted awareness in him. Evidently, he needed to have his head examined. The last thing he should be feeling toward her was desire, but damn if he didn't have a sudden, heated urge to make her say his name with a different kind of contempt. The kind he'd wring from her cruel mouth while she was spread beneath him in carnal surrender.

The impulse was so strong, so powerfully vivid, it took him aback.

"Where is Jordana?" Nathan demanded. "If you've hurt her, I swear I will make you regret it."

"She's safe. Safer with me and our people than she could ever be among your savage race." Although the answer was directed at Nathan, Selene's attention hadn't wavered for a moment off Darion. A smug kind of challenge lit her gaze. "Didn't I warn you once that you wouldn't want to stand against me?"

"You did," he admitted evenly. "And didn't I warn you that only a fool believes she can never lose?"

Anger flared in those oceanic eyes. "So arrogant. I didn't think it possible for anyone to exceed your father's ego, but once again you manage to surprise me."

He smiled at her, baring the tips of his emerging fangs. "I'll take that as a compliment."

Several of his comrades threw incredulous looks in his direction, but Darion hadn't been able to curb his baiting remark. Selene was an ageless queen with a lethal temper, but she was also a woman. As powerful as she clearly was, Darion was willing to bet there were few willing to call her on her shit. Possibly no one.

He hated to do it while Jordana's life was in Selene's hands, but he actually believed her when she assured them Jordana was being kept safe within the Atlantean realm.

That didn't change the fact that they needed to get her back.

"Where is Lucan Thorne?" Selene demanded. "I'm not about to waste my breath on anyone less than the Order's leader."

Darion felt the ripple of unease move over the other warriors at her query. They couldn't let anyone discover Lucan's compromised condition, least of all the immortal who'd made little secret of the fact that she'd like nothing better than to wipe the Order and all the rest of the Breed off the face of the Earth.

"If you have something you want to say, Selene, you can say it to me. Now, let us see Jordana. We need to know she's as safe as you claim."

"You do not make demands of me, vampire. If you want to see Jordana again, there is only one way. Give me the crystal the Order stole from me."

More than one of the warriors at Darion's back emitted a low snarl. Although Selene's price didn't come as a shock to him, it wasn't something he or any other member of the Order was willing to surrender. Even Nathan remained quiet, though Darion could hear the grinding of the warrior's molars as he glowered at Selene's face on the monitor.

Darion shook his head. "You need to get your facts straight. The Order didn't steal that crystal from you. It belongs to Jordana. Why don't you ask her if she wants you to have it?"

Her face flashed with disbelief. "We are not negotiating, Darion Thorne."

"No?" he asked, lifting a brow. "Then why'd you call? After our last virtual chat, I figured you might decide to lose my number."

If she could have reached out and strangled him, Darion felt certain she would have. Selene's eyes flew wide with outrage, then narrowed on him with the heat of searing blue lasers. "I tried to tell Jordana she means nothing to you and your ilk. You turn your backs on her so easily just to keep hold of a little power."

"Come on, now, Selene. It's more than a little power or we wouldn't be having this conversation. And remind me again how you are any better? You're willing to bargain your own kin like a pawn to get what you want."

Nathan hissed a dark curse. "For fuck's sake, Dare. You are gambling with my mate's life."

Darion didn't consider what he was doing as gambling. Rather, he was running through a few mental chess moves in his head. A plan was taking shape, one with enormous risks to be sure, but better than handing Selene a second crystal.

He let her simmer for a long moment, then said, "Here are my terms. You bring Jordana to us personally, then we can talk about who should have the crystal."

"Bring her to you?" She laughed. "Absolutely not. And I'm through with talking to you or anyone else. Once the crystal is returned to me, I will release Jordana. Not a moment sooner."

Nathan grabbed his arm. "Goddamn it, what choice do we have? There isn't a blood-bonded male in this room who wouldn't trade this whole fucking world for his mate's life. Darion . . . all of you . . . don't ask this of me. Just give the bitch what she wants."

"You should listen to him," Selene said calmly. There was challenge in the haughty stare that was trained on Darion. She was confident she'd already won.

Which meant he had her exactly where he wanted her.

Darion released a slow sigh. "All right, you'll have your crystal. Since you and I are getting along so well, I'll even bring it to you myself."

"No," she replied tersely. "Not you."

*Shit.* Not the response he had been hoping for. His plans hinged on getting past the veil that barred him from her hidden realm. He'd let himself get too distracted by sparring with her and trying not to notice how ridiculously hot she was, when perhaps he should have been trying to exude a little charm instead.

"The Order's leader will bring it to me," she insisted. "Just him. No one else."

Several heads turned in Darion's direction, more than one of the Order elders eyeing him with dubious anticipation. For obvious reasons, there was no way in hell they would be sending Lucan anywhere.

But that's not what the Atlantean queen had stipulated.

Selene's smile broadened as the silence stretched out. "Are we agreed, then?"

Darion inclined his head, fighting his own satisfied grin. "Agreed."

"Excellent." Her chin hiked up. "My guards will be waiting with a boat tomorrow night in a small port near Athens. I'm sure Zael remembers the one. He can explain how to find it."

Zael nodded, but he looked none too certain about this unexpected—and perilous—arrangement.

"Oh, and one more thing," Selene added. "If the Order thinks to deceive me in this, it will come at the cost of your leader's head."

Her icy stare bore hard into Darion as she spoke. Then, as abruptly as she had appeared, she was gone.

As soon as the war room monitor went blank, Darion's comrades surrounded him with incredulous remarks and more than one question regarding his sanity.

Only Nathan seemed even a little relieved. He put his hand on Darion's shoulder, torment still raw in his voice. "Tell me what I can do. Just promise me I can be the one to sever Selene's head from her neck."

"You can't actually be considering doing this," Tegan said, frowning.

Darion shrugged. "You heard the lady. She wants the Order's leader to deliver the crystal in exchange for

Jordana. Until my father resumes his place at the head of our table, his duties fall to me."

Chase cursed. "He wouldn't expect this of you, Dare. None of us do."

Dante nodded. "There has to be another way."

"I say we go on the offense," Niko suggested. "Zael, you've said the crystals house massive power. Can't we use the one we have to attack the barrier around the Atlantean realm so we can get inside?"

A grave shake of his head. "To do that, we would need the power of more than one crystal. And once the veil has been torn down, it cannot be repaired. We would be leaving the entire realm vulnerable to future attacks, regardless of what happens to Selene."

Brynne's gaze was tender on her Atlantean mate. "No matter how any of us feel about Selene's actions today, none of us want to see innocent civilians hurt."

Darion gave her a confirming nod that was echoed by the rest of the warriors. "This is the only way."

Zael turned a troubled look on him. "If we give her that crystal, there's no telling what she'll do with it. We can't even trust she'll release Jordana as she's agreed to."

"I know," Darion said. "That's why we're not going to give it to her."

Nathan's expression darkened. "What do you mean we're not? How else are we going to bring Jordana home?"

Darion met the questioning faces of his friends and comrades. "I have a plan."

# CHAPTER 18

He hoped to hell it was going to work.

To say his plan was risky was putting it mildly. Darion arrived in Athens the following evening, disembarked from the Order's private jet, and made his way on foot to the tucked-away marina in a small port off the Mediterranean Sea where Zael had instructed him to go.

Only one vessel waited at the dock, a large white sailboat that practically glowed beneath the starlit night sky. Two big men stood on the deck of the boat, another waited on the dock. Atlantean soldiers, all of them, garbed in belted, light-colored tunics with close-fitting pants tucked into tall boots. Long swords gleamed at their sides.

Darion strode toward the boat, his own weapons bristling from the belt around his waist. He'd opted for his black combat fatigues, seeing no reason to pretend this pre-arranged audience with their queen was anything close to friendly.

The soldier waiting on the dock scrutinized him as he approached. "Lucan Thorne?"

Darion inclined his head, never more thankful for his uncanny similarity to his father. He had his mother's eye color and a darker shade of her chestnut hair, but even then the differences were minimal.

The soldier indicated the dagger and pistol Darion carried on him. "Turn over your weapons."

Darion shook his head. "Since you've all come dressed for war as well, I'll keep them."

The Atlantean's gaze slid to the box Darion carried under one arm. The lidded titanium container held the small, egg-shaped crystal back at the D.C. command center. Tonight, it held a lesser bit of Atlantean treasure, though one that was critical to Darion's plan tonight.

Before departing on his journey, he and Zael had replaced the true crystal with Zael's teleportation amulet. The smaller bit of crystal inside the box put out just enough otherworldly energy to indicate there was something inside.

More importantly, the amulet would be Jordana's guaranteed ticket home. All Darion had to do was find a way to put it in her hands and she could escape in a heartbeat.

As for the second part of his goal once he was on the other side of the Atlanteans' veil, he was going to have to improvise.

All he knew was he intended to leave with Selene's crystal. Whether he obtained it by force or by stealth, he couldn't be sure until the opportunity was at hand. Either way, his options were thin at best.

Rather like his odds of actually making it out of this mission alive.

Fortunately, he'd always thrived on challenge.

"I'll be keeping a hold on this too," he told the grim-faced guard. "Make one wrong move and I'll send it to the bottom of the ocean."

The threat was apparently enough for Selene's men. The soldier gestured for Darion to step aboard the boat, then, within moments they set sail into the darkness.

He guessed they'd been at sea for more than an hour when the salty night air began to thicken into a fine, swirling mist.

The sailboat cleaved through it for what felt like a strange suspension of time. The three Atlantean guards who had remained silent for the duration of the journey now hastened to adjust the sails and slow the vessel.

Along the starboard side, a pristine white dock began to materialize out of the dark, churning mist. The soldiers tossed ropes to others waiting amid soft yellow lantern light to help them bring the vessel in and secure it.

"This way," one of the Atlantean guards said to Darion once they had docked.

They led him up a silky sand beach that gradually inclined toward a citadel that sparkled under the starlight. Darion hadn't known what to expect of Selene's Atlantean realm, but it wasn't this cozy settlement of white stucco cottages, elegant temples, and lush public gardens filled with fruit trees and fragrant flowers.

There was no stench of fire and ashes in the air. No bloodshed or death. No Rogue-infested streets filled with terror and misery. The contrast between his world and this one took him aback.

Despite that it was Selene who prompted his intrusion tonight, he almost felt unclean stalking up the pleasant paths in his black combat gear with violence on his mind.

But it was Selene who invited this confrontation.

Her actions would determine how it ended.

Flanked by the soldiers from the boat and dock, Darion stared ahead, where situated on a green hill at the heart of the island paradise stood a soaring palace of white stone crowned with multiple tile-topped, turreted towers.

The Atlantean royal palace.

Even he had to admit it was stunning.

Impressed or not, his tactician's mind counted dozens of ways for an army to attack. The island realm and its palace had no visible defenses beyond the veil that protected them. Yet Selene was willing to expose those weaknesses to an outsider in exchange for another crystal.

Was she simply that confident in her own power once she had the second crystal she was expecting to receive tonight? Or was it certainty that once her prize had been delivered the only place Darion would be taking Atlantis's secrets was to his grave?

He would find out soon enough.

The soldiers closed in tight around him and marched him through an opened gate, into the center of the gleaming palace's ground floor.

Pale lamplight illuminated the airy interior of the cathedral-like chamber in which he stood. White walls glowed with a pearly iridescence. Mosaic tiles crafted of opalescent stone and shells glistened under his black boots, and high above his head a glass-domed ceiling sheltered what appeared to be no less than eight spiraling floors of arches, chambers, open-air galleries, and columned arcades.

The melodic sounds of fountain water trickling gently into a reflection pool that stood as the centerpiece of the incredible space was almost soothing.

Darion couldn't pretend he wasn't impressed. Not to mention surprised.

This tranquil haven was the lair of Atlantis's tyrannical queen?

"Keep moving," one of the guards muttered behind him. "Her Majesty is waiting."

The swords that had remained sheathed on the boat and on the march to the palace came out now that he was inside. The soldiers urged him none too gently up one of the wide staircases that climbed the perimeter of the palace tower, drawing the curious out of chambers and other spaces to gape at the Breed warrior in their midst.

When he reached the second floor, he was brought into another spacious chamber even more opulent than the one that greeted him downstairs. Tall marble columns circled the interior of the enormous room with its glistening walls and masterful sculptures.

Every detail had been designed to draw the eye toward the sparkling, jeweled throne and the woman who was seated upon it with imperial grace and a lethal, watchful stillness.

Selene.

*Holy hell.*

If Darion had thought her beautiful before, he hadn't been prepared for the sight of the Atlantean queen in the flesh.

When she'd appeared on the command center's monitor, she had worn her long platinum-blonde hair unadorned and in loose waves, a simple gown of peachy silk floating against her pearlescent skin. Plain enough, though far from ordinary.

Tonight, she was resplendent.

And garbed like an immortal queen prepared for war.

She sat, head held high, wearing a golden crown sparkling with precious jewels and pearls. Her lustrous hair was gathered into a long, braided rope that hung in front of her right shoulder and coiled into her lap like a viper. Another gown with filmy skirts flowed from her tiny waist to the floor of the dais, this time in rich shades of violet with a bodice and tall, open collar of cerulean blue. A corset-like piece of golden armor hugged her torso and accentuated the perfect swells of her small breasts as she sat, regal and utterly silent, watching Darion as her guards shoved him toward the center of the huge chamber to face her.

He told himself the reason for his spiking pulse was simply adrenaline. No different from the way his body reacted any other time he strode into combat. Anticipation of the first strike against an enemy. Impatience to come out victorious on the other side.

Anything but the sharp jolt of desire that burned through his veins as he stared up at Selene in all her furious glory.

"Darion Thorne." There was disdain in every syllable, and if she had tried to keep her disdain for him out of her cool expression, she hadn't succeeded. Her arctic blue eyes narrowed on him. "I knew you couldn't be trusted at your word."

He smirked, unable to resist provoking her. "You said you wanted the Order's leader. Here I am."

Suspicion drew her pale brows together. "You? Where is Lucan?"

Darion wasn't about to give her that answer. "Where's Jordana?"

"First, my crystal." She glanced at the titanium box he held under his arm. "Guards, bring it to me."

Darion tightened his hold on it as the soldiers at his back and sides began to close in on him. "That wasn't our deal, Selene."

"You've already broken our deal simply by coming here," she fired back.

Darion shook his head. "And you were never going to release Jordana either way, were you?"

"Do not suppose you know anything about me, vampire."

Without warning, she lifted her hand and a bolt of light arced the length of her court and wrapped around him like a rope. He couldn't move, couldn't break loose.

Fuck. He knew Atlanteans and their light were powerful, but he'd never seen anything like this. Like her.

She sent another bright stream at him. The titanium box was snatched from his grasp and delivered straight to Selene's waiting hands.

She didn't even attempt to mask her smug satisfaction at besting him. Her triumphant smile transformed her face into a vision that was almost sweet, almost playful.

Then she opened the box and looked inside.

She lifted her crowned head, fury in her glare. "What is the meaning of this?"

Darion felt the guards tense beside him, ready to act on their queen's command. But he stood firm, unwavering. "I didn't trust you at your word either, Selene. Since you haven't brought Jordana here for the exchange, obviously, I was right to doubt you."

She took out Zael's amulet and let the empty box fall discarded at her slippered feet. Her fist closed tight around the crystal. Light surged between her fingers, then went out just as suddenly.

When she opened her hand, only a small puff of stardust remained. She let it spill off her fingertips, minuscule flecks of glitter that swirled on an unseen breeze.

Darion groaned inwardly, watching Jordana's only means of escape fade into nothingness.

And he still couldn't move. The bonds of light Selene had caged him with held more firmly than chains.

She stared with open amusement as he struggled. "I knew better than to think one of the Breed would have even a speck of honor."

Darion scoffed. "That's a hell of a lot of haughty indignation from a woman who's holding an innocent member of her own family hostage."

Selene moved to the edge of the cushioned seat on her elaborate throne, practically crackling with outrage. "You are an arrogant, crude creature, Darion Thorne. I'd be well within my rights to kill you where you stand. Didn't I warn you deceit would carry a steep price?"

"Yeah, you did, but killing me won't bring you any closer to getting the Order's crystal, will it?"

He saw her hesitation. As murderous as she might feel toward him, was she actually prepared to let her fury overrule her reason?

Darion seized on that small glimmer of hope. "You want a hostage? Here I am. Just let Jordana go."

"I want what belongs to me and my people." She vaulted to her feet as her voice began to rise. "What I want is the crystal you agreed to bring me."

Darion frowned, questions forming in his head. "If the crystals mean so much to you, why didn't you take the colony's when you had a chance? You could've had it as easily as you took Jordana the other day. According to Zael, you didn't even try."

A ripple of shock went over the guards. Unspoken, but Darion could feel the tension vibrate from the other Atlanteans. They didn't know Selene had been at the colony—or that she could have recovered the crystal.

Why was she keeping that secret from her people?

What did she have to hide?

She stood rigid at the top of the dais stairs. A curt nod to her guards. "Leave him with me."

One of the soldiers sounded unsure. "Your Grace?"

"I said go, Yurec. All of you." A flick of her finger tightened Darion's bonds even more. "This male poses no threat to me."

Once the guards exited, Selene made her descent from the dais. She moved with fluid grace, her steps confident as she slowly approached Darion.

He didn't know what she intended. With her moving in so close to him, his grasp on strategy and negotiations was usurped by the undeniable flood of awareness and attraction that swamped him as she drew to a pause in front of him.

He'd been wrong about her beauty. Nothing about her was cold, not even her startling blue eyes. She was searing in her loveliness. Creamy skin and silken hair that wasn't merely platinum but shot with the finest gossamer strands of silver, gold, and copper.

Her tall, leanly curved body radiated undeniable heat, even if it seemed to be primarily in anger toward him. And her scent, an intoxicating combination of sea, sand, and sky, made his thoughts scramble and his veins go taut with desire.

Not even the bonds that might choke the life out of him at any moment were enough to curb the arousal that flared through him like quicksilver as he drank in every inch of Selene's extraordinary face. His fangs throbbed in his gums, stoking a hunger that rose as swiftly as the rest of his unwelcome responses to her.

He cleared his throat, trying to wrestle his wits back. "Why didn't you take the colony's crystal when you had the chance? As I understand, they've lived in fear of you discovering their location and destroying them by taking their crystal, but you left it. Why?"

She drew in a breath, her fine brows rankling slightly. "I don't have to explain myself to anyone. Certainly not you."

But Darion caught the spark of something soft in her gaze. Perhaps this close she couldn't hide it. At least, not from him.

"You chose to leave the crystal with them, even though they stole it from you when they fled the realm all those centuries ago. You've chosen to leave the crystal with them this whole time, haven't you?"

An agitated, cornered look swept over her. Christ, she almost looked afraid. Terrified of being discovered.

"Do not mistake my benevolence toward my people for weakness," she all but hissed in his face. "And don't think I will have any where you're concerned, Darion Thorne."

He saw her crystalline blue gaze narrow with contempt before a blast of white light slammed into him.

Then everything went dark.

# CHAPTER 19

Selene stared down at the immense Breed warrior lying unconscious at her feet.

She was trembling inside, her heartbeat racing.

She told herself it was outrage. That the lightheadedness she felt, the difficulty catching her breath, was due to the depth of her fury. She would have willingly blamed the strange sensation on the fact that she had spent too much of herself the past few hours—first, in leaving the realm to find Jordana, and now, having wielded her light against Darion Thorne.

Those things had taxed her, but the truth was something far more alarming.

*He* had done this to her.

The handsome, dark-haired Breed male with the sharp mind and reckless tongue. The Order warrior who had dared to walk into her court on a lie, even when he had to know the brash move might cost him his life.

As queen, she had every right to end him here and now.

As a woman, she couldn't deny that every particle of her being stirred with unwanted awareness the instant he'd stepped into the room, a broad wall of hard muscle and menace, garbed from head to toe in black and armed with his crude weapons of war. Bold. Unflinching. Radiating undeniable strength, even after she'd wrapped him in her bonds of light.

Darion Thorne was arrogant and fearlessly defiant, a clear threat to her and every citizen in her realm, yet she couldn't help but be intrigued by his uncommon courage.

Neither of their previous confrontations had prepared her for facing him in person. To say he was attractive was pitifully inadequate. His intelligent brown eyes were closed now, shuttered by thick dark lashes that fell against lean, angled cheeks that tapered to a strong, stubborn jaw shadowed with black whiskers. He was a big male, broad-shouldered and covered in muscle, from his powerful arms to his long legs.

Everything about him spoke of darkness when she inhabited a world of light. His mere presence in the realm should have been an affront to her senses.

But that wasn't what she felt when she'd watched him from the dais. How she wished she could claim it had been.

Even now, she shook with a reaction that had little to do with anger or offense.

Scowling at his unmoving bulk, she stepped around him and gestured to the captain of her palace guard who waited outside. "Yurec, take him to the east tower."

"Yes, Your Grace."

Selene didn't wait to see her men collect Darion and remove him. She needed a moment of solitude, a chance to catch her breath, which was still racing in time with her galloping pulse.

Darion Thorne had only been inside her palace for a few minutes and yet nothing felt the same. Anxious energy buzzed throughout, attendants and guards whispering in the shadows of the open-air galleries and colonnades about the dark stranger their queen had permitted past the veil. With the exception of her legion soldiers, few of the realm's inhabitants had ever so much seen an outsider, human or otherwise.

They were right to be concerned. At the moment she was questioning her own sanity.

A Breed male inside the realm.

What had she been thinking?

Selene strode briskly under the high arches of the corridor, heading for the stairs that led up to her residence floor. She entered the sprawling private chambers, seeking out one of the many tranquil salons nestled within the royal suites. She didn't slow her pace until she was safely ensconced inside.

Her ceremonial crown weighed like it was crafted of lead. The fitted golden vest cinching her waist and lifting her breasts was a constriction she couldn't bear for another second.

She pulled frantically at the laces that held it closed, unable to breathe until the damned thing fell away. Her crown came off next, ripped from her head and tossed onto a cushioned, velvet chair.

She was only inside for a handful of moments before a rap sounded on the main door outside. There were few with the permission to disturb her, so she was hardly surprised to find Sebathiel waiting on the other side.

He held the titanium box Darion had brought with him. Seb's brows rose in question as he extended the box to her. "I found this on the dais."

She took it from him without comment.

"May we talk, Your Grace?"

"Come in," she replied tonelessly, pivoting away. She strode farther into the room with Sebathiel trailing behind her.

"You should have told me you were planning this," he said with concern and no small measure of disbelief. "I should have been with you to confront the warrior."

"I handled him well enough on my own."

"So I heard," Seb replied. "Yurec told me he's taking him to Soraya's tower."

Selene winced before turning to look at Sebathiel. When she spoke, her voice was quiet with remembered pain. "Don't call it that."

She should have torn down the charred ruin ages ago, but she just . . . couldn't. No matter how the sight of it still cleaved her heart, she'd kept it standing. It was the only thing she had left of her cherished daughter after Jordana had been stolen away from the realm.

Now, the awful tower had another use.

"It's not like you to take these kinds of chances, Selene." Sebathiel stepped closer to her, studying her too closely. "It's one thing to hold Jordana here, but an outsider? A Breed male who's not only an Order warrior but the son of Lucan Thorne?"

"What's done is done, Seb."

He glanced at the empty titanium box in her hands. "I have to say I'm shocked you haven't killed him."

"The night is young," she said, placing the box on a nearby table.

"If you wish, I will get rid of him for you."

"No." When Sebathiel's brows rose at her swift refusal she added, "We still need the Order's crystal.

Now, I have new leverage to persuade them to give it up."

"I'm still not convinced that keeping one of the Breed here in our realm is wise."

"Then it's a good thing I don't need to convince you," she replied. "I'm doing what I need to for *my* realm. For *my* people."

Ordinarily, that chilly tone and none-too-subtle reminder of his station would be enough for Sebathiel to back down. Tonight, it was clear his apprehension over Darion's presence troubled him even more than the thought of displeasing his queen.

"Your Grace, do you truly want to invite war with the Order?"

No, she did not. Particularly when she still had just one crystal in her possession. The last thing she wanted was to place her people in harm's way or jeopardize the world she'd given so much and strived so hard to create for them all.

Unfortunately, she may have already lit the flame in taking Jordana.

Tonight, Darion Thorne had left her in an impossible position. Without the crystal she'd demanded, she couldn't let him or Jordana go free without looking weak and ineffectual as a ruler, not only to the Order but more importantly, to her own people.

She had failed them catastrophically once.

She could never fail them again.

While she might put on a resolute front for Sebathiel and the rest of her court and citizenry, deep down she feared it was only a matter of time before war collided with Atlantis's shores.

Whether it came from the Order or other enemies on the outside remained to be seen.

The only thing she could be certain of was without more crystals, the realm could not hold out against anyone for long.

She would never willingly take away the colony's, but what if she had no choice? She didn't want to think about that awful prospect. And even if the Order decided to use theirs against her, there was still another thing to consider. The matter of the unusual disturbance in the region of the Deadlands.

There was no question that crystals had caused the detonation. One crystal alone could not produce that kind of power. The only questions were how had the explosion occurred, and how long before someone decided to use the crystals for their own destructive means?

Possibly even the Order.

"Has there been any word from General Taebris and his search party?" she asked Seb.

He gave a grave shake of his head. "Nothing yet."

She frowned. "It's been days since they departed for the region. Do you suppose anything's wrong?"

"They've got a large territory to search, Your Grace. These things take time."

She nodded, but couldn't dismiss her niggling sense of foreboding. "I hope you're right, Seb."

"We could send another group after them to join the search," he suggested.

"No, not yet." As impatient as she was to locate and recover the crystals, the risks were immense.

Sending more of her men without being certain of the first team's progress might only be putting additional lives in danger.

Not to mention thinning the realm's small army even further.

"Perhaps Nuranthia can shed some light on the team's whereabouts, Your Grace?"

Selene nodded. "Yes, perhaps. Send her in with her bowl on your way out, Seb."

His face registered a note of surprise at her polite dismissal, but he merely lowered his head in acknowledgment. "Of course, Your Grace."

A few moments after he had gone, the seer appeared in the open doorway carrying one of her golden bowls. Selene motioned her inside and waited as the woman poured a pitcher of clear water into the basin.

At Selene's request, the seer opened a window onto the swath of barren, ghostly forest in a forgotten corner of the Siberian wilderness. There was no sign of Taebris or the soldiers who accompanied him. Only an empty woodland utterly devoid of life.

"Perhaps I can illuminate a different area for Your Grace?" Nuranthia asked after several fruitless minutes of staring into the water with no sign of her men.

Selene shook her head. "No, that will be all."

"Yes, Your Grace." She reached out to collect her bowl.

"Wait, Nuranthia." The seer froze. "Before you go . . . there is something else I want to see."

"As you wish, Your Grace."

The seer listened without so much as a flicker of reaction before conjuring the vision her queen had commanded.

Then Selene peered into the water at the window Nuranthia had opened for her. It was a vision into the east tower cell.

Selene watched for a long while, observing Darion Thorne as he lay unconscious on the cold stone floor, and wondering if she had made a colossal mistake by allowing the handsome, dangerous Breed warrior into her world.

# CHAPTER 20

D arion's head felt like it had been split open with an axe and put back together again.

Everything ached. He tried to move and found he was lying on cold stone. He hurt everywhere, but he was alive. At least for now.

The damp smell of hewn rock hit his senses at the same time he peeled open his eyes and realized he was in some sort of cell. Though this was unlike any prison he'd ever seen before.

Three walls were made of stone, with a thick iron-banded door sealing him inside. A pale glow radiated all around it, but that wasn't the strangest part of the room.

One entire wall of it was open to the elements, looking out onto a world blazing with the full intensity of a noonday sun.

*Holy shit.*

Daylight.

Instinct brought him up in a scramble of screaming limbs and throbbing skull. He was well within the shadows of the surprisingly large, empty cell, yet the sight of all that sunshine was hard to ignore.

A gull swept past on a shrill cry as it arced toward the thin clouds overhead. Evidently, wherever Selene had sent him, he had to be many stories off the ground. One of the steep towers of the palace grounds, then?

Compared to the opulence of the rest of the palace, the one he'd been left in held the neglect of a tomb. Scorch marks scarred the pale stone walls and floor with angry smudges of black soot. Cobwebs hung in the corners, riffling in the warm breeze flowing in from outside.

Darion forced his limbs to take him to the edge of the shadow cover so he could get his bearings on his location. As he moved, he noticed his weapons and boots had been confiscated. His black combat fatigues stuck to his skin like they'd been pasted on, only adding to the discomfort of trying to move.

Cautiously, his retinas burning with the effort, he peered out at his surroundings.

He was in the uppermost chamber of a ruin on the east side of the sprawling palace compound and courtyards. No less than ten stories stood between him and the ground. An easy jump for him, but not with the white-hot sun high in the sky overhead.

Shielding his face with his arm, he glanced higher, up toward the clouds . . . and noticed something odd.

Despite all the sunlight pouring down over the realm, Darion could see a crescent moon and a blanket full of stars glittering faintly above the canopy of light.

*What the fuck?*

The door to his cell swung open, and in walked a tall Atlantean male. Not a soldier, despite the long, sheathed blade that hung at his side. Golden-haired and outfitted in fine teal and white robes, the male looked like some manner of official. In his hands he carried some folded linen clothing.

His shrewd blue eyes registered Darion's curiosity about the sky outside. "It's real enough. Feel free to test the light if you like. I've never seen a Breed vampire burn up before."

Dare flashed his fangs. "Maybe another time. Where's Selene? We were in the middle of a conversation when she rudely cut me off with a lightning bolt to the chest."

"Her Majesty has no interest in speaking with you."

"Who are you then, her royal mouthpiece?"

The male sneered. "I am Sebathiel. High Chancellor and adviser to Her Majesty."

Darion grunted. "Were you the one who advised her to abduct Jordana and ransom her back to the Order in exchange for our crystal? Some family, eh, Seb?"

He bristled visibly, as if Darion had struck an unseen mark. "Do not test her wrath," he snarled. "You'd be wise not to test mine, either."

Sebathiel tossed the clothes at him. "Put them on."

An ecru linen tunic and tan pants fell at Darion's feet, along with a pair of plain leather sandals. He eyed the shoes and garments, glancing at the Atlantean with some skepticism. "You gonna stand there and watch?"

The big Atlantean crossed his arms, neither speaking nor leaving the room.

Darion shrugged. "Suit yourself."

He took off his combat gear only because even he couldn't stand the stench and stiffness of it. His muscles still complained with every flex and movement, but he ignored the aches and took his time stripping down and then donning the strange-feeling, too-snug Atlantean attire.

"How long have I been up here?" he asked Selene's man.

"Three days."

The news came as a shock. Three days unconscious in an enemy prison cell. Three days without securing Jordana's release.

Three days without feeding.

No wonder his body felt so sluggish and out of sorts. Selene's blast had been debilitating enough. Another few days without fresh, living blood to drink would be the beginning of his end. Human blood, since he didn't expect any of the Atlantean males were going to offer up a vein to him anytime soon, and drinking from an Atlantean female would activate a mutually unwanted blood bond between them.

So, yeah, if he didn't find a way back to D.C. with Jordana soon—with or without the realm's crystal in hand—he was fucked.

He held out his arms, baring his teeth and fangs in a parody of a smile. "Now that I'm all presentable, why don't you send Selene up here so we can finish our chat?"

Sebathiel grunted, his stare dark with contempt and something else Darion couldn't quite describe. He didn't answer, just turned and strode for the door.

If Darion thought attacking the male or threatening Selene with her High Chancellor's death would help his odds of freeing Jordana, he would have considered it. At the moment, he wasn't sure if anything—other than her precious crystal—held any value for the Atlantean queen.

Sebathiel walked out and locked him inside. Darion stepped forward to have a closer look at the glowing light that emanated from around the door. He tested the lock with the power of his mind, but it held fast.

The light refused to bend. He touched his fingers to it, then leapt back on a hiss at the searing heat that scorched him.

Shit.

No way out through the door, and unless Sebathiel was lying the only thing waiting on the other side of Darion's cell was death.

He had to be sure. Walking back to the line separating shadow from the unusual sunlight outside, he extended his hand. As soon as his fingertips moved into the light, they began to blister and smoke.

"Son of a bitch." He yanked his hand back into the cool shadows, his fangs punching out of his gums at the excruciating pain of the burn.

And then he saw her.

In another tower across the palace courtyard from him, Selene stood in a garden bursting with lush flowers and citrus trees. Watching him.

Darion stared back. He let his smile spread slowly, lip curling away from his teeth and fangs as he lifted his hand in a flagrant salute.

He could practically feel her icy fury stabbing him across the distance.

Even if she unleashed another bolt of Atlantean power on him right now, it would be worth it just to see the incredulous look on her royally outraged face.

But she didn't blast him into next week.

With a glower, she pivoted, giving him her back as she stormed into the shade of her solar, her gauzy silk gown rippling like a sail in her wake.

# CHAPTER 21

J enna lifted her eyelids and found herself staring into the sweet, freckled face of a little boy.

"Uh . . . hello," she said, her throat scratchy from sleep. Her tongue didn't want to cooperate in forming words. "Who—who are you?"

"I'm Caleb." Stated as if it was common fact, and accompanied by small smile.

She was groggy and confused, a bit disoriented, none of which were helped by the presence of a kid she'd never laid eyes on before. Still, she couldn't resist the tender brown gaze that studied her as though he'd known her forever.

"Hi, Caleb," she murmured thickly. "I'm Jenna."

"I know. Brock told me." The boy turned his head and shouted over his thin shoulder. "Brock, come quick! She's awake!"

Brock was already in motion even before Caleb's urgent summoning. He raced into the bedroom and crouched at her side. His handsome face was drawn with concern as he searched her eyes, his strong hands tender as he smoothed her sticky hair away from her cheeks.

No, he wasn't merely concerned.

He was scared as hell . . . about her.

"Jenna, thank God." He leaned in and kissed her with a desperation that rocked her. "You've had me so fucking worried, baby."

"You just said a bad word," Caleb pointed out.

Brock blew out a jagged laugh that held the raw edge of a sob. "Yeah, I did. Sorry about that, kid."

Even as he spoke, he took Jenna's face in his hands and kissed her again, as if he couldn't keep from touching her.

His worry-filled eyes searched her bleary gaze. "Are you okay?"

She swallowed, testing her parched throat. "I'm not sure. I feel all right, but my head . . ."

A shiver ran through her, even though she wasn't particularly cold.

"Caleb, go get the blanket off the sofa for me."

The boy ran out to the other room. Jenna stared up at her mate. "You have a new friend?"

He smiled, lifting one bulky shoulder. "Looks that way."

"He's Breed," Jenna said, less a question than a fact. "From one of the area Darkhavens?"

"Yeah," Brock said. "It's a long story. I'll catch you up soon. There's a lot to catch you up on."

"I don't think I like the sound of that."

His grim expression didn't do anything to dispel the note of dread creeping over her. "Right now, I'm just really glad to see you awake, beautiful."

She frowned up at him, confusion deepening. "Was I sleeping very long?"

"Jen, you've been in some kind of coma for the past five days."

"A coma," she echoed, stunned. She remembered a feeling of exhaustion coming over her, how she'd gone to bed to lie down—just for a short nap. "Brock, something's not right."

He squeezed her hand, exhaling a troubled sigh. At the same moment, Caleb returned with the blanket.

"I brought the fluffy one," he said, handing it over to Brock.

"Thanks, buddy."

Jenna managed a smile as she thanked him too. "How old are you, Caleb?"

"I'm six."

"Six." Jenna glanced up at Brock, and his tender eyes said he knew where her thoughts had gone.

Back to Alaska, a long time ago.

Back to when Jenna's own daughter, Libby, had still been a happy, vibrant six-year-old child.

Caleb's little hands helped Brock tuck the blanket around Jenna's shoulders and under her chin.

"Are you warmer now, Jenna?" the boy asked, earnest with concern.

She nodded. "I am. Thank you."

Brock put his hand on Caleb's shoulder. "Do me a favor and go tell Tess and Gideon that Jenna's awake, okay?"

"Sure."

Once the boy was gone, Brock resumed his gentle caress of Jenna's cheek. "Everyone's been worried about you."

"I'm fine," Jenna said. She was starting to feel her senses coming back online with every passing minute. But something seemed . . . off.

Brock frowned at her troubled look. "What is it?"

"I don't know. My head feels strange. It feels like someone's been rummaging around inside my skull like it was an old trunk."

As she spoke the words, a horrifying realization settled over her. A certainty she could not deny—no matter how much she wanted to.

"Brock, it was him. The Ancient." She drew in a sharp breath. "Oh, God. He's been in my head, in my memories. Everything I've been cataloging and recording in my journals for the past twenty years . . . he knows it all."

# CHAPTER 22

S elene inhaled a steadying breath before dropping the seal of light on the door to Jordana's chamber.

The two female attendants who accompanied her carried trays laden with fruit, cheeses, bread, and juice. It was enough to feed a family, but Selene had no idea what Jordana liked and she wanted to make sure there was ample food to tempt her.

Not that she would eat any of it.

Jordana had refused everything Selene brought her so far, including her every attempt to talk and get to know her granddaughter. The young woman was headstrong and unyielding, traits that evidently had passed down through all three generations of their line.

Jordana had been seated on the end of the large bed when the door opened. Now, she moved against the far wall, putting as much distance as possible between herself and Selene.

Her hands were unbound. Selene had removed the ropes of light the same night Jordana had arrived, mainly out of love and compassion, but also because her granddaughter now understood that Selene was the stronger of them by far.

At least for now.

She couldn't pretend the past three days weren't taking a toll. How long could she expect to wield her light without depleting herself beyond repair? Holding locks in place and wielding binding ropes were child's play, but maintaining full daylight over the realm in order to keep Darion Thorne imprisoned in the east tower wasn't something she'd been prepared for.

His dark smirk and infuriating salute a few hours ago still grated on her. Even more, she hated that he'd caught her watching him from across the courtyard.

His piercing stare had felt like a physical thing, heated and uninvited. Impossible to forget, no matter how much she wanted to.

"Good morning, Jordana," she said, corralling her thoughts away from the aggravating Breed male.

"Is it morning?" Jordana glanced at the small window in the chamber. "How can you tell? Does night never fall in this place?"

Selene offered a small smile. "The light is necessary. We've brought you a few things to eat. I hope you'll find something to like."

"You shouldn't have bothered. It's impossible to have an appetite while I'm being held prisoner by a mad, treacherous queen."

Selene felt her attendants quake at the insult, one of them drawing in a sharp gasp. She calmly glanced their way, dismissing them with a mild tilt of her chin. They scurried out of the room, closing the door behind them.

Selene took a step forward and Jordana backed away even farther. Her hands came up defensively, her palms glowing with Atlantean light.

Selene paused, exhaling a soft sigh. "Are you that afraid of me, my child, or do you hate me that much?"

"I haven't decided. And I'm not your child. I'm not anything where you're concerned."

The mistrust in her eyes carved a deep wound in Selene's heart. "You are safe here, Jordana. I promise, I have no intent to harm you . . . not ever."

"Then let me go. I want to go home to Nathan. I want to be with my mate and the rest of my family."

"Your family," Selene murmured quietly. "I am very sorry to tell you, that *family* of yours doesn't place as much value on you as you apparently hold for them."

Jordana's chin came up in challenge. "What are you talking about?"

"I offered to let you go. All the Order had to do was bring me the crystal that belongs to me."

"You did what?" Her expression was incredulous, her tone edged with disgust. "Tell me they didn't agree to that."

"They did agree, Jordana, but then they sent a ruse instead. All they delivered was lies."

"What are you talking about? Who did they send here?" Panic rose in her voice. "Was it Nathan? Is he here? No, he can't be here . . . I would feel him in my blood."

Of course, she would. Because Jordana had bound herself to a Breed warrior by blood and vow. As unfathomable as it seemed, it was obvious she loved her mate deeply. It was a feeling Selene had never known in all of her immortal existence.

She slowly shook her head. "No, he was not the one they sent. It was Darion Thorne."

"Dare came for me? Where is he, Selene? I want to see my friend right now."

"That won't be possible."

"Oh, God. What have you done?"

"Don't worry, he's alive . . . for now. But he's not going anywhere. He betrayed me and there is a price to be paid for that. He had a chance to bring me the crystal, but he brought only deceit, despite knowing your freedom was at stake."

Instead of reacting with disappointment or hurt, Jordana let out a sharp laugh. "I'm glad Darion didn't give in to your demands. I'm *relieved*. No one trusts you with another crystal, least of all any of us. All you'll do is use it to make war on the Order and our world."

"That's not true." Selene frowned, taken aback by the accusation. "It's the Breed who threatens us, our peaceful way of life. They're no better than the monsters they came from, terrorizing and killing, turning their streets red with bloodshed and violence."

"Not the Order," Jordana replied vehemently. "All we want is peace. We'll fight for it. We'll die for it if that's what it takes."

*We.* Not they. Had the warriors and the male she'd taken as her mate corrupted Jordana's reason so much she couldn't accept the truth? Or was her faith in their honor simply that strong?

Jordana paced forward a step. "If you value peace as much as you claim, then let me go. Release Darion and me now."

Selene stared into those pleading blue eyes that looked so much like Soraya's. Even if she wanted to give

Jordana her freedom, she couldn't. Darion Thorne had tied her hands with his betrayal.

"I'm sorry," she said gently. "I cannot do that. I won't reward the Order's deceit. It would only encourage more of the same."

"Or it might help show them that you could possibly be an ally, not an enemy."

Selene sighed, loathing this impasse that stood between her and her only kin. "You are free to walk about the palace and grounds as you wish, Jordana, but go no farther. You won't get past the veil."

"What about Darion?"

"What about him?"

"He can't survive here, Selene. The unrelenting light is one thing, but unless you mean to starve him to death, he'll need to feed. Without nourishment—without drinking blood from an open vein—he'll die."

"How long?" Selene asked, curious in spite of herself.

"A week, possibly less."

He had been in the east tower for three days and counting. If she wanted to bargain him back to the Order for their crystal, she needed to keep him alive. No matter how he irritated her simply with his presence, she didn't intend for him to die.

Selene recoiled at the idea of Darion's fangs tearing into someone's throat, but she could see Jordana truly was concerned about him. She cared for him, had called Darion her friend.

If she could give Jordana nothing else, she could give her this.

"Tell me what he needs," she murmured stiffly.

# CHAPTER 23

Darion was seated in the shadows of his cell, resting his back against the cool stone wall when the heavy door swung open, and a pair of palace guards stepped inside.

The larger of the two, whom Selene had called Yurec the night of his arrival, gruffly gestured for him to get up. "The Queen demands your presence."

He stood, glad for the break in his endless boredom if nothing else. "She missed me already, eh?"

The quip earned him a hard jab in the back as the two Atlantean soldiers all but shoved him out of the room. As they marched him down the spiraling steps, he studied every inch of the palace, cataloging unsecured chambers and open passageways with an eye toward his eventual escape.

He didn't expect he'd be allowed to live for much longer if Selene didn't get what she wanted. Then again, if he didn't find some way to slake his blood hunger soon, it wouldn't matter what she wanted. He had no wish to die, but he'd be damned before he tried to appeal to her mercy.

Yurec walked him into the opened doors to the massive throne room. Selene waited inside again, but not alone.

Two more guards held an aged, portly human male. His graying hair was matted from salt air and sea spray. His simple clothing reeked of sweat and fish. He squirmed and struggled between his captors, eyes wide with fear as he spoke rapidly in a language that sounded to Darion like Greek.

"What's going on, Selene?"

"I brought you something from outside the veil."

The old man jerked around at the sound of Darion's voice and began pleading incoherently to him.

Darion could smell the human's terror and uncertainty. As much as he disapproved of what he was seeing he smirked up at Selene, seated calmly on her throne at the top of the dais.

"A present for me? I didn't realize you cared."

Her pretty mouth flattened. "I imagine the Order will be less willing to trade the crystal for you if you're shriveled up and dead of hunger."

He couldn't deny his surprise. Or his bone-deep relief at the thought of easing some of the fierce gnawing of his thirst. "I appreciate your concern, but I'm not usually one for public feedings. Why didn't you bring this little gift of yours up to my cell?"

"I never step foot in the east tower." Her reply was sharp and immediate—almost an unwilling reflex.

She kept her expression schooled, but there was no taking back her knee-jerk response. Unless he missed his guess, Darion would have sworn he noted a flicker of emotional pain in her glacial blue eyes.

Selene gestured to Yurec to bring Darion forward. The old fisherman struggled some more, whining now as one of the guards holding him grabbed his head and bent it to the side, exposing his neck to Darion.

Hunger spurred him, his gaze burning amber at the sight of the pounding carotid that raced under the tanned, grizzled skin.

He forced his gaze back up to Selene, turning the heat of his sparking irises on her instead of the blubbering human.

"This isn't my usual fare," he said, his voice a deep growl. "For future reference, I prefer female necks. They're softer under my fangs, sweeter on my tongue."

Selene's fingers tightened on the arms of her jeweled, gilded throne. "I'm not interested in your preferences. This isn't about satisfying anything but your basest needs."

"And how would you know what those might be, Your Grace?"

She swallowed visibly, looking uncomfortable. "Just get it over with."

"That's something I'm not used to hearing."

He smiled, giving her a good long look at his fangs. After all, this spectacle was taking place on her command. He wasn't about to let her off easy. And for some twisted reason, he enjoyed seeing the haughty female squirm.

He had the strong urge to make her do a lot more than that.

She glowered at him, pulling her shoulders back and sitting ramrod straight.

"Enough." She lashed out with her light, using it to push the old man out of the guard's grasp and toward Darion. "I want this over with. Now."

The human stared up into his transformed face and screamed. Darion's pulse sped, banging so hard it was all Darion could hear. His eyes burned, filling his vision with bright amber. He couldn't see his *dermaglyphs*, but he knew the Breed skin markings were certain to be a riot of seething, dark colors under the loosely laced collar of his linen tunic.

His fangs crowded his mouth.

"Don't be afraid," he murmured, but the old man kept howling in terror, pleading for help.

He wouldn't recall any of his ordeal once Darion was finished with him. A trance and a mind scrub would erase all the fear the old man was feeling. Assuming Selene let the human live, he'd return to his boat or his village without a single memory of where he'd been or what he'd endured in the Atlantean queen's court. It seemed the least Darion could do for him.

But for now the man was petrified with fright.

Darion struck fast and hard. With his hand splayed on the gray head to hold it steady, he bit into the fleshy throat.

Selene gasped, one hand flying to her chest. But she didn't avert her eyes for a moment as Darion began to drink.

Warm red cells flooded his mouth.

He stared at Selene, gripped by the thought of having her tender neck yielding under his bite. Her blood flowing over his tongue. Her body naked beneath him as he took his fill from her vein and gave her pleasure back tenfold as he drove his cock deep inside her.

The fantasy was so powerful, so shockingly vivid, he snarled with the savagery of his desire.

She had to know what he was thinking. He couldn't keep the intensity of his arousal out of his hot gaze.

He drank some more, waiting to see Selene break away from his profane stare. But she didn't flinch. She seemed as unable—or as unwilling—to sever their visceral connection as he was.

And goddamn if it didn't make him burn with the need to have her even more.

# CHAPTER 24

S he couldn't look away from Darion as he fed.
 She watched transfixed, riveted when she should
be repulsed.

Aroused when she should be appalled.

What was wrong with her?

It was impossible to look away from his scorching
gaze. No longer the absorbing brown eyes that made her
wonder if she might find any softness inside him, but
shocking amber that burned as hot as an open flame. His
pupils had winnowed down to the narrowest vertical slits
as he drank greedily, his sensual mouth latched onto the
human's throat.

The tunic he'd been given to replace his own clothes
hung open at the collar, the linen laces unfastened and
loose. It revealed only a wedge of his smooth chest, but
what little of it she saw drew her attention almost as
magnetically as his eyes.

Breed skin markings curved and tangled across his
chest, alive with dark colors. Changing shades of deep
red, indigo, and gold, twisting and pulsing.

He was as alien to her as anything she had ever witnessed, beautiful in a disturbingly erotic way.

Yet for all Darion's coiled power, he seemed to be holding it in check with the aged mortal. His grip on him was almost gentle. The man's legs had given out the moment Darion struck, and instead of letting him sag or fall to the floor, Darion carefully held the old man's body upright with one arm.

It wasn't hard to imagine what it might be like to be pinned under all that power. Utterly at the mercy of those sharp, unforgiving fangs.

It should have unsettled her, even terrified her.

In many ways it did.

Because instead of the sick feeling she had anticipated, watching Darion slake his hunger electrified every cell in her body. Arousal spiraled, unbidden, a deep, liquid warmth she could hardly bear.

As if he sensed what she was feeling, he made a hungered sound while those fiery eyes consumed her with unrelenting heat.

Finally, she couldn't take another moment. If playing spectator to his hunger wasn't jolting enough, her strange reaction to Darion's penetrating gaze was.

She rose, making her way down the steps as swiftly as she dared without breaking into a run.

She fled immediately for the stairs leading up to the royal chambers, her heartbeat hammering at every pulse point on her body.

She had hardly been inside her quarters long enough to catch her breath when the air stirred behind her with dark energy. She spun, astonished to find Darion standing there.

Alarm rang through her. "How did you— What did you do to my men?"

"Relax, Selene." That low voice of his seemed even deeper with his sharp fangs gleaming behind his lips. "Yurec and the others are fine, aside from the headaches they'll have when they come to."

"Get out, or I'll call more of my guards."

"Go ahead." He had the audacity to grin. "I'm running on all cylinders now, and fuck knows I need to work off some serious aggression right now."

She swallowed, refusing to shrink away from him as he strode farther into her personal space. Her hands came up out of reflex, palms warm with the waking of her power. After holding the light outside the palace and on the east tower cell door these past several days, she didn't know if she would have enough reserves left to do him any harm now. She had never intended for him to remain in the realm all this time. How long she could hope to continue holding him prisoner, she wasn't sure.

That didn't mean she wouldn't use whatever she had to protect herself now.

He glanced at her closed fists and raised a dark brow. "Thinking about lighting me up again? Be careful. You said yourself I'm worth more to you alive than dead."

"I'm beginning to have my doubts."

He smiled. A real smile, one that reached those amber-flecked, brown eyes. Some of the fire in them was banked now, but the embers continued to smolder as he stared at her. "We started off on the wrong foot, Selene. I don't see the need for us to be enemies."

Was he serious? With a narrowed glare, she scoffed. "That's all we can ever be. You and your kind embody everything I despise. You're brutal, and you have a complete lack of honor. You're cold-blooded killers who thrive on war and bloodshed."

He paced forward as if testing her mettle. "I am brutal, Selene. That much I'll grant you. But only to my enemies."

She lifted a brow. "Is that intended to coerce my cooperation?"

"I don't need to coerce you," he said, taking another step. "You asserted that I and my kind are brutal killers. I'm simply agreeing with you on that. But only when it's to stop worse brutality and suffering."

"I'm supposed to believe that when your word means nothing?"

He tilted his head. "Ah, right. Now, we arrive at my complete lack of honor."

"You proved it yourself when I demanded to negotiate with Lucan Thorne and instead you showed up."

"No, Selene." He slowly shook his head. "Your demand was the Order's leader. Here I am."

She frowned, not only at the way he had used her words against her, but also at the confusing implication he was making. "You have taken his place? Why?"

"Only for the time being," he replied, his expression openly grave. "My father was . . . injured recently in an attack by Opus Nostrum. You'd better pray you had nothing to do with it, *Your Grace*."

She drew back in genuine shock. Even a small note of sympathy for the obvious pain the assault had caused him. "No, I don't have anything to do with that organization. One of my people, an exile who fled to the mortal world decades ago and went by the name Reginald Crowe, tried to involve me in his schemes with

Opus Nostrum, but I had no interest. Their battles are their own, not mine."

Before she was tempted to soften any further to his or the Order's conflicts or tribulations, she reminded herself that Darion had still deceived her. "So, you twisted my words to suit your purposes. There's little honor in that . . . or in the fact that you came here without the crystal we agreed to."

Far from contrite, he gave her a knowing look. "Tell me you wouldn't have done the same thing."

He was right, of course. She would never surrender her own crystal. She couldn't, or everyone who depended on her to protect them as their queen would be put in jeopardy of attack.

Another step closer carried him within inches of her now. "I'm not without honor. Neither are any of my brethren in the Order. We're not cold-blooded killers, Selene."

"Tell that to the fisherman whose throat you just ravaged before my eyes."

His wicked mouth curved with dark amusement. "The man is alive and his throat is intact. I tranced him while I drank from him. After I finished, I scrubbed his memory of this entire day. He's resting downstairs with Yurec and the others. You can feel free to toss him back wherever you found him."

"You didn't kill him?"

"That would seem awfully rude, considering his tired old red cells probably saved my life."

Selene suppressed her sigh of relief. She did not want to warm to Darion. It would take far more than some meager kindness shown to a random mortal to convince her he was anything but what she knew the Breed to be.

"So, you have a little mercy in you. Is that supposed to make me forget where you come from?"

He arched a brow. "You've got something against Washington, D.C.?"

Dammit, the male was infuriating. "Am I supposed to ignore the fact that you and your ilk are the spawn of Atlantis's destroyers?"

"No," he answered soberly. "I don't expect you to ever forget that, or to forgive it. But I'm not a monster."

There was precious little space left between them, but one more step closed the gap entirely. She couldn't think with him so near. She couldn't summon a sharp reply or a demand that he step back to a respectable distance.

She didn't want to do either of those things.

"I don't believe you're the monster you're feared to be either, Selene."

Her lungs felt constricted as she stared up at him. She couldn't seem to slow the frantic pace of her pulse, feeling it drum in her breast, in her throat, in other places she didn't want to consider. Especially not when Darion's smoldering gaze felt hot enough to incinerate her clothing.

"Do you want to know what I think?" he asked, his deep voice vibrating straight to her marrow.

She was certain she did not want to know, but she couldn't find words to say so.

He slowly lifted his hand, as if giving her the chance to deny him. Faith help her, she couldn't have refused his touch if her life depended on it.

He stroked his fingertips along the line of her jaw. "I think you're lonely, not evil."

She bristled, hearing his quiet remark like a physical blow. "You don't have the first idea—"

His mouth met hers in a kiss that not only silenced her outrage, but scattered it.

She almost expected his lips to carry the bitter metal tang of mortal blood, but all she tasted was spicy, warm male and something elusive that made her senses spin out of control as Darion's tongue thrust past her teeth and into her mouth.

She couldn't deny the pleasure.

She couldn't pretend she didn't crave more of him with an intensity that astonished her.

How could this man she should despise as her enemy stoke such a swift and staggering need inside her? He was the last man she should crave, yet his kiss ignited a want in her unlike any she had ever known before. Heat unfurled in her core, threatening to melt away her sanity.

He drew her against his muscled length, cradling the back of her skull in the palm of his big hand as his kiss went deeper. The sharp tips of his fangs grazed her tongue, and where their bodies pressed together she could feel the hard evidence of his arousal.

This was wrong. It was reckless.

Desire like this could be the ruination of everything she stood for, everything she had strived for so long to protect.

Selene moaned, knowing she should push him away.

She couldn't.

Her fingers tunneled into his dark hair, urging him closer as she licked her tongue against his. A low groan vibrated through him, as ominous as thunder at the head of a storm.

He pulled back only for a moment, his handsome face fierce with desire and not a little anger. "Fuck," he uttered harshly. "Why did it have to be you?"

Selene didn't have an answer. She was grappling with the same staggering disbelief.

All she knew was she needed to have his mouth on hers again.

With her hand at the back of his corded neck, she pulled his head forward for her kiss.

# CHAPTER 25

He was burning up already, and now her kiss poured gasoline on the flames.

Selene had been angered when he told her she was more lonely than evil. He'd thought for sure she would torch him with her light.

He could still feel her rage at him, but her desire felt even stronger.

Possibly as strong as the need he was feeling for her.

Christ, he was consumed with it. Consumed with the taste of her kiss, the feel of her hands clutching him as their mouths met and tongues tangled in raw demand.

Selene was a volatile adversary, no doubt about that. But she was also a woman. One who burned like an inferno against him.

He cursed himself for feeling this need for Selene. He was no stranger to lust or the pleasures of beautiful women, yet feeling Selene in his arms was a revelation.

Fuck. Of all people, she was the woman he had to have?

There was no ice in her now, and her heated response to his kiss was almost enough to make him forget the reason he was there in the first place.

His mission for Jordana, the Order, and the welfare of the world itself depended on securing Selene's crystal.

Darion didn't want to be Selene's enemy; he meant that. But there was no way in hell they could be lovers while she was holding Jordana against her will and was one temper spike away from ashing Darion with her Atlantean light.

Strong logic to be sure, but damn hard to hold on to when every cell in his body was on fire and hungry for her.

Soft curves crushed against him. Her kiss was equal parts soft and demanding, a heady combination that only made him impatient to know how it would feel to be inside her.

His fangs surged against her questing tongue. His pulse was a hammer beating in his veins, sending licks of flames into every nerve ending. His cock strained against the Atlantean clothing he wore, a flimsy barrier between his rampant need and the woman driving him to the brink of madness simply with her kiss.

He cupped her breast over the bodice of her wispy silk gown, groaning at the feel of her taut nipple that hardened to a pebble beneath his caress. She moaned at his touch, then sucked in a shuddery breath when he ground his stiff erection against her abdomen.

Darion's warrior mind was desperate to reel him back to the reason he'd come to Selene's realm—to get the crystal, no matter what it takes.

Even if he had to seduce it away from her.

He hadn't ruled that out when he left D.C. with the Order's titanium box in his hands. But that wasn't what this kiss was about. No matter how he wished he could deny it, what he was feeling was real.

Unless Selene was a diabolical liar, she was caught up in the same overwhelming desire for him.

He broke their kiss only to trail his mouth along the delicate curve of her jaw line. Her head dropped back on a sigh, exposing the creamy column of her neck.

Ah, fuck.

A darker hunger bloomed inside him, despite the fact that he had taken more than enough nourishment from the briny old fisherman.

Darion's gaze rooted on the throb of Selene's carotid. A low growl rumbled in the back of his throat as he struggled to get a grip on the galloping pound of his heart. His breath sawed out of him, ragged with warning.

Selene froze. Her wild gaze shot to his in stark alarm.

And at that same moment came the urgent pound of booted footfalls approaching in the hallway outside the closed chamber door.

Selene broke away, shoving Darion back with a stricken look on her face.

Her guards pounded on the door. "Your Grace, the prisoner is on the loose."

"He's in here," she shouted, her voice huskier than normal.

At the same time, she bound him with a sudden stream of light that Darion didn't even try to fight. He doubted the half-dozen guards who burst into the room could hold him back if he truly meant to have her, but Selene's bonds held fast.

Several of the armed Atlanteans surrounded him while the rest formed a wall between Darion and their shaken queen.

"It took you long enough to get here," she told them tersely, refusing to look at him now. "Take him back to the tower."

Darion wondered if the guards were blind to the fact that she was breathless and red-cheeked, and he was seething with obvious lust and something even more dangerous to her wellbeing.

Selene pivoted away without a word, disappearing into an antechamber of her royal quarters.

As her men hustled Darion toward the door, his gaze strayed to a small pedestal table where a gleaming silver box sat. No, not merely silver. It was the titanium box he'd brought with him from D.C. The one he'd intended to use to smuggle out the realm's crystal when he eventually made his escape.

If not for his bound arms, he might have been tempted to make a lunge for it now.

Instead, he walked forward as Selene's guards shoved him into the hallway to take him to his cell.

# CHAPTER 26

Lucan peeled open one eye, struggling against the heavy sedatives that clung to him.

His throat felt as if he'd swallowed a box of razor blades. His gut was empty, hunger clawing at him with sharp talons. It was all he knew now—that raking, ceaseless drive to feed.

*Bloodlust.*

His sanity was threadbare, but not so far gone that he didn't recognize the addiction that coursed through every starving cell in his body.

He shuddered with the ferocity of his thirst. The hollowness and agony knew no end. Feeding it would only prolong the inevitable and worsen the suffering.

His *and* Gabrielle's.

Through the searing amber haze coloring everything in his vision, he glimpsed her on the narrow cot that had been set up outside the cell that contained him inside the command center. She had been there continuously for days, sometimes speaking words of love and encouragement to him through the fog of his madness and drug-induced rest, other times weeping softly into her pillow when she didn't realize he could hear her.

He had other scattered recollections too. Spotty bits of conversation spoken over him while he'd been heavily sedated. Tess and her son Rafe voicing frustration as they'd tried—and failed—to heal him with their shared abilities. Gideon and other members of the Order speculating about how much Red Dragon he must have ingested, and their grimly murmured fears that he may never fully recover.

He had no illusions about what lay ahead for him.

Death.

Be it from starvation, madness, or his own hand, his end was coming—likely sooner than later. He was Rogue, and there was virtually no coming back from that.

In front of him, a wall of ultraviolet light bars glowed with pale blue outlines, a warning that any attempt to escape would be fatal. Not a quick death like a UV bullet shot into his bloodstream or a nick from a titanium blade, but an incremental killing that would take several long minutes to finally reduce him to ashes.

If he didn't know Gabrielle would not only witness it, but feel it too, he would have already fried himself on the bars.

Even now, he contemplated the most efficient way to do it on the chance she might ever leave him alone in the room.

She must have sensed him coming back to consciousness. Her head lifted from the cot and she peered at him where he sat, his back against the cool wall of the cell, his knees bent and his head slumped toward his chest.

"Lucan?" Her soft, gentle voice nearly undid him. "You're awake."

Her movements were careful, her beautiful face pinched with discomfort, as she slid off the mattress and approached the bars. She eased down onto her knees, folding her legs beneath her.

"Lucan, can you hear me?"

As much as he wanted to resist her tenderness, there was a part of him lurking far beneath the grasp of his Bloodlust that couldn't deny her anything.

He lifted his head, staring at her through the matted hanks of black hair that hung over his forehead and eyes. A deep, rumbling vibration was all the sound he could muster.

Her hand came up to her lips to stifle her small sob. Through his daze, he couldn't tell if it was sorrow, pity, or relief that made her suck in that jagged breath.

"You've been asleep for several days," she whispered, her sweet brown eyes welling with tears. "I wasn't sure you were ever going to wake up."

That same hand that had been hovering at her mouth reached out now, fingers curling around one of the UV bars. She wasn't Breed, so the same light that would ash him had no effect on her.

A sad smile curved her mouth. "Can you forgive me for letting them put you down here? We didn't know of any other way. There wasn't anyplace else where you could rest and heal that would be safe for you . . . for everyone."

He felt a scowl furrow deep into his brow as he considered all the ways he remained a danger. To her, to his son and his brethren, the family and friends he would love until his last breath.

She moved closer to the bars. "The important thing is you came back to us. You came back to me. That's a miracle all of its own. Now, we just need one more."

He snarled, gutted by her hopeful optimism. That had always been her way. It had been the thing that had brought him through countless doubts and dark moments over the years.

But hope and optimism weren't going to pull him through this.

Worry knit her brows. Based on the sharp scraping of his thirst, he knew it wasn't only concern that drew her features into a pained expression.

"Lucan, you haven't fed all this time. I know you're starving because I can feel it."

She slid her hand between the bars, turning her arm until her wrist hovered just feet in front of him. He could smell the intoxicating, familiar fragrance of his Breedmate's bloodscent. The urge to lunge forward and take that tender limb to his fangs was overwhelming.

He fought to resist it, knowing if he drank even a sip, her blood would make him crave more. It would only prolong the inevitable and worsen his insatiable thirst.

Worse was the idea that he might injure her.

That was something he could never bear.

Gabrielle seemed undeterred. She stretched her arm inside even farther, straining to reach him. "Let me help you, please."

The roar that escaped him shook the thick walls. He forced himself into motion, flashing to the opposite corner of the cell. He crouched there like a wraith, vibrating with bone-deep fury. Not for her, but for how fiercely he wanted to take what she offered.

"Go," he rasped. "Leave me, Gabrielle."

"Never." There wasn't so much as a hint of trepidation in her voice. Only unwavering resolve. "I told you that a long time ago, Lucan Thorne. You promised me eternity, remember?"

The memory slammed into him, as fresh and vivid as the night they pledged their lives together. The bittersweet anguish of those vows felt like a curse to him now. All he had left to offer the woman he adored was misery and pain.

The awful weight of his guilt exploded out of him. *"I said get the fuck out of here."*

She flinched at his furious outburst, but she didn't budge. "I know what you're doing. You want me to leave so you can do something awful." Slowly, she withdrew her arm from the cell. She shook her head, her gaze locked on him with nothing but love and stubborn tenacity. "We've been through hard things together before, Lucan. I'm never giving up on you, on us."

Even through his rage and madness, he recognized her unbreakable resolve. Nothing he said or did was going to persuade her to abandon him. Not even Bloodlust. Not even the agony he had shackled her to through their blood bond.

The very qualities that had attracted him to her from the beginning were the ones that infuriated him now. Her hard-headed determination. Her courage. Her loyalty toward everyone she cared about. Her unshakable belief in him.

He'd thought she'd already seen him at his worst before she'd humbled him by becoming his mate. Never in his worst nightmares had he imagined he'd one day put her through this.

He couldn't bear to see her looking at him so tenderly in spite of the jagged pain his disease had to be causing her. He would rather be put back under sedation and hope to not wake up again.

Gabrielle could feel that too.

Her hands gripped the bars as if she were taking hold of him. "Don't you dare fucking give up, do you hear me? We'll find a way through this. We have to. Until then, I'm not going anywhere and neither are you."

The sedation was wearing off fast now. The waves of hunger that had been scraping at his insides now dug talons into him. The shredding pain wasn't anything he couldn't bear, but Gabrielle doubled over sharply, crying out.

He couldn't take it.

Tipping his head back, he bellowed Gideon's name.

The warrior rushed in from somewhere else, skidding to halt when he saw Gabrielle in utter agony. "Oh, shit."

Lucan leapt up, stopping only inches from the UV bars. "Put me back under. Do it now, goddamn it."

# CHAPTER 27

A full day had passed, yet Selene was still reeling from what had happened between her and Darion.

It wasn't bad enough that she had allowed a prisoner of the realm—a lethal enemy—to knock out several palace guards and stroll into the royal chambers without penalty. He had also kissed her, awakening a shocking desire she was loath to admit even now.

Although it was impossible to deny, at least to herself, when just the memory of his mouth on hers ignited spirals of pleasure in her veins and caused a low, smoldering heat to bloom deep in her core.

Clearly, she was the worst kind of fool.

Had it not been for the soldiers who'd discovered their comrades unconscious in the throne room and rushed to make sure she was safe, Darion likely would have had her carotid caught under his fangs and ripped from her throat.

Except he wasn't a killer. She'd witnessed that firsthand with the fisherman he'd drunk from, and in the fact that—true to his word—Darion had left the man uninjured and dozing soundly until he'd been returned to his little skiff by Atlantean soldiers and sent on his way none the wiser.

As for the way Darion had treated her, it hadn't been murder blazing in his eyes as he'd stared at her neck. Nor was there any hint of malice in the fevered look on his face when they'd kissed. Selene had only seen wanting in his molten amber gaze.

Want for her, and for a taste of her blood.

She pressed a hand to her breast, trying to calm the gallop of her heartbeat. She didn't want to think about Darion or his unsettling kiss anymore. She had important business to attend to with Jordana.

Selene arrived at her door alone today. She knocked politely, waiting for her granddaughter's response before entering.

Jordana eyed her warily, though it seemed they were making some small progress. The breakfast tray and cup of honeyed tea she had sent up to the room a couple hours ago weren't sitting untouched like all the others.

Instead of moving as far away as she could, Jordana rose from the cushioned seat at the window and turned to face Selene as she entered.

"Good morning," Selene said, offering a mild smile.

"What do you want?"

The reply was less combative than curious. Selene was willing to accept that as a positive too. "I came to tell you that I'm releasing you."

"Releasing me," Jordana echoed, suspicion shadowing her narrowed gaze. "Is this some kind of trick?"

Selene shook her head. "Not a trick."

There was something more she'd been reliving since her unsettling encounter with Darion. Something he'd said. An observation that lingered in her mind—and her heart—as much as his kiss.

That she was lonely.

Was that what had spurred her rash decision to abduct Jordana and forcibly bring her to the realm? Selene had told herself she'd been motivated by love, by a profound need to give love to the child who was her only heir and family.

It was love she felt toward Jordana. Unconditional, unbreakable.

But had it been a selfish need to fill a void in her life?

She would never have so much as considered the possibility until Darion confronted her with it. She didn't want to accept it now, either.

All she wanted was to try to make things right with Jordana.

If she wasn't already decades too late.

"There is a boat waiting at the dock to take you back to the mainland. My guards will ensure your safe passage back to America."

Jordana swallowed. "You're really setting me free?"

"Isn't that what you want? To return to your life with this Breed male of yours, Nathan?"

"Yes." A breath gusted from between her lips, halfway to a sob. "More than anything, that's what I want."

"He makes you that happy?"

"Nathan is my home. He's my heart and soul, all I ever need."

LARA ADRIAN

Selene studied her, watching the changing emotions play over Jordana's face as she spoke. Relief. Elation. A tender yet profound yearning.

"You truly love him."

"Yes." Jordana's chin lifted, gaze resolute. "And Nathan loves me every bit as deeply."

Selene smiled, moved by the depth of her conviction. The power of her certainty. "I'm glad for you, Jordana. I know you may not believe me, but it's true."

"What about Darion?" she asked. "Are you letting him go too?"

"No. He will remain here until I have the Order's crystal."

Jordana frowned. "They'll never agree to it. Release Darion along with me and prove you're not our enemy."

"All that would prove is that I am unwilling, or unable, to stand against them. I assure you, I am not."

"Is everything a test to you, Selene? Some fight you're determined to win?" Jordana shook her head, frustration seeping into her tone. "What are you so determined to prove?"

Selene didn't have an answer for that. This wasn't how she wanted her last conversation with her granddaughter to go. She hadn't been expecting some cathartic washing away of all her sins, but she didn't want to argue with Jordana, either.

She stared at her, looking at the beautiful woman who faced her now. So fearless and confident. So compassionate and strong.

So like her mother, Soraya.

"You were so small and precious when I saw you for the last time," she murmured. "You looked exactly like her, Jordana. I see so much resemblance, even now."

Jordana folded her arms in front of her, standing utterly still, saying nothing. Selene couldn't even tell if she was breathing.

"I'd never seen Raya happier than when she was holding you in her arms."

"Then why did you tear my family apart?" Bitter words, her chin trembling as she said them. "Why couldn't you let my mother and Cass be together?"

"I allowed my own wounds to color my actions," Selene admitted. "I didn't trust Cassianus to love her. I didn't want my daughter to be hurt, to be betrayed."

"He wouldn't have done that."

"How could I know that? He was the captain of my palace legion. He of all people knew Raya was not to be touched. I had made him personally responsible for her protection. He broke realm law and he betrayed his pledge to me."

"Broke the law?" Jordana scoffed. "They fell in love. You tore them apart."

Selene nodded, her head heavy with regret. "I believed I was acting out of a mother's love, a mother's need to protect. I know how wrong I was now, but at the time . . ." She inhaled a fortifying breath to say the rest. She had never confessed any of it before, but she wanted no secrets between her and Jordana—even if they never saw each other again. "Cassianus and Soraya left the realm before her pregnancy began to show. She gave birth to you somewhere else."

"A villa on the Amalfi coast in Italy," Jordana said. "Zael told me everything. How Cass and my mother lived there for a while after I was born, but she missed her homeland. She missed this place. Zael also told me what happened after Cass brought me and my mother back to the realm. He told me what you did the minute they arrived. You called for Cass's execution."

Selene closed her eyes for a moment, reliving the awful memories. "Soraya had been innocent until him, untouched. After they fled and returned, when I saw you in her arms I feared he had seduced her, possibly even forced her into bearing his child to satisfy his own ambitions in my court."

Jordana gaped at her, incredulous. "Even then, you couldn't see they were deeply in love?"

"I didn't know what that looked like," Selene admitted quietly. "Real love. I had never known it myself."

She still didn't. She knew what faithless promises looked like. She knew how heated whispers of desire and devotion could dry up in an instant if there was something greater to be gained somewhere else.

She knew how a foolish heart could be led into believing someone truly cared, only to turn around and find it had been cut open and left to bleed out while her enemies moved in to destroy her.

What Soraya and Cassianus had, what Jordana clearly shared with Nathan . . . Selene had gone her entire existence without ever knowing a moment of it herself.

Jordana regarded her with sympathy in her gaze, even pity. "You destroyed everything they had, Selene. You destroyed everything I had at the time too, because I didn't get to know either one of them. My mother burned herself alive in one of these palace towers, and twenty-five years later Cass was cut down in the streets of Boston on your order."

"If I could take it all back, Jordana, I would. I've regretted this every minute of every waking hour since that awful day I lost my daughter."

Jordana shook her head. "You can't take it back. If you were sorry for what you'd done, why did you send your legion soldiers to take Cass's head all those years later? Was it punishment for the fact that he escaped with me, or the fact that he also stole one of your precious crystals when we fled the realm?"

"By the time my legion caught up to him, I had already given up on ever seeing you or that crystal again. I should've called off the order. It was one of my generals who continued to hunt for Cassianus. I didn't know Taebris and a few of his men had tracked him to Boston until they returned with the news of his slaying." Selene wanted to reach out to Jordana, offer some comfort for the hurt in her eyes, but what good would it do? "I am sorry . . . for everything."

"Sorry doesn't change anything. Remorse can't bring them back."

"I know," Selene murmured. "But I hope telling you might help you understand. Just as I hope releasing you will at least lessen some of your hatred toward me."

"I should hate you," Jordana said quietly. "I want to. All I feel for you is pity, Selene. Your bitterness and mistrust robbed all of us . . . including you."

"Yes, it has." Selene nodded soberly, her throat raw with grief and self-condemnation. "I don't expect it, but I hope in time maybe you'll find a way to forgive me."

Before Jordana could see the emotion welling in her eyes, Selene turned away and walked to the opened chamber door. With shoulders squared and a steeliness in her voice that she truly didn't feel, she called for her guards.

"Please, take my granddaughter down to the dock now."

"Yes, Your Grace."

# CHAPTER 28

Movement down at the beach caught Darion's attention as he sat in his tower cell.

The large sailboat that had brought him to the Atlantean island was departing. Crewed by several soldiers from Selene's legion, it also bore a single passenger: Jordana.

She stood on the deck, facing the island while the men heaved the vessel away from its moorings.

Had Selene set her free?

Darion got up and walked to the border of shadow and sunlight, watching as the white sails began to unfurl into the warm winds off the water.

At that same moment, Jordana must have spotted him standing in the tall tower. Her hand went up slowly, and even across the distance he could see the conflicted look on her face as she waved goodbye to him.

All he felt was relief to see her go.

Her freedom was the most important part of the mission he'd had when he left for the Atlantean realm.

Now, all that remained was finding some way to either persuade Selene that he and the Order weren't her enemies, or hatch a plan to locate her crystal and somehow smuggle it off the island before she was tempted to use it against them.

He hoped to hell Selene would eventually come around, because the alternative plan held nothing but obstacles and nearly impossible odds of success.

As the sailboat moved farther into the distance, Darion glanced across the palace grounds to the private garden off Selene's royal chambers. She was there, sunlight illuminating her as she tended to a rosebush bursting with bloodred blooms. Her long platinum waves were gathered up off her shoulders today into a complicated arrangement of loose twists and pearl-studded plaits, topped with a delicate coronet. The soft curves of her lean body were draped in filmy blush-colored silk and long skirts that were nearly translucent in the golden sunlight overhead.

Darion's mouth watered at the arrestingly sensual sight of her. He had been tormented by the memory of her soft lips and pleasured moans ever since he kissed her. His body still burned for her, arousal still smoldering in his veins. Seeing her again lit a match to the embers.

As for Selene, all her focus seemed rooted on the long-stemmed flowers she carefully snipped and placed into a vase of clear water. She didn't look his way, but Darion knew she felt him watching her. The almost rigid way she moved despite her innate grace, the way she seemed to deliberately avoid acknowledging her awareness of him . . . all of it gave her away.

He smiled to himself, far too pleased to realize she wasn't as unaffected by him as she wanted to pretend.

Overhead, the peculiar sunlight blazed. If not for the threat of certain incineration, it would have been tempting to leap across the distance and pay the haughty immortal queen another unannounced visit.

Maybe there was another way.

He'd been noticing the persistent glow that sealed his cell door closed had been dimming now and then over time. Even now, the ring of white light that had burned so brightly when he'd first woken up a prisoner in the tower seemed slightly guttered.

Darion sent a mental command to the locked latch on the thick stone door. It yielded to his mind with a quiet, metallic snick. He took full advantage, moving swiftly. Opening the door on the pair of sentries posted outside, he quickly tranced them both, dragged them into the cell, and closed them inside.

Using the speed of his Breed genetics, he flashed through the abandoned east tower of the palace to Selene's chambers, stirring no more notice than a cool breeze as he passed the handful of oblivious attendants and soldiers along the way.

He strolled through her living quarters and out to the shade of an ivy-covered pergola at the edge of her cheery little garden where she had just finished arranging the flowers.

"Good to see you took my words to heart."

She whipped around, startled. After the way their last encounter ended, he expected her to raise the alarm with her guards again now.

But she didn't call out for protection.

Her chin lifted and she regarded him with a cold, imperious look that might have frozen any other man or mere mortal. It only made Darion smile.

"I saw Jordana sailing away," he said.

"What of it?" she asked tersely.

He took a step forward, just to the edge of the light. "I have to assume you freed her to prove a point, but was it to demonstrate you're not evil, or that you aren't lonely?"

"You have no idea what you're talking about. And I have nothing to prove to anyone, least of all you."

He shrugged. "I didn't say it was me judging you. I suspect you're harder on yourself than anyone else could be."

"I released Jordana because it was the right thing to do—for her and for the realm. Thank you for informing me of your current upgrade in status, by the way. It's good to know I have something of even greater value to your comrades now." She gave him a self-satisfied smile. "If Jordana wasn't worth surrendering their crystal, I expect you will be."

Darion chuckled. "Think again. You and I had better get used to seeing a lot more of each other, because the Order isn't going to take that deal. I won't let them take it."

She smiled at him in challenge. "You had better hope they will, if you ever want to feed again."

Her threat had no teeth—unlike him. "You really want to put me to the test? There's only one thing more dangerous than a pissed off Breed male, and that's a starving one."

He stared at her throat, which was highlighted by a ray of sunshine. The beam of light glittered almost like stardust, thin and sparkling, fragile somehow. Almost as if it were an unearthly, silvery illusion.

He thought back to the illumination around the door in the tower. How it had degraded over time, weakened. Until today, when he'd been able to break through it and escape the tower cell.

And there was the strange effect he noticed in the sky from time to time, when he could plainly see the moon and a night full of stars hanging just above the canopy of sunlight that had drenched every square foot of the Atlantean realm from the moment Selene had taken him prisoner.

"It's you." He'd had his suspicions before, but now there was no doubt. "You're creating all of this light, aren't you? Keeping night from falling so I can't set foot outside the palace walls."

"Stay where you are," she commanded, a breathlessness in her voice. "I promise you, my light burns as hot as any sun's."

"Yes, I know. I've already tested it for myself. It must take some effort, even for you." The weakened glow around his door was evidence of that. "How long do you expect you can hold it, Selene?"

"Longer than you can last without blood."

He shook his head. "I don't believe you want me dead. You may wish you wanted that, but you don't. That kiss the other night said a lot about what both of us want . . . and it doesn't have anything to do with a fucking crystal."

On a huff, she stalked forward, stopping just out of arm's length. "I am the queen of this realm. How dare you imply—"

"I'm not implying it. I'm stating it plainly, Selene. You wanted me to kiss you. You want it now. I can hear how fast your heart is beating. I can scent how hot your skin is beneath all that silk and royal propriety. When you're looking at me like that, it has nothing to do with that crown on your head or the realm you rule."

"Shut up," she murmured.

But he was only getting started. "I can see the flush in your cheeks, Selene. Every time you lick your lips—like you just did now—I'm not thinking about the Order or my duty to them. All I'm thinking about is how much I want to feel my mouth on yours again. I know you're thinking about it too."

She drew in a shallow breath, shaking her head. Her voice dropped to a whisper. "I said shut up."

"Am I wrong? If I am, prove it to me. Come stand out of the light where I can touch you. Show me how wrong I am."

She didn't move. She stood there in that shimmering nimbus of her own creation, staring at him in silence, looking so forlorn and lost he couldn't stand it.

Darion reached out into the light and took her hand in his.

His forearm was bare under the loose-woven sleeve of his tunic. The skin burned instantly, scorching from even that scant exposure.

He didn't care. His Breed cells would heal in moments, and he hardly registered the pain as he drew Selene toward him, into the cool shadows of the pergola.

The pulse point in her wrist throbbed under his grasp. Their bodies brushed against each other, her curves soft against all the places he was hard. She breathed rapidly, her blue eyes dusky with desire.

Darion stroked his free hand along her cheek, down onto the side of her neck. His touch pulled a ragged sigh out of her, but her heart was still galloping like a wild horse. The feel of her—the strength and softness of her—nearly undid him where he stood.

His fangs surged, and the erection that had been raging even before her body brushed against him was now as hard as stone and greedy to be inside her.

"I came here prepared to fight an enemy," he murmured, his voice rough with need. "I came here expecting to feel contempt for you, not this. Christ, anything but this."

He lowered his head and kissed her, hot and hard and deep.

She melted against him, no resistance in her at all. The hand he'd been holding slipped out of his loose grip and came to rest against his chest, right above the thundering pound of his heart. She moaned as he took her deeper into his kiss. Her fingers curled into the fabric of his tunic as she clung to him, her mouth as fevered as his.

He growled against her lips, a low, possessive sound. The intense kiss they'd shared before was only a pale prelude to this one. Darion wanted to devour her. He wanted to uncover every sweet inch of her body and make her his.

But he needed to hear her tell him she wanted that too.

"If you say you don't want this," he rasped thickly, pulling back from her kiss to search her gorgeous blue eyes. "Ah fuck . . . even if you lie when you say it, tell me to stop now and I will."

She stared at him, panting through her kiss-bruised, parted lips. Her little crown was askew, her pale blonde hair falling loose from its confinements. She was immortal and ageless, a formidable queen, but she looked as innocent as a kitten in his arms.

She shook her head in response to his demand.

"Not good enough," he growled. "I need to hear you say the words."

"Yes." The word rushed out of her like a curse, like a prayer. "Yes, I do want this. *You.*"

The dark sound of satisfaction he made was unearthly, even to his own ears.

A large marble table with a sculpture of a sea nymph stood beside them under the pergola. Gripping Selene under her fine ass, he lifted her onto the edge of the table. His hand went to one perfect breast as he kissed her again, his fingers kneading and caressing over the top of the silky bodice of her gown, coaxing the tight peak of her nipple until it was like a pebble to his touch.

He needed to feel her softness without the barrier of clothing. Slipping his hand inside, he moved the fabric away and lifted her bare breast in his palm. On a groan he bent his head and suckled her, careful to keep his fangs from nicking her tender flesh.

No easy thing when everything Breed in him drummed with the urge to possess her in every way.

His hands shook with the force of that want as he pulled her bodice down off her arms and bared her torso to his hungry gaze. She was beyond lovely. Creamy skin so flawless and delicate it radiated an unearthly luminescence, as though she were made of starlight and moonbeams.

He touched her with reverence, his hand looking too big and rough against her skin. He marveled, not only at the extraordinary beauty seated in front of him, but at the fact that she wanted him.

"Selene," he uttered hoarsely, lifting his admiring gaze to the desire-drenched eyes that watched him with a hunger that rocked him. "I've never seen anything as perfect as you."

She started to shake her head, but he stopped her with another kiss. This time, he took his time, despite the savage arousal spurring him with every hard beat of his pulse.

He hadn't come there to seduce her, but he couldn't keep his hands or mouth away from her now. After kissing her breathless, he moved on to lavish more praise on her breasts.

Selene's short nails dragged down his back as she arched into him. When she brought her hands back up again, she drew the hem of his tunic up at the same time. He shrugged out of it, eager for her touch on him too.

He stood still and let her trace the *glyphs* that spread out over his chest and shoulders. Her fingertips on his skin markings left a trail of fire in their wake, stirring the *glyphs* into moving, variegating colors.

"Amazing," she whispered, then leaned forward to trace the same paths with her tongue.

He went taut as a bowstring, his head tipped back on his shoulders with a strangled groan hissed through his teeth and fangs. His arousal was beyond bearing, a hard, pulsing demand.

When he brought his chin down again, his vision burned with amber, and he didn't have to hear her quiet inhalation to know how fierce and feral he must look to one of her kind.

Selene didn't shrink away. No, not her. She didn't turn her head in horror, or try to avoid seeing what he truly was.

Breed.

The enemy race she professed so vehemently to despise.

She reached up and curved her hand against his face. Then brought his head down with singular purpose and took his mouth in a ravenous kiss.

Their hands moved hungrily now, hot breaths mingling.

Darion reached down and lifted her long skirts, pushing the yards of diaphanous silk up around her thighs. Then he sank down to his knees in front of her.

She wore delicate panties made of lace beneath the regal gown. As much as he tried to be gentle, his fingers rent the fragile lace. Impatient with himself and his need, he shoved the frilly thing aside then lowered his head and pressed his mouth to her sex.

She tasted sweeter than he could have imagined. He was drunk on her at the first stroke of his tongue over her satiny flesh. He slid a finger into her wet heat at the same time, reveling at the pleasured sounds she made as he stroked her.

But he wanted more.

He wanted to obliterate any claim she may try to make that she wasn't every bit as consumed by need for him as he was with her. He drove her to the crest of a violent climax and then tumbled her over the edge with his name on her lips as she shattered against his mouth.

She was still panting with the force of that release when she reached down and grabbed a fistful of his hair, pulling him up the length of her gorgeous body. Her eyes glittered with unearthly blue fire.

Holy hell. She was the hottest thing he'd ever seen.

Her mouth curved, her expression one of pure hunger and demand. "I need you inside me."

She didn't have to say it twice.

# CHAPTER 29

Never in her entire existence had she ever felt so alive. So emotionally free and untethered from the burdens of her role as queen.

With pleasure exploding through every cell and fiber of her being from the release Darion had just given her with his wicked mouth and amazing tongue, all she felt was bliss. Right now she was, simply, a woman.

The woman Darion was looking at as though none other existed for him. Not in this moment. Not ever before, if the intensity of his fiery amber gaze could be believed.

She wanted to believe it.

She wanted to believe every second of bliss he'd given her was real.

She just wanted to have more.

*More of him.*

Her demand to have him inside her was met with his slow grin, one that sent a lick of fire curling through her veins. He rose from his crouch between her spread thighs. His strong body was impressive under normal circumstances. Seeing him like this, with his bared torso and muscled arms covered in intricate patterns of Breed skin markings that pulsed and churned with dark colors, she couldn't keep herself from staring in open wonder.

Instead of seeing him as part of an enemy race so different from her own, Selene was captivated. Awed. Desperate to feel him against her . . . inside her.

She pulled the tie on his linen pants and together they shoved the fabric off him. There were more *dermaglyphs* here, bold arcs accentuating the lean cut of his hips, the sinew of his powerful thighs. His cock jutted from a thatch of dark curls, capturing her attention even more than the mesmerizing beauty of his *glyphs*.

She took his thick length in her hands, marveling at the silken strength of him. As she stroked and caressed him, his arousal surged impossibly harder, throbbing against her palms and fingertips.

He tipped his head back on a strangled moan, the tendons in his neck like cables, all of his skin markings intensifying and filling with deeper shades of indigo, wine, and gold.

On a ground-out curse, he brought his gaze back to hers. She stared at his molten eyes, his fangs that gleamed like daggers behind the sensual curve of his lips. There was no mistaking what he was, this member of a race that had been at war with hers for eons. She looked at him and all she felt was raw, primal desire.

"God, Selene . . . when you look at me like that," he snarled, shaking his head.

He didn't finish whatever he meant to say.

He shot forward and took her mouth in a bruising, possessive kiss. His big body pressed her down beneath him on the marble tabletop. His pelvis wedged between her opened thighs, his cock like a length of heated steel against her wet cleft.

She was on fire for him. There was no stopping the cry that boiled out of her as he entered her. He was so big, invading her so thoroughly she could scarcely breathe from the pleasure of it.

"Are you all right?" he asked, braced on one hand above her. He moved only incrementally, driving her mad with the careful strokes. "Is this okay?"

At first, all she could manage was a wobbly nod and a broken gasp. "God, yes. Oh, God . . . it's so good."

He kept his eyes locked on hers as he picked up the pace of his thrusts, murmuring words of praise for how soft she felt around him, how beautiful she was, and how much he craved her.

It was all fuel to the fire of her senses, ratcheting up her ecstasy as his deep strokes and slow withdrawals brought her careening toward the peak of another climax.

She clung to him, digging her fingers into the bulky curves of his shoulders as she gripped him tightly with her thighs and her sex.

"Can't get enough of me, can you?" He grinned, smugly arrogant.

What would have pissed her off only an hour ago instead inflamed her with unabashed need. "Shut up and fuck me harder."

He chuckled darkly. "Yes, Your Grace."

Faith, did he ever oblige.

He rocked into her with relentless power, giving more pleasure than she could take. The wave of bliss that crashed over her was so shocking and profound it brought hot tears to her eyes. She cried out as she came, shuddering with the force of it.

Darion drove deeper then, his tempo urgent before he snarled her name and hurtled off the edge of his own release.

They didn't let go of each other, not even when the last aftershocks had ebbed. Selene rested her cheek against his shoulder, grappling with the confusion of emotions and bliss that spiraled through her as Darion held her in his arms.

He drew back abruptly, and she saw that his shoulder was wet with her tears. A scowl furrowed his brow. "Did I hurt you?"

"No." Embarrassed, she swiped impatiently at her damp eyelashes and cheeks. "It's not that. It's just . . . I've never felt . . . I didn't know it could be so . . ."

She was babbling. And dammit, those tears were still leaking out of her.

Smiling, Darion leaned forward and kissed her. This time it was a tender meeting of their mouths, his lips infinitely soft.

"Incredible," he whispered in between kisses. "I believe that's the word you're looking for."

It was incredible. *He* was incredible.

Now that it was over, she suddenly felt awkward and vulnerable. Holding his naked body against her—inside her—felt overwhelmingly intimate. Terrifyingly so.

But it was much worse than that.

She didn't have a single regret for what they'd just shared, but she couldn't afford to let herself sink into his tender caresses and pretty words. She couldn't allow her heart to get caught in a trap. She had made that mistake before and it had come at the cost of thousands of lives.

She wanted to believe Darion was different. She wanted to believe that so desperately right now, it nearly scared her to death.

She put her hand against his chest and eased herself out from beneath him. She couldn't look at him, fearful he would see how deeply he affected her.

"Hey, where are you going?" he said, confusion in his deep voice as she started to straighten her skewed bodice. His knuckles coaxingly brushed her arm. "We're just getting started."

Selene forced herself to move away from his tender touch. She slid off the edge of the table, arranging her long skirts. "You should get dressed. Someone may come to the door."

"You should've thought about that before," he joked as he drew his pants up and loosely fastened the tie. He was smiling as he took her shoulders in his hands and turned her around to face him. "God, you look so beautiful like this, all flushed and in disarray. I want to muss you up all over again."

She didn't let herself return his smile. It was nearly impossible to maintain a cool facade when he was looking at her with renewed hunger in his glittering eyes.

She was too shaken by the tangled confusion of her emotions to her let down her guard, despite the pleasure they had just shared.

"Please go now, Darion. I have duties to attend, so I'd like to get on with them."

He stared at her, all the humor and tenderness fading from his handsome face. "What are you doing?"

"It was just sex," she said, which wasn't untrue. Still, it felt like the worst sort of lie as it slipped off her tongue. "Pleasurable or not, it changes nothing between us."

He was silent, but the fire in his gaze took on a darker edge.

"Go," she said again. "Unless you prefer me to call for my guards to come and take you out of here."

His scoff was brittle, incredulous. Sharp with bewilderment. "No, Your Grace. I wouldn't want you to go to the trouble. I'll show myself out."

Cursing under his breath, he grabbed his discarded tunic and stalked away from her.

# CHAPTER 30

*What the hell just happened?*

Darion walked away from Selene in a state of confusion and frustration.

And yeah, he was plenty pissed off too—all of it self-directed.

She was ready to freshen up and take on whatever vague royal duties she claimed were so immediately pressing, and he had been sent to the exit with his dick in his hand.

It didn't help his mood that he was still hard for her, still aching to get back inside her heat even after her cold dismissal.

What happened between them had been incredible sex. Neither one of them could argue that. But apparently for Selene, that's as far as it went.

He didn't want to believe that.

Hell, he *couldn't* believe it.

He saw the emotion in her face. He felt it in the way she clung to him, the way she stared into his eyes while they moved in tempo together. For a moment while he'd been inside her, he'd felt as if the rest of the world had stopped all its madness and there were only the two of them.

Not a Breed warrior and an Atlantean queen. Not enemies pitched against each other over the possession of some otherworldly crystals. Not a man bound to the night and a woman who burned so hot she could have been made of sunbeams.

Just Selene and him.

For a moment, he'd been able to imagine spending the rest of his life in her light-drenched realm, if only for the chance to feel her naked beneath him.

The urge to turn around and force her to admit her lie was nearly overwhelming.

He cooled his heels.

Because maybe he needed the reminder that they were, in fact, still adversaries. She had her world and he had his, where his brothers-in-arms were steeped in combat with Opus Nostrum and his parents were suffering the shared horror of Bloodlust.

Darion had come to Selene's realm on a mission, and that mission was only half fulfilled with Jordana's release.

He had no wish to deprive Selene and her people of their crystal's protection, but he would be a fool not to consider all of his options and plan accordingly in case he needed to.

Selene had made that fact clear enough just now.

As he stalked through the living area of her quarters, his gaze locked on the small titanium box he'd spied the last time he was there. The container had been specially crafted to carry a crystal safely and virtually undetected.

Darion didn't know where the realm's crystal was located. He hadn't even attempted to look, he'd been so distracted by the Atlanteans' lovely, hot-as-sin queen. And even if he had found it, since he wasn't Atlantean, he wouldn't be able to touch the crystal without lethal ramifications.

Ramifications that would be neutralized if he had that titanium box.

Selene's sharp insistence that she never steps foot in the east tower began to ring in his ears.

Except for the few guards she posted outside his cell, no one ventured up to that empty ruin.

Darion paused, hissing a curse under his breath. He was too skilled in combat and strategy to ignore a valuable tactical advantage when it was sitting right under his nose.

He wrapped the box in his tunic, then flashed from the royal chambers to the tomblike east tower to stow the box somewhere for safekeeping.

Even though by rights it belonged to the Order, to Jordana, guilt pricked him for taking it.

He only hoped he wouldn't be forced to use it.

# CHAPTER 31

Jordana arrived home to D.C. the following day to find the headquarters gripped in bad news and worry.

Rogue violence showed no signs of abating. Not even Darkhavens were safe against the scourge of Red Dragon. Brock and Jenna had recently taken a foundling boy into their care after his parents had fallen victim to the terror Opus had set loose on the city.

On top of that, Jenna was dealing with upsetting problems of her own. A strange coma had taken her down for days while Jordana was gone. She'd awoken with the certainty that the Ancient had not only escaped the Deadlands with the pair of crystals from his wrecked craft, but had somehow been rummaging through her mind while she slept.

As for Lucan's condition, it was worsening by the hour. Tess and Rafe had been unable to reverse his Bloodlust, even with the power of their combined healing abilities. He hadn't fed in nearly a week, although everyone understood the hunger brought on by Red Dragon couldn't be sated no matter how much blood he consumed. When he wasn't heavily sedated, he was combative with everyone who attempted to reason with him.

Worst of all, he was withdrawing from Gabrielle.

Jordana could hardly bear having to tell Darion's mother that her son was currently imprisoned in the Atlantean realm and being ransomed for the crystal. Nathan had stood at Jordana's side as she had explained the situation to all of the Order upon her arrival. The long walk down to the Lucan's holding cell where Gabrielle had been living—and barely sleeping—the past few days had seemed like walking toward a gallows.

Gabrielle listened without speaking, and it wasn't until Jordana and Nathan left the room that they heard her crying brokenly into the pillow on her cot.

"I should've stayed," Jordana murmured into Nathan's chest. "I should have refused to go unless Selene released Darion too."

"No." Nathan lifted her chin on the edge of his strong hand. "Don't even think it. Darion would have pushed you onto that boat himself rather than have you stay another second under that sadistic witch's control. She'd better pray I never get my hands on her after all she's done."

Jordana winced a little at the venom in her mate's deep voice. "This may sound crazy, but I don't want to see Selene suffer."

Nathan drew her close and tenderly kissed her forehead. "That's because you're the kindest, most forgiving person I know."

"No," she said, meeting his serious gaze. "She's done awful things. Selfish things. But I don't think there's anything that anyone can do to her that would be worse than living with her own regret and sorrow for the cost of her actions. She has nothing, Nathan. Nothing but her people and her realm."

He grunted, skeptical. "If she had her way, she'd also have two crystals and the power to obliterate anyone or anything that dares to piss her off."

"I'm not sure anymore if that's true. Selene could've had the colony's crystal instead of taking me. She could've had her vengeance on the entire community that rejected her rule. Instead she left it with them."

"Only to have a bigger prize—you."

"And yet she let me go." Jordana was going to need a lot of time to come to terms with all her conflicted feelings about Selene, but she was certain about one thing. "Selene isn't driven to destroy. I think she's desperate to protect the things that matter to her."

Nathan's scowl relaxed somewhat, but his warrior's gaze remained sober. "I trust your judgment, but even if you're right, that doesn't make her any less dangerous."

Jordana couldn't argue that point, especially when Darion was still a captive on Selene's unbreachable, sun-drenched island.

As she and Nathan continued walking up the corridor, Micah and his Atlantean mate Phaedra rounded a corner up ahead of them. Tegan's son sent a grave look at Nathan.

"You coming to the war room?"

"Why? What's going on?"

"The daywalker teams are in place and moving in on Opus targets."

Jordana turned a confused look on her mate. "What kind of Opus targets?"

"The inner circle. Thanks to Darion, we were able to deploy Gideon's worm and it went off without a hitch.

For the past few days we've been working on nailing down Opus locations and getting our assassin teams deployed."

"Explain it to her on the way," Micah urged. "It's just about showtime."

Jordana hurried alongside Nathan to catch up with Micah and Phaedra. The four of them entered the war room where the long table was already encircled with nearly every Order elder and their mates. Under normal circumstances, it would have been something of a celebration having practically the entire commanding arm of the Order gathered in one place.

But these were far from normal circumstances, and it was impossible not to notice the absence of Lucan, Gabrielle, and Darion at the table.

Jordana and Nathan moved toward the back of the room to stand beside some of their friends and comrades. Mira and Kellan who'd come in from Montreal with Nikolai and Renata. Niko's mate held their sleeping infant son Dmitri in her arms as the couple stared riveted like everyone else at the large monitor dominating one wall of the room.

Jax stood next to a grim-faced Rafe, whose daywalker mate Devony was part of the team video-feeding in from the operation. The Chase twins, Aric and Carys, and their mother Tavia, daywalkers all, were also represented by their live camera feeds on screen. Rounding out the eight-person team were Zael's mate and Tavia's sister, Brynne, as well as Aric's special unit consisting of daywalkers Lachlan, Jade, and Grayson.

Opus had both Breed and human members pulling the strings of their terrorist operation. They also had an army of Rogues and a seemingly endless supply of Red

Dragon at their disposal, but one thing that wouldn't stop the kill squad from coming after the leadership of their underground cabal was ultraviolet light ammunition.

Jordana stared transfixed, her heart in her throat as each Order warrior on camera began to move in on their targets in different corners of the world.

Like a lethal symphony, one after another the daywalkers slipped past locked doors and security systems in pursuit of their unsuspecting prey.

Lachlan was first, entering the bedroom of a Breed dignitary in Costa Rica and severing his head while he slept.

Carys's target was a Louisiana businessman. The Breed male got into the driver's seat of his Bentley, unaware that death waited directly behind him. Before the Opus operative could start the engine Carys fired her weapon from the seat behind him, painting the inside of the windshield with his gray matter and skull fragments.

More stealth assassinations followed. The daywalkers were swift, expert, and effective.

Finally, only Aric Chase on location in Prague was left to complete his mission.

"Something doesn't feel right," he whispered into his headset as he approached a side door of a non-assuming house in an unremarkable residential neighborhood. "We sure this is the right location? The whole place feels empty."

Gideon confirmed the intel to Aric, exchanging a wary look with Sterling Chase, who watched his son as though the commander were seated on a bed of nails.

Aric stole down a stairwell to the basement of the house. His camera feed displayed an impressive communication center with a dozen or more computers. He moved deeper into the cavernous space, rounding a corner on silent feet. His camera slowly panned to a storage room in the far corner of the basement.

The door was closed, a keypad lock blinking a warning of a breach.

"Careful, son," Chase murmured.

Aric reached for the latch. Swung open the door with one hand, his other holding his blade.

"Ah, fuck."

The grisly image of a decapitated Breed male lying in a large pool of blood filled the war room monitor. Someone had already taken the Opus operative out.

But that wasn't the only thing that made Jordana, Nathan, and everyone else gathered in the room stare in mounting dread at what they were seeing.

Whoever had killed this Opus Nostrum leader hadn't done it with any kind of blade.

The head had been cleaved from the male's neck with a brutal strike.

A strike from a hand that was tipped with sharp talons.

"Oh, my God," Jenna gasped, coming out of her seat. "It was him. The Ancient did this."

Every head in the room turned in her direction.

"Babe, are you sure?" Brock asked.

She nodded, her face blanched. "Nothing else could do that."

"Guys," Aric said, stepping over the corpse to aim his camera at a crate that sat inside the storage room. "This doesn't look good."

The crate had been torn open by the same taloned hand, exposing what had to have been hundreds of cylinders packed inside. All but a handful of them had already been removed.

Aric reached inside and took out one of the remaining cylinders. He unscrewed the cap and cursed as he peered inside.

Very carefully, he tipped the canister and poured out a small amount of what it held.

Fine, dark red powder drifted to the floor.

"Is that what I think it is?" Gideon asked.

"Yeah." Aric's voice was grim. "What the hell does the Ancient want with a shitload of Red Dragon?"

# CHAPTER 32

"On your feet," barked the largest of two big Atlantean guards who'd barged into Darion's cell the next day. "Her Majesty wants to see you."

He took his time standing up. "Here I was just about to get a little shut-eye," he said, with a sardonic smile.

The soldiers glowered, shoving him out the door ahead of them. They had no idea that his boredom was an act. If they had come to get him just a minute sooner, they would have found his cell vacant and their prisoner on the loose somewhere inside the palace.

Since Selene had ordered him back to his cell, he'd been making good use of his time. The light she had been holding around the door to lock him inside was fading even more after their encounter in her garden.

Darion had used the opportunity to slip out and explore where he could. It wasn't easy avoiding detection from the various attendants and guards, but even his limited reconnaissance had given him a decent understanding of the palace layout and the purposes of its various chambers and public rooms.

What he hadn't yet been able to discern, however, was the location of the crystal.

The soldiers marched him down from the east tower and across to the larger, main tower that contained the throne room and Selene's court. She wasn't inside the expansive space, but her voice filtered out, along with someone else's, from the adjacent solar.

"It's been too many days, Your Grace. I suggest we send a second search party to the area."

"I'm just as concerned as you are, Seb. Something's not right. But if anything has happened to Taebris or his team, sending more men will only put them at risk as well."

Sebathiel started to argue further, but one of the guards cleared his throat and Selene's adviser stiffened at the interruption. He looked at Darion with the same disapproval he might give a flea-bitten mongrel standing in the queen's presence.

With a courtly bow to her, Sebathiel then strode out of the solar on a current of contempt, his long robes billowing in his wake.

Darion smirked. "He doesn't like me much," he said, his gaze rooted on Selene.

It was next to impossible for him to notice anything else at all when she was in the room. Breathtaking as always, today she was resplendent in a pale blue gown and her shimmery hair loose around her shoulders and arms. But there were shadows in her eyes, Darion noticed.

Her conversation with Sebathiel obviously had her pensive, even worried, but her face seemed to carry a weariness too. She seemed on the verge of exhaustion, despite her regal poise.

A flick of her hand dismissed the guards. Once they had gone, she regarded Darion with a carefully schooled stare.

"Seb doesn't like anything that threatens the realm."

"Or that threatens you," Darion added.

She gave a mild nod. "That's what makes him my most valuable adviser. Sebathiel has lasted longer in that post than anyone else because he would do anything to protect the realm, and his queen, from any threat."

"Is that how you see me too? A threat to the realm? A threat to you? I thought we were moving past all of that yesterday but you seem to have other thoughts."

He studied her face, noting the hint of color that flushed her cheeks, the way she struggled to hold his stare now.

She drew in a shallow breath, her voice just above a whisper. "What happened yesterday was a mistake."

"Didn't feel like one to me." Despite her insistence, he spotted the lie in her gaze and in the anxious way she licked her lips.

His body responded instantly, making the urge to close the distance and pull her into his arms nearly overwhelming. He stayed put, though not without effort.

He could still feel her in all of his senses—the sweet taste of her, the velvet softness of her skin, her hair, her sex. Her scent still lived inside his head, as did the husky sound of the hot demand that had boiled out of her while he'd been buried to the hilt inside her body.

All of those things were the truth. Not her abrupt determination to deny it.

He shook his head. "I don't believe yesterday felt like a mistake to you, either."

She frowned. "I didn't send for you to talk about any of that. I've decided to move you out of the east tower, into the main palace."

"An upgrade?" He grinned. "I was just starting to enjoy having the whole east tower ruin to myself."

She didn't laugh, not that he expected her to. No, his remark only seemed to make the shadows in her eyes go darker, until her expression seemed haunted with private pain. Her voice was quiet, toneless now. "You'll stay in the chamber Jordana vacated on the fifth floor. It will be easier to keep you under closer watch—and under heavier guard—if you're here in the main tower."

Darion didn't mean to add to her distress, but he had to know. "Why don't you ever go to the east tower?"

She flinched as if she'd been struck. "It's a ruin. There's no reason for me to step foot in that place."

He lowered his voice, realizing it was sorrow, not anger in her sharp reply. "It wasn't always a ruin, though, was it?"

She may wish to draw a clear line between what they should be to each other and what they were becoming, but the simple truth was he cared about her. If he had learned anything about Selene since he'd arrived on her shore, it was that she was a complicated woman whose emotions went a hell of a lot deeper than she wanted to admit.

As strong as she was, her heart was weighed down with a heavy burden of pain.

It tore at him to see her struggle to carry that burden on her own.

"What happened, Selene?"

At first, he didn't think she would answer. "My daughter perished in that tower."

"Ah, Christ," he uttered quietly. "I'm sorry."

"It was a long time ago." Her reply was toneless, as if it took all she had to keep her voice from breaking. "I should've had the damn thing torn down. Anyway, it's not fit for anyone now, including you."

It was a small truce, but he'd take it. And it was clear that Selene wasn't going to give him more than that. At least not now, with the large throne room open to the rest of the palace while he and Selene stood in the open-air shelter of the adjacent solar.

Outside the columned arches and domed roof there was yet another garden. Although Selene's light washed over the lush fruit trees and colorful flowers, he couldn't help but notice that today it was . . . thinner. Less golden and vibrant than it had been upon his arrival.

Selene squared her shoulders and made to step past him. "I'll have Yurec take you to your new quarters now."

Darion took her arm in a loose grasp. "Wait."

He took note again of the fatigue in her face. There was no doubting the enormity of her power, but was holding the light for so many days becoming too much for her?

Or did her fatigue have something to do with the sober conversation she'd been having with Sebathiel? Darion didn't have to wonder what an Atlantean search team might be after, but the knowledge that they had possibly run into trouble was as much a concern to him as it clearly was to Selene and her adviser.

"What happened to the men you and Seb were talking about?"

Her gaze went wide. "Unhand me."

Darion let go, but continued to block her way. "Talk to me, Selene. Where did you send your soldiers?" He saw the spark of reluctance in her face, the mistrust. "I heard Sebathiel say you sent a search party. I think we both know what they're looking for."

"I didn't send them to D.C., if that's what you're thinking."

It hadn't been what he was thinking. There was only one place he wanted to contemplate even less than the Order's headquarters. "Tell me you didn't send them to the Deadlands to search for the missing two crystals."

Her face said it all. "I sent soldiers several days ago. They haven't returned."

Darion cursed. "Even if they do come back, they won't have what they're looking for. The crystals are gone."

"Gone?" Her cheeks went even paler. "The Order found them?"

"You'll wish we did," he said grimly. "This whole fucking world should wish we'd been the first to get them off that wrecked alien craft."

Selene staggered backward, reaching for a bowl-topped pedestal for support. Darion caught her elbow, steadying her. "I was right," she whispered. "Their ship *was* out there in that taiga all this time. They had it cloaked?"

Darion nodded. "It also had a DNA lock on it. If it was breached, a trigger would detonate the crystals and blow up the ship and everything else on the planet."

She closed her eyes on an inhaled oath. "There was a detonation. So, if the Order didn't get the crystals off the abandoned craft, then who did?"

"Selene, the ship wasn't empty. There was an Ancient on board. He'd been injured, but kept alive in stasis. The Order sent a team in to kill him and take the crystals, but we failed. The Ancient escaped with them, but not before attempting to annihilate our team along with his ship."

She stared up at him in dread. "Why are you only telling me this now?"

"Why didn't you tell me you sent a search party to the Deadlands?"

Some of the fear and horror in her face dissolved, replaced by shock and quiet regret. "General Taebris, his team of soldiers . . . I may have sent them to their deaths."

She didn't draw away when he gently stroked her cheek. "Seems like we both could benefit from some mutual trust."

His touch seemed to soothe her, but worry remained sharp in her eyes. "Do you realize the power he has? One crystal can provide light and protection. So can two, but if used together as a weapon they can create darkness and wreak unimaginable destruction. That's what your forebears did to my Atlantis."

Darion nodded soberly. "I'm sorry for what they did."

"So am I. It cannot happen again. And if the Ancient were to obtain all five crystals? Darion, he could turn this whole planet into a lightless, blood-drenched hell for all eternity. He would be a king—a god—and there would be nothing anyone could do to stop him."

It wasn't mere hyperbole. As much as Darion wanted to hope it might be, Selene's grave expression left no room for doubt.

A fierce determination filled him as he cupped her face in his palms. "Then we'll have to do whatever it takes to make sure he never gets close to the remaining three."

She nodded, swallowing hard.

As he struggled to resist kissing her, there was a short burst of light in the throne room behind them. The air shuddered, lifting the hairs on Darion's arms and the back of his neck.

Instinctively, he pushed Selene behind him for protection.

At the same moment, an immense Atlantean male materialized in the center of the large court. His clothing was torn and covered in blood and gore. He dropped to one knee on the marble floor, breath heaving.

Selene gasped. "Taebris."

# CHAPTER 33

Selene ran to the throne room with her heart in her throat.

She waited to see the rest of the legion soldiers teleport back with their general . . . but no one else came. And Taebris looked like he'd emerged from the mouth of hell.

"Taebris, are you all right? What happened to everyone?"

He lifted his head, breath heaving. "They're all gone, Your Grace. I barely made it out alive."

Sebathiel rushed into the throne room now too. His face sagged when he saw only Taebris, and the mighty general's haggard condition. "The other men?"

Selene shook her head, grief thick in her throat. "Tell us what happened, Taebris."

"We were attacked within moments of our arrival in the Deadlands. Your Grace, our worst fears are true. The enemy ship had been hidden in those woods. All that's left of it is a scar in the earth, but it was there. And one of our enemies is still alive."

She closed her eyes as she absorbed the awful news, even though Darion had prepared her to hear it. "Did you locate the crystals?"

Taebris shook his head. "No, Your Grace. And we weren't the only ones looking for them. There were more Atlanteans who'd been slaughtered in that wasteland before we were attacked. The colony must have sent them ahead of us."

"Oh, no." Selene pressed a hand to her breast, but it didn't ease the ache of the horror she was imagining.

Her people were strong, all of them gifted with their own light. They were more than capable warriors and defenders, but their enemy was brutal. Her men and the group from the colony had gone in unaware of the predator who lurked in the Deadlands, poised to strike.

Sebathiel exhaled a curse. "What about the rest of the men? Did any of them survive?"

"I don't know. The bloodbath went on for so long. I got separated from my team. I lost my amulet in the scuffle and was on the run for days. Finally, I was able to circle back and take another off one of the fallen to teleport back just now."

At Selene's back, Darion grunted. The sound was caustic, edged with skepticism.

For the first time, the general's gaze slid to the Breed warrior in their midst. His eyes registered both alarm and animus. "What the fuck is one of their kind doing here?"

Selene intervened. "It's all right, General. This is Darion Thorne. He is . . ." *Faith, what was he to her now?* No longer just her prisoner, regardless of the circumstances that brought him into her world and kept him there.

In that short time he'd gone from her adversary to her lover. If her heart wasn't so reluctant to let anyone in, she might even be tempted to call him something deeper than that. All she knew was that the man she had tried so hard to despise and mistrust was becoming someone she believed in. Someone she had begun to care for, regardless of the circumstances that had brought them together.

"Darion is here with my approval," she finished. "You may speak freely in front of him."

Taebris practically seethed with suspicion. "He's with the Order, for fuck's sake."

"Yes, he is," Selene replied tersely. "And your queen has just informed you that you have no reason to fear him."

"Fear him? He's a filthy blood drinker. I should cleave his head from his shoulders before he turns on all of us like the evil that spawned him."

Darion took a step forward, his body vibrating with menace. "And you're a general who abandoned his men to save his own ass."

Sebathiel cleared his throat, casting a glower between the other two men.

"Enough," Selene said. She pivoted to face Darion, placing her hand on his chest and giving him an infinitesimal shake of her head. His dislike of Taebris was instant, and even she had to admit she found it markedly disappointing that her general had admitted to letting himself get drawn away from the rest of his unit in the heat of battle.

"Tell them what you told me a few minutes ago."

Darion glanced at her, a note of hesitancy in his hard expression. Then he nodded. Selene turned back to Seb and Taebris, watching their faces go from astonished to dread-filled as Darion explained about the Order's discovery of the alien craft and their failed efforts to recover the pair of crystals from the lethal predator who'd been awakened after long centuries of sleep.

"If I had known all of this," Selene told Taebris, "I never would've sent you and your men into that kind of danger unprepared."

His scowl remained as he glanced from Darion to her. "We'll need a goddamned army to go after him, if we have any hope of winning those crystals."

Seb nodded grimly. "Even with all of the realm's legion behind us, we still have but one crystal. We'll be no match for the power of two wielded against us. You know this, Your Grace."

She did know. Her entire being was filled with the dread of that knowledge. The hopelessness of it.

"We need to find the colony," Taebris said. "We need their crystal. I have spies who can find someone willing to talk. If unwilling, I have other soldiers specialized in more persuasive methods."

Sebathiel looked pointedly at Selene. Taebris had been gone before she'd ventured to the colony to take Jordana a few days ago. But Seb knew where she had gone. Selene had never told him she'd been aware of the colony's hidden, protected location from the day the exiles fled with their crystal, but after her abduction of Jordana there had been no reason to tell him. Seb knew the truth: She could have taken the colony's crystal that day, but she hadn't.

She waited for him to betray her secret to the general, but Seb held his tongue.

"No," she said. "The colony needs their crystal as much as we need ours. I will not leave them unprotected just to save the rest of us."

"Even if we did have a second crystal, the best outcome we could hope for is a stalemate," Sebathiel warned. "The worst being mutual destruction."

"Then we need three." Darion's deep voice drew everyone's attention. He looked only at Selene, his brown eyes solemn and intent. "If we ally together—the realm, the colony, and the Order—can we combat the power of the Ancient's two crystals?"

"Yes." She nodded, unable to curb her surprise, or the hope that bloomed to life inside her. "With three crystals in our control, he can't touch us. But you said yourself, the Order would never agree to part with theirs."

"Let me worry about that. Do you think you can convince the colony?"

Before she could answer, Taebris scoffed. "I can't believe what I'm hearing, what I'm seeing. Your Grace, has the world turned upside down in the short time I've been fighting your battles in the Deadlands?" He barked a caustic laugh. "Tell me you're not actually considering an alliance with the Order."

"Careful, General," Sebathiel urged in a low voice. "You are speaking to your Queen."

Another scoff, this time with more venom. "This wouldn't be the first time our Queen has allowed a snake into her bed. Need I remind anyone that thousands of Atlantean lives were washed away and our entire settlement lost because of her misplaced faith in another man?"

Darion's growl rumbled like thunder. Selene felt him coiled with hard menace, about to spring on Taebris. But her own fury erupted before he had the chance.

Light arced from the center of her glowing palm, slamming into the general and lifting him off his feet. He struggled, face turning red, then purple, as her light twisted around his thick neck. It took more strength than she truly had, but she held him there, her entire body shaking with the ferocity of her outrage.

When she finally let him drop, the big soldier wheezed and sputtered on the floor, moaning from the powerful blast.

"That you are still living is a testament to my mercy," she told him coldly. "Do not forget who you serve, General Taebris."

Seb stared at her agape, but unmoving. Darion looked like he wanted to stalk over to Taebris and finish him off.

Selene's head pounded from the energy she had just spent. It had been a rash, risky thing to do when she was already taxed from all the days of holding the light to keep Darion trapped inside the palace.

Now, she had nothing left.

With her arm throbbing, the skin's pallor fading toward a sickly gray hue, she cradled her limb against her body and strode out of the throne room as swiftly as she dared without breaking into a desperate run.

# CHAPTER 34

Darion had the urge to end Taebris for the disrespect he showed Selene.

He might have given in to that temptation, but he couldn't ignore how urgently she had fled the room after delivering her punishing stream of light. Was she upset by her general's insults, or had wielding her power injured her somehow?

A cool breeze blew in from the solar in her wake. Darion glanced that way and his concern multiplied. The pale sunlight that had washed over the garden outside— the light Selene had been holding for days without end— was extinguished completely now, replaced by instant, inky-black night.

*Ah, Christ.* "Selene."

"Let her be," Sebathiel said, but Darion ignored the command.

He ran out of the throne room, but she was nowhere to be found. Palace attendants gaped at him anxiously as he tore up the steps that led to the royal chambers.

The door was open. Darion rushed inside and called out her name. "Selene. Are you all right?"

No answer followed. He shut the door behind him and stalked through the main living area, past the moonlit garden and the marble table where he'd had his first taste of Selene. She wasn't there, either.

"Selene!"

Only silence. He rushed through her enormous bedroom and down a short corridor toward a thick stone door that stood ajar at the far end.

A glow radiated from inside the small chamber. As he approached, his skin warmed and a strange hum began to vibrate in his veins, in his marrow. The fine hairs on his nape lifted, prickling with warning . . . and wonder.

Because there she was.

Seated on the floor, she leaned against a slim marble pedestal veined with gold, holding in her lap the egg-shaped treasure that was the Atlantean realm's crystal.

Light radiated from the core of the crystal, illuminating Selene's hands and face and hair. The glow filled the small chamber, the power so immense Darion could only stare in complete awe.

Not only for the crystal, but the woman holding it in her palms.

"This is where you've been keeping it."

She said nothing, just stared at him, no doubt waiting to see what he would say, what he would do.

He took a hesitant step over the threshold. "I saw how you acted after you hit Taebris with your light. I saw the dark skies outside. Are you all right?"

"I will be," she replied quietly.

Darion's concern deepened as he glanced at her arms. Her skin was colorless, nearly gray. Blue veins formed spiderweb patterns that spread from her hands to her shoulders, and onto her delicate chest. Some of the breath in his lungs seized up.

"You need the crystal to heal after you use your light?"

A faint, confirming nod. "It's more than that," she admitted softly. "I need the crystal in order to live. I cannot be separated from it for very long before my own light—my life—starts to dim and weaken."

The understanding hit him like a physical blow. "Your life is tied to the crystal?"

"Yes. As the last Queen of the Atlantean race, the crystals are part of me, just as I am part of them. It was my cousin, Sindarah, and her mate, Maenos, who created the crystals for our world eons ago. Your ancestors have been after them nearly as long as that."

Darion walked to where she sat and sank down beside her as she continued to heal. Her skin was becoming less translucent as he watched. "How long can you survive without needing light from the crystal?"

She gave him an ageless, yet weary, smile. "With only one to restore me, less and less, as the decades pass. It is irreversible now."

A tightness formed in his chest as he considered what she was saying. "There's no way to change that?"

"There are rumors, but I only know of one way. That is to have a crystal living inside me."

He swore under his breath. "That's why you want the Order's crystal. You can't deprive the realm of this one, and you won't take the colony's away from them, either. You've been sacrificing your own life to keep both the realm and the colony safe."

He stared at her, astonished not only by the depth of her honor, but by the goodness of her heart. Her motivation to win back another crystal wasn't steeped in vengeance or the wish to retaliate against her enemies. She needed it to keep herself and her people alive.

"You amaze me," he said, unable to resist the need to touch her beautiful face. His fingertips tingled with powerful energy as he stroked her cheek. "I've been so wrong about you. Selene, you are the most extraordinary woman I've ever known. You are a compassionate, true leader who cares about all her people, even the ones who are no longer aligned with you."

"No." She winced slightly, glancing away from him. "What Taebris said was right. I am to blame for thousands of deaths. The first paradise I built for us in this world fell because of me. Because of my foolishness." She lifted her gaze to him. "Because of my unbearable loneliness."

Darion recalled the words he'd said to her not long after they'd met. He told her he believed she was lonely more than evil. He hadn't meant it as a barb, but now he could see the wound had been festering inside her ever since.

"Selene, when I said that, I didn't mean to hurt you."

"You were right. Back then, before the wave that destroyed my paradise, there was a man. A human. He fell off a boat in the midst of a storm and he'd been drowning just off our shores. I couldn't bear it. I sent a crew out to rescue him. They brought him through the veil, to our island. He was a shepherd from the mainland, and his name was Endymion. I was besotted with him, so much so, I let him stay in Atlantis for months after he recovered. I trusted him. Worse, I let myself believe we were in love."

"I know his name," Darion said. "Cass hid the crystal he took inside a sculpture for more than twenty years after he fled with Jordana. It was a piece depicting a shepherd boy who fell in love with the goddess, Selene. A shepherd named Endymion."

Selene exhaled a soft, wry laugh. "Cassianus always did love his art . . . and his irony."

"I've heard some of what Endymion did," Darion said. "He stole two crystals and escaped with them. Then he gave them to the Ancients who used them to send a tsunami to destroy Atlantis."

She nodded. "There's a part of me that wishes I had perished along with the majority of my people. We had survived so much to flee our home and make our new one here, only to see it annihilated because of me."

Darion cupped her cheek in his palm. "No, not because of you. Because someone else used your love against you for his own gain. It's not your fault."

"Tell that to the dead. Tell it to the survivors who still blame me for what happened, even if they won't say it out loud as Taebris did."

"Take nothing he says to heart," Darion snarled. "The man is a coward. If you hadn't schooled him with your light, I would've done it with my bare hands."

She smiled. "You would defend my honor, Darion Thorne?"

"Any minute of any day, Your Grace."

She held his solemn stare, her enchanting blue eyes searching his gaze. "You are a good man."

"Took you long enough to admit that." He leaned forward and kissed her, just the barest brush of his lips against hers. A thought had been nagging at him for a while, and before he fell any further he needed to know where he stood. "Tell me about Sebathiel. He's not only your High Chancellor and adviser."

Not a question, yet he still felt a small kick to his gut when she shook her head.

"No, Seb is not only that."

"Are you in love with him?"

Her eyes went wide. "No. I never have been."

"I think he'd like to change that if he could."

"He's my . . . friend." She let out a quiet sigh. "He is also Jordana's grandfather. Soraya was our daughter. Before you ask, no, Seb and I were not lovers. Not like that. After Endymion's betrayal, I couldn't trust anyone. I couldn't risk misjudging someone's heart again, and I refused to let any man seduce me with pretty lies or flattery. So, I remained alone. For a long time, I convinced myself I was happier that way. But being alone meant never knowing the joy of a child. That was one yearning I couldn't bear."

"So, Sebathiel generously volunteered to assist?" Darion didn't want to imagine any other male's hands on Selene, but especially not the tall, golden Atlantean she seemed to trust more than anyone to this day. "How noble of him to offer his services to his Queen."

Selene tilted her head. "Is that a note of jealousy I hear?"

Darion scoffed under his breath, but he could hardly deny it.

She smiled and went on. "Seb and I made an . . . arrangement. He is a good, loyal man with his own ambitions. I wanted a child and he wanted a large temple and lofty post. It was a transaction that worked for both of us."

"Did Soraya know he was her father?"

Selene shook her head. "He kept that secret for me. I wonder sometimes if things might have ended differently if she'd had a father in her life. I kept so much from her, thinking I was protecting her—shielding her from future heartaches. I did everything out of love for her. That love ended up destroying many lives. None worse than hers."

"Tell me what happened," he gently coaxed.

"Soraya and Cassianus secretly fell in love. They hid it from me, from everyone, for a long time. Eventually, she became pregnant. Being of my line, she was able to breach the island's veil without detection. One night they fled together. They returned months later, she carrying Jordana in her arms. The deception hurt me more than I wanted to admit, even to her. I lashed out in anger, calling for Cassianus's execution. Soraya begged me for mercy. Finally, I agreed—but on one condition. She had to give him up and take a mate of my choosing from the court."

Darion swallowed, hearing the remorse in Selene's voice. Her pain was raw, even all this time later.

"Soraya refused. She was so angry with me, so bereft at the thought of losing Cassianus. I didn't know how deeply they loved each other. I had never known that kind of love myself to recognize it in them. After placing Jordana in the palace nursery, Raya went up to her private quarters and set a terrible fire. It consumed the entire tower."

Darion exhaled a low curse. "The east tower."

Selene nodded. "No one could put it out. It burned for hours and hours. If I could've reached her, I would have saved her with this crystal. I would have sacrificed myself and the rest of the realm for the chance to heal her, but she made sure there was nothing left of her to save."

Tears welled in Selene's eyes then spilled down her cheeks. Darion gathered her close, wrapping his arm around her shoulders as she wept against him. He placed tender kisses to her brow, gently swept away the hot tears that dripped off the tip of her nose and chin.

"Jordana hates me now too. She'll never forgive me for the deaths of her parents, or for taking her away from her beloved Nathan like I did."

"Jordana's not someone who hates," Darion assured her. "Jordana's heart is too giving and open. You'd see that if you told her everything you just shared with me."

"I'll never have that chance. I won't ever be able to make up for what I've cost her, or to see Jordana's happiness for myself."

Darion lifted her face on the edge of his fingertips. "I will help you find a way."

He didn't know how he might accomplish that yet, but as he kissed her, he was determined to make it happen.

Selene drew back then, and Darion watched as the gray cast faded away and the pearlescence of her skin returned. The blue veins vanished, and a soft glow limned her from head to toe.

Extricating herself from his embrace, she stood as gracefully as ever, her strength restored. Carefully, she placed the crystal back atop the pedestal, where it hovered on its own power just above the marble surface.

She turned back to face him, her expression sober, hesitant. "Now you know all my secrets. Including the location of the realm's crystal."

"Your trust is safe with me, Selene. You are safe with me." He stood too, then stepped toward her. "I give you my word that you can trust me."

He reached for her hand, which she held lightly fisted at her side. Uncurling her fingers, he spread open her hand where the soft glow of her inner power revealed the teardrop-and-crescent-moon symbol nestled in the center of her palm.

"Only a woman with this same mark somewhere on her skin—this Atlantean mark—can form a blood bond with a member of the Breed," he told her, tracing the outline with his finger. "Atlantean and Breed have always had this connection. Our worlds may have started off at war, but it doesn't have to stay that way. Tell me you trust me, Selene."

She swallowed, her eyes lifting from their joined hands to his solemn gaze. "Yes. I trust you, Darion."

He smiled slowly, bringing her palm to his mouth. He placed a kiss there, his lips lingering as a fierce desire rolled over him.

Selene stepped into his arms and then her mouth was on his.

Darion lifted her up, hooking her legs around him as he carried her out of the crystal room and into the chamber where her large bed waited. He placed her on top of it, then slowly peeled off her silken clothes and delicate sandals, pausing to trail his mouth over every inch of her skin.

His own clothes came off more hastily. Selene helped him get free of them, their hands moving urgently, lips seeking each other in breathless impatience.

When he finally entered her body, he sank as deep as he could go, reveling in her soft, hungry moans and tiny gasps as they began to move together. His arousal was a wild demand, making his fangs punch out of his gums and his *glyphs* pulse with dark colors.

*Mine,* he thought as he watched Selene spiral toward release.

The silent declaration became a mantra, a wish, a promise.

*Mine.*

Tonight had changed everything, brought his world into sharp focus. And what he'd realized is that somehow, Selene had become an integral part of that world. The thought of her extraordinary light being extinguished for any reason put a cold dread in his veins.

He couldn't stop the possessive need that gripped him as she cried out in pleasure. A vision unfurled in his mind's eye—an image of Selene at his side, not just as an ally, but as his woman.

His lover.

His mate.

He only hoped that when the time came, the Order and the colony would stand with them in the war that was surely coming, sooner than anyone wanted to imagine.

If he couldn't broker an alliance, then Darion was prepared to stand with Selene on his own.

# CHAPTER 35

Tegan and the other warrior teams returned to the D.C. headquarters from patrols just before dawn.

The mission to take out Opus Nostrum's inner circle was already making a difference, with fewer Rogues prowling the streets and no new nests turning up in major cities.

It would've been good news, if not for the shocking discovery Aric Chase had made in Prague. An untold amount of Red Dragon had fallen into the Ancient's hands. The only question was, what did he intend to do with it?

The Order was on guard in anticipation of a rise in Rogue infestations and attacks around the world, but the opposite seemed to be happening.

Tegan couldn't help but dread that the lull in violence might actually be the calm before a very bad storm.

He entered the command center with Micah, giving his warrior son a hearty clap on the shoulder. "Nice work out there tonight."

"Thanks." Micah's smile and eyes were so much like his mother's it never failed to warm Tegan when he looked at the boy who had grown into one of the best warriors the Order had ever seen. The fact that Micah had also found a mate in Phaedra, a woman who adored him as much as he loved her was more than any parent could wish for their child.

Even Tegan, who had spent the majority of his five hundred years convincing himself he didn't need soft things like love or happiness in his life.

He might still be in that bleak place if not for Elise.

She met him in one of the command center corridors as he and Micah were on their way to stow their combat gear and weapons. Elise held a small tray of food in her hands.

Tegan paused, greeting his Breedmate with a heated kiss that earned a chuckle from their son as Micah continued on to stow his gear. "Get a room, you two."

"Good idea," Tegan said, smiling at his beautiful mate.

Elise smiled, but there was worry in the faint lines that bracketed her lips. "I'll be up at the residence shortly. I wanted to see if I can get Gabrielle to eat something."

Tegan frowned. "Still no appetite?"

"No. She hasn't taken even a bite of food since Lucan . . ."

She seemed reluctant to say the words. No one wanted to acknowledge the disease that was devouring Lucan's sanity bit by bit each and every hour. Bloodlust was doubly heinous, because while it ate away the mind, the body wasted away from a thirst that could never be quenched.

The fact that Lucan and Gabrielle were going through something as awful as this drove home the reality of just how precious and fragile life could be, even for the Breed.

Tegan stroked his mate's cheek. "Come on, I'll go with you. I want to look in on Lucan."

"I should warn you, the situation's not good, Tegan. I'm really worried for our friends."

"I know," he said. "So am I."

That worry went even darker and colder as he and Elise stepped into the chamber that contained Lucan's holding cell. Gabrielle slumped on the edge of a small cot, looking beyond exhausted. She had been sedated off and on for days, and it was starting to show. Her cheeks were drawn and sallow. Her gaze was bleak as she glanced up at Tegan and Elise.

"Oh, Gabby," Elise exclaimed softly, setting the tray down on the cot as she took a seat beside her. "I brought you some of your favorite things to eat."

While Elise comforted her friend, Tegan glanced into the ultraviolet-enhanced cell at Lucan. He sat in the far corner, his black hair wild and drooping into his face like a dark thicket. His eyes blazed, but the life in them was starting to dull.

Elise rose from the cot, looking at Tegan in concern. "I'm going to take Gabrielle to freshen up for a minute," she said, assisting Lucan's mate to her feet.

Gabrielle moved sluggishly, but she grabbed Tegan's sleeve as Elise started to hustle her toward the door. "Swear you'll stay with Lucan while I'm gone. Don't take your eyes off him, Tegan. Promise me."

Tegan nodded. "I promise."

She sagged into Elise as the two women stepped out.

Tegan approached the UV bars of the cell. He cursed under his breath, realizing that Lucan looked even worse now than he had when Tegan saw him earlier in the day.

"If you're just gonna stare at me in pity, get the fuck out." The sound that came out of Lucan could hardly be called a voice. It was unearthly, a low, throaty growl that seethed with madness.

"It's not pity," Tegan replied. "It's respect. Concern for my friend, my brother."

A caustic snarl grated out in response.

"I hate like hell to see you like this, Lucan. I wish to fuck I could help you."

The dark head came up at that. "You wanna help me? There is something you can do."

"Name it."

Lucan got to his feet and prowled toward the bars, his body hunched forward, lips curled away from his teeth and enormous fangs. He nodded at the weapons belt Tegan still wore around his hips. "Take out that long blade, then open this door and slice my head from my shoulders."

Tegan recoiled. "Fuck no. Jesus Christ, Lucan. No."

"Do it," he uttered viciously. "If you truly consider me your friend—your brother—then for fuck's sake . . . do this for me." He panted, whether from the effort of speaking or the fury clearly erupting inside him, Tegan wasn't sure. "Make it quick, Tegan, so she doesn't suffer any pain. Damn you, do it now! Before she comes back."

Tegan shook his head. "I can't do it. Don't ask it of me."

Lucan glowered at him, nostrils flaring. "You used to hate me, T. Surely, you remember. How could you forget? I was the one who killed your first Breedmate,

Sorcha. Don't tell me you wouldn't love a little payback?"

"No," Tegan insisted. "You couldn't be more wrong about that. I don't want payback. I forgave you a long time ago for that. What you did was a mercy—for her and for me."

"Then have some fucking mercy for me," Lucan raged. "Have some for Gabrielle. End this for me. You know damned well you would demand the same of me if the tables were turned."

Tegan couldn't deny it. He wasn't sure he could have held on as long as Lucan already had. And yes, if it were him caught in the downward spiral of Bloodlust and hurting Elise every minute he continued breathing, he would have begged someone—anyone—to make it stop.

His hand came to rest on the grip of his long blade while he grappled with the impossible request. He couldn't imagine the Order without Lucan at the helm. He didn't want to think about the hole it would leave in his own life if he lost his closest friend.

There had been times when the two of them might have both wanted to kill each other, but their friendship was unbreakable now. They had grown as close as any brothers could be.

And as much as he wanted to end Lucan's suffering, Tegan couldn't give up the selfish hope that his friend would be able to overcome even this. Tegan refused to give up hope, even when he felt in his heart it was futile.

Lucan moved closer to the bars. His face was a mask of utter torment and despair. "Tegan . . . please."

He swore tightly, and let his hand fall to his side. "I'm not giving up on you, Lucan. Don't you fucking give up, either. You hold on as long as you can. You can beat this. If anyone can, it's you."

Lucan stared at him. "You really believe that?"

Tegan gave a firm nod. "Yes. I do."

The chuckle that slipped past Lucan's cracked lips was brittle. He looked at Tegan with a deep disappointment in his blazing amber eyes. "That's the first time you ever lied to me."

Then he turned away and slunk back to the corner, dropping into a slow crouch as Elise and Gabrielle returned to the room.

# CHAPTER 36

D arion left Selene's bed while she slept, slipping away stealthily then flashing to the fifth-floor chamber in the main tower.

After their incredible night together, there was nothing he would have enjoyed more than waking Selene up that morning with his mouth, his hands, and his very interested cock, but his extended presence in the royal chambers was likely raising enough eyebrows as it was.

Being Queen, she didn't have to explain herself to anyone, but that didn't mean Darion wanted to cause any more conflict than he already had. Sebathiel had disliked him on sight, and after what happened with Taebris in the throne room, Darion was racking up far more enemies than allies in the Atlantean realm.

Not so with Selene.

Aside from the trust forming between them on the personal side, they were also unified in their plan to approach the Order and the colony about joining forces to go on the offense against the Ancient. All they had to do was hope they could convince everyone else— including Selene's general and the rest of her legion.

While he showered in the chamber's adjoining bathroom, Darion calculated dozens of different scenarios for how the three factions could work together. Each one he envisioned had him standing side-by-side with Selene.

Damn. He was falling hard and fast. As stunned as he was to realize how much she was coming to mean to him, in a way it didn't surprise him at all. They'd had a sharp, undeniable connection from the first moment their eyes met. Granted, they'd also been at each other's throats from the start, but that only seemed to make their passion now all the deeper and more intense.

It wasn't merely passion he was feeling toward Selene, either.

He cared for her. More than cared.

Every minute he spent with her made it that much harder to imagine a day when they would part.

And that day would come.

It had to.

His life was with his warrior brethren. If his father didn't recover enough to resume his role as leader, Darion owed it to him to keep the Order alive.

It was a possibility he didn't want to accept, and not only because it would mean leaving Selene for good.

He stepped out of the warm shower and toweled off. Pulling on his linen pants, he loosely tied the drawstring as he strode barefoot into the main area of the chamber.

Taebris was there, along with two other legion soldiers Darion had never seen before. The three Atlanteans stood inside the closed room, all of them wearing long swords at their sides and murderous intent in their eyes.

"Ever hear of knocking?" Darion asked, taking note of the glow building in the trio's closed fists.

Taebris's lip curled in a sneer. "How's she taste, blood-drinker? Got your fangs in her yet, or did you start with something else?"

Darion's fury spiked. "Fair warning, Taebris. If I knock you down, you won't get up again."

He scoffed. "I always suspected our royal bitch liked getting her skirts dirty. Spreading her legs for a human wasn't filthy enough. Now she's rutting with the likes of you." He glanced at his comrades. "Kill him."

Both soldiers unleashed their light on Darion, slamming him against the far wall. The window at his back was open to the elements—and to the bright morning sunlight shining outside. Real sunlight. He could feel the heat of it on his bare back and head.

The Atlanteans kept pushing with the glow from their palms. If he stopped fighting against it, the force of that light would send him flying into the sun-filled courtyard below.

Taebris grinned from his position just inside the closed door. Darion couldn't break out of the relentless hold. He sent a mental command to the thick stone door. It flew inward, knocking into Taebris.

His shout of surprise drew the attention of his comrades. Only for a moment, but that was all Darion needed.

The light faltered, and he spun away from the punishing stream. Moving at his full speed, he snapped one soldier's arm. The male howled and went down on one knee. Darion pulled the guard's sword from its scabbard at the same time and swung it into the Atlantean's neck.

Light exploded from the severed wound and from the male's palms as the body and head both fell to the floor.

The dead soldier's comrade fired more light at Darion. He dodged it, coming up swinging with the sword. Taebris joined in now, both of them pinning Darion to the stone wall with excruciating light. He fought the intense power that held him trapped, finally managing to bring his blade up in front of him.

Light sparked against the Atlantean blade's surface. Taebris sent more, until a sharp beam of his light ricocheted off the blade and struck the soldier instead. He lit up like his comrade as his corpse hit the floor.

Darion immediately rolled out of the way of Taebris's light. He flashed behind the general with the long sword in hand. With a roar he cleaved the Atlantean's head from his shoulders.

Light filled the chamber with Taebris's death. When it cleared, Darion turned around and found Sebathiel standing in the open doorway, staring in abject horror at the carnage around Darion's feet. And at the bloodied weapon in his hand.

Other palace inhabitants started to gather around Sebathiel. Attendants and courtiers, other members of the palace guard.

And then, Selene herself.

The small crowd parted to let her pass. Only Seb held her back from entering the room where Darion stood. Seb's hand rested on Selene's shoulder, while his free hand glowed with growing light.

Selene sucked in a sharp breath. "Darion."

He dropped the sword at his bare feet. "Taebris and these other men tried to kill me. I only acted in self-defense."

Sebathiel's face was hard with suspicion. "A likely excuse when none of them are alive to dispute it."

Darion kept his gaze on Selene. "It's the truth. I will never lie to you."

She nodded, and then she went to him, slipping from under Seb's protective hand while he and the rest of the spectators watched in shocked silence.

"I believe you," she said, worry in her lovely face. She touched his bare chest with tender fingers. There were burns on his skin from the light, along with a few minor cuts and abrasions. Her brows knit as she inspected him. "You're injured."

"I'm fine. I'll heal."

She gave him a tight nod, then turned to address the crowd. "The dead must be attended. The rest of you, disburse. There is nothing more to say or do here."

Four men stepped in to deal with the bodies of the fallen, while everyone else went back to whatever they had been doing.

"You too, Seb." Selene ordered quietly, when Sebathiel continued to study Darion with misgiving in his eyes.

The adviser nodded to her in deference, then turned and strode away.

# CHAPTER 37

Selene brought Darion up to her quarters, ignoring the whispers and astonished gazes of her people.

Taebris and the other two soldiers' deaths would fly like wildfire through the palace and the settlement outside the tower walls. So would the equally shocking news of their queen's plainly intimate regard for Darion.

Let them talk and stare.

Let them think her a fool.

All that mattered to her now was the fact that Darion had been attacked and nearly killed under her own roof. Obviously, he'd handled the assault with proficient, lethal skill, but seeing him standing in the midst of all that carnage had opened up a hole of stark panic in her breast.

"I'm fine," he said as she steered him to one of the velvet sofas in the living area.

She went into the bathroom and returned with a cool, wet cloth. Seating herself beside him, she pressed the soft compress to some of the burns and abrasions on his chest and arms.

While she tended him, his fingers began to play in her unbound hair, distracting her with the pleasurable feel of his touch. "Stop fidgeting."

His chuckle vibrated through her, warm with amusement. "Selene, I'm already healing."

And so he was.

The burns seemed to absorb into his skin. The minor cuts and lacerations stopped bleeding, the wounds knitting tightly closed before her eyes.

"If you want to continue touching me, you won't hear me complaining," he said, his brown gaze dancing with amber sparks.

"How can you make jokes? Darion, you were almost killed."

He scoffed lightly. "Three against one is an easy fight. You should see some of the things the Order runs up against on our patrols."

Selene frowned. "I'm certain I wouldn't want to. It was bad enough seeing what I did just now. I had no idea Taebris would dare something so heinous."

Darion stroked her cheek. "I have a feeling he would've proven to be a problem with or without my presence here. He wasn't worthy of you, Selene. I'm sorry for the spectacle it caused today, but I'll sleep better knowing he's no longer part of your legion."

She nodded in agreement. Taebris was no loss, particularly after the way he'd failed his fellow soldiers in the Deadlands. For his attempt on Darion's life? If the general wasn't already dead, Selene would have ended him personally.

"Hey," Darion said gently. "Why are you trembling?"

She swallowed. "I can't stop seeing you standing there in the middle of all that death. I could hardly breathe when I realized what must've happened—that three of my own men would have murdered you in cold blood. That is not the Atlantean way."

"It's not the Breed way, either."

There was a time when she would have been certain it was. Not anymore. Darion had helped her see past those old misjudgments and paranoias. He had opened her eyes and her heart. His honor and his honesty had allowed her to have faith in him, to let herself care for him. And she did care, deeply.

"My being here is causing friction between you and your people, Selene. Seb too." His expression was thoughtful, his brows furrowed. "I know what having your people's trust means to you. I know how hard you've worked, the things you've sacrificed to preserve this way of life. I don't want to make that difficult for you."

"You aren't. They don't understand yet, but they will. My people need to know that I trust you, and that I intend to ally the realm with the Order."

Darion nodded, smoothing the pad of his thumb along her jaw line. His stare was intent, solemn. "This isn't just an alliance to me. What we have together has nothing to do with the Order or the realm. This is only about you and me . . . us."

"Yes." The word escaped her on a soft sigh. "I feel the same way. I've been so afraid to let down my guard for so long, Darion. Part of me still is."

"Don't be," he murmured. He captured her face in his hands, bringing her forehead to rest against his as he held her gaze. "I don't want you to ever be afraid when you're with me."

His lips brushed over hers in a tender, unhurried kiss. She melted into him, into his comforting words. In the short time Darion had been in her world, he had made her believe that she could trust him. That she could let herself feel all the incredible emotions he stirred within her. That she might one day be safe allowing herself to love.

To love him.

She opened her eyes as he drew back from her mouth. His eyes held her warmly, his strong hands reverent and protective. Somehow, this dark Breed warrior who was so formidable, so expertly lethal, had become her safe harbor.

Her haven.

"I woke up this morning and you were gone," she whispered. "I thought for a moment I might have been dreaming that you'd been in my bed."

"No dream," he said, lifting her chin on his knuckles and trailing soft kisses down her throat. "It was real. *This* is real."

The tips of his fangs grazed just above her skin, yet enough to send spirals of fire licking through her veins. She moaned as his mouth drifted down onto the curve of her neck and shoulder.

His breath fanned across her skin, hot and erotic. "I know I have to leave soon, go back to the Order to argue for our alliance, but damn . . . I don't want to be away from you. When you're in my arms like this, I never want to let go."

On harsh growl, he moved over her, pressing her down on the sofa beneath him. His hands moved down her body, lifting her skirts as he caressed her naked thighs.

Selene watched him, mesmerized at the changes that played over his face and skin as his arousal swamped him. His gaze scorched everywhere it lit on her, molten with desire for her. His *dermaglyphs* felt alive beneath her fingertips, surging with dark, exquisite colors.

His fangs, which had at one time filled her with fright now stoked an intense, undeniable yearning she hardly dared to think, never mind speak aloud.

He reached down, his hands working to push his pants out of the way. Then he was hard between her legs, his rigid length teasing the wetness of her core before he entered her.

He took her mouth in a possessive kiss as he plunged deep, then began to move with aching slowness inside her.

"You've ruined me for anyone else," he uttered against her parted lips. "I will never want another."

She gazed up at him, awash in sensation and overwhelmed by the depth of all she felt for him. "There's never been anyone like you for me, Darion. I've never felt so alive as when you're looking at me like this . . . when you're filling me so completely."

He smiled a wicked, sexy smile, fangs gleaming. Faith, she couldn't get enough of him. He looked so wild and darkly beautiful, all of his attention, all his desire, focused on her as their bodies moved in perfect tempo, gazes locked.

Selene gave herself over to him completely, lost in the bliss of what they had found in each other.

What she was feeling went beyond mere desire or affection. She knew that with a certainty that shook her.

She was falling in love with him, and she only hoped she could trust her reckless heart not to lead her into disaster.

She prayed she could trust Darion's word as well, because she wasn't only placing her heart in his hands, but the fate of her entire realm.

# CHAPTER 38

Is this the book you want, Jenna?"

Caleb stood across the archives room from where she was working on some notes. He held up one of her journals that seemed nearly as big as he was.

She smiled at the sweet boy. "Yep, that's the one."

He brought it over to her, setting the thick book on the table beside a dozen others. She and Caleb had been hanging out together quite a bit the past couple of days. Tonight, while Brock and the other warriors were on patrol in the city, it was more a matter of simply enjoying Caleb's company rather than needing his help with her work.

She and Brock both adored him. Over the years they'd had more than one conversation about how much they would love to raise a child together. Getting to know Caleb had only given those conversations a new sense of clarity—and urgency. Neither one of them was eager to tell the little boy that no family had come forward to claim him, even after the Order had put out feelers with the Breed community at large. The thought of sending him off to one of the area Darkhavens to live with total strangers was unthinkable. Brock felt so too. They just had to decide when to sit Caleb down and ask him if he might want to stay with them on a more permanent basis.

She reached over and tousled his silky hair. "You're not bored sitting down here with me, are you, kiddo?"

He smiled. "Nah-uh. I like books."

"Me too." She went back to the new journal she was starting, and paused as an odd chill swept over her. Her skin suddenly felt damp and clammy, her head a bit woozy.

"Are you okay, Jenna?" Caleb's voice took on a distant tone, as if an unseen breeze was carrying it away.

"I think so," she said, although she actually wasn't sure at all. "Will you do me a favor, please? I'm just a little cold, so do you mind running up to the residence to fetch one of my sweaters for me?"

He nodded vigorously, then hurried away.

The strange sensation stayed with her, and sitting wasn't helping. She got up and carried a small stack of unused journals back to the bookcase. She barely made it over there when she was overcome by nausea, as though waves were rocking under her feet.

She gripped a shelf to steady herself—and at the same time a vision jolted into her mind's eye.

A cool, damp darkness all around her.

Waves rolling against the prow of a large sailboat moving at high speed across a wide body of water. Salt water. She could taste the sea's brine on her lip, could feel the sting of it in her eyes.

On deck, a crew of dozens skulked under the thin moonlight. Big bodies garbed in everything from street clothes to rags, taking orders from a captain who stared with singular purpose into the distant horizon.

*She* was that captain.

It was his otherworldly eyes her mind was connected to now.

Mist began to cling to her face as the boat continued on its course. The captain pointed his finger toward the bow, a silent order to the crew manning the tall sails.

*Almost there.*

He knew this in the way the air was shifting, feeling thicker as the boat neared the perimeter of an unseen barrier.

It was time.

The captain bent to retrieve a metal box he had stowed near his booted feet. He lifted the lid and out poured pure white light.

His crew gasped at the sudden illumination, some of them swiveling their heads in alarm at the impossible brightness he had uncovered. Fangs glinted behind mouths gone agape in confusion and alarm. Their amber eyes glowed like lanterns in the mad faces of the Rogues.

"Steady," the captain commanded them in the primitive tongue he knew they would understand.

The mist surrounding the boat glittered in the light pouring off the pair of crystals he held in their titanium box. The waves cut away beneath the prow as the vessel sped forward.

The veil couldn't hold.

It shuddered . . . then broke, burning away to nothing under the power of the two crystals.

Up ahead, beneath a blanket of starlight, lay the island.

The distance was closing swiftly.

On deck, the monstrous crew awaited their captain's order.

Only a few hundred yards to the beach, he gave it.

"Kill them all."

Rogues leapt from the decks to the water, rushing the shore. More poured out from belowdecks, hundreds of snarling beasts, a never-ending tide of death.

And then, the slaughter began.

Screams went up as the Rogue army swept in, killing everyone in sight. Men. Women. Children.

Holding the box of crystals in his arms, the Ancient leapt in one soaring motion from the deck to the beach. Atlantean soldiers rushed at him, but none could touch him. Weapons and light bounced away, useless against the shielding power of the crystals.

He strode forward, leaving the sounds of agony and death in his wake.

"Jenna! Jenna, can you hear me?"

Caleb's panicked voice yanked her out of the awful vision.

She sucked in a jagged gasp, as if she'd been on the verge of drowning. Her stomach roiled from actual nausea now. And a bone-deep dread.

She could hardly draw breath to speak.

"Oh, God. The Ancient . . . he's got a third crystal."

# CHAPTER 39

D arion woke to the feel of Selene jolting out of his
arms as they slept naked in her bed.

A strangled, mournful sound wrenched from her
throat. "Oh, no. No!"

"What is it?" He vaulted up next to her, moving onto
his knees as he tried to discern what was wrong. "Are
you hurt?"

Another awful cry tore out of her. "No . . . this can't
be."

She scrambled off the bed as though caught in a
nightmare, but it was obvious she was wide awake. Wide
awake, and gripped in unseen pain. She rushed to the
window and looked out at the night sky as if searching
for some answer in the darkness.

"No . . ."

Darion yanked on his pants and flew to her side as
her legs slowly collapsed beneath her. She sagged against
his chest, weeping.

"Talk to me," he urged her gently. Her distress
carved at his heart like a blade. "Tell me what's wrong."

Hot tears soaked his bare chest. "They're all dead."

"Who?" He struggled to comprehend the depth of her sudden grief. Part of him still hoped she had been caught up in a terrible dream, even though her reaction felt too real for him to believe that. "Who's dead?"

"The colony," she choked out. "Darion, something's happened . . . all I feel is a great void, their light is gone."

She broke down sobbing, great racking heaves. He held her in his arms, but she was shivering, shaking uncontrollably.

Someone pounded on the door to the main apartment outside.

"Your Grace!" Sebathiel's deep voice called. He pounded again. "I heard you cry out. Are you all right?"

She was too distraught to respond. Darion got up, grabbed a blanket off the bed and wrapped it around her as he assisted her to her feet. She was still crying as he walked her over to sit on the edge of the mattress while he then went to answer the door.

Sebathiel's typically disapproving look held a lethal edge when he saw Darion inside. "Where is she?"

He didn't bother to wait for an answer. Darion stalked ahead of the Atlantean into the bedroom where Selene was still sitting shell-shocked and trembling on the bed.

She looked up at her adviser, her eyes full of tears. "Seb, it's the colony . . ." Mutely, she shook her head, as if the words refused to leave her tongue. "They're all dead."

He staggered back, visibly shaken. "Are you sure?"

Her head wobbled in confirmation. "The colony's veil is down." She glanced from her adviser to Darion, looking so helplessly lost and broken it was all he could do to resist wrapping his arms around her regardless of their audience. "The crystal . . . it's gone."

Darion hissed a low curse. It couldn't be possible. If it was true, that the colony had been killed and their crystal seized, it was too awful to contemplate.

Sebathiel swung an accusing look at Darion.

"Is this the Order's doing?" he demanded. "Was this all part of your plan—to seduce our queen before you steal our crystal while your comrades are taking the colony by force?"

"What the fuck are you talking about?" Darion recoiled at the very thought. "There is no such plan. The Order would never attack the colony. I'd stake my life on that."

"I'll personally hold you to that vow," Seb snarled. "Although, Her Majesty may want that satisfaction for herself after she hears the truth about how you've been deceiving her."

Darion met Selene's questioning look. "He's lying. I haven't deceived you about a thing. I never will."

"Oh, really?" Seb asked. "Care to explain this?"

He'd been holding something behind his back when he came in. Darion hadn't realized it until Seb threw the titanium box at him. Darion caught it in his hand, his heart sinking with regret.

"I found it in the east tower tonight, Your Grace. He clearly wanted to hide it where he thought no one would look. Particularly you."

Darion cursed under his breath. "Selene . . ."

She turned her bleak, confused gaze on him. "That box was here in my private chambers."

"He obviously stole it, then squirreled it away until he could use it to hold the realm's crystal once he was ready to make his escape."

Selene swallowed. "Darion, is it true?"

"No."

She tilted her head, her expression pained. "No, you didn't take the box? Or no, you weren't planning to use it to steal the crystal from me?"

He could hardly bear to hold her wounded gaze. As if her pain over the colony and its lost crystal wasn't enough, his stupid mistake was going to break her heart. But he couldn't lie to her, not even to lessen her hurt.

He tossed the box onto the bed.

"Yes, I did take it."

Seb scoffed. "At least you're man enough to admit it to her face."

Darion ignored the jab. Hell, he had it coming after all. The only thing that mattered to him in that moment was Selene, and the broken look on her face. "Everything's different now. I would never take the crystal, no matter what. And I would never allow any harm to come to you, the realm, or the colony. I promise you, Selene."

Her face slowly lost all expression, closing up before his eyes. Her gaze dulled as she looked at him in her awful, mistrusting silence.

"When?" she asked woodenly. "When did you take the box from my chambers?"

He swallowed, feeling the noose of his own actions tightening around his throat. "That day in your garden. After—"

She held up her hand to silence him. A faint glow was building in the center of her palm, the one reaction she couldn't seem to shutter from his view.

Without speaking, she stood up, pulled the blanket tighter around her. She wouldn't look at him now.

He understood her anger and her misgivings. What he couldn't bear was feeling her emotional withdrawal. He could almost see her walls going up again, higher than ever before.

"Selene, nothing is the same since I came here. The only thing I want is you."

He stepped closer to her, reaching out to touch her arm. The imperious look she gave him stilled his hand.

"Sebathiel," she stated calmly. "Please have a boat and crew readied to depart the dock for the mainland as soon as possible. Darion will be on it."

# CHAPTER 40

It was all she could do to hold herself together.

The people of the colony were dead. Grief overwhelmed her at the total, unthinkable loss. The exiles may have broken away from her and the realm, but they were still her people.

Had been.

They were all gone, and whoever had snuffed out their collective light now had the colony's crystal too.

Selene didn't want to consider it might be the Order. Not after Darion's many assurances that he and his brethren were on the side of good, that they could be trusted as an ally to both the colony and her. But if not the Order, there was only one other possibility left to consider. It was even more harrowing to imagine it was the Ancient.

As for Darion, maybe he did have a change of heart since coming to the realm and spending time together with her, but that didn't alter the fact that he'd taken the titanium box from her quarters with the intent of escaping with her crystal.

And she had been fool enough to trust him with its location besides.

Now, with her heart torn open and her soul mourning all of tonight's staggering losses, she didn't know what to believe.

Or whom to trust.

The only thing she was certain of was that she couldn't bear to let Darion stay another minute when he was still the only one she wanted to turn to for comfort and strength while her entire world seemed to be crumbling around her. He needed to be gone, so she could think clearly and focus on what she had to do to save her people.

He stepped toward her. "Selene, please listen to me. For fuck's sake, talk to me."

"You heard Her Majesty," Seb interjected. "You're leaving."

Darion swung a vicious look at him, fangs bared. "This doesn't concern you, Seb. It's between Selene and me. Get the hell out of here and let us talk. Now."

Seb didn't seem eager to challenge him, and the last thing Selene wanted was more violence on top of everything else that had happened tonight.

She nodded at Seb.

He frowned. "Are you sure you want me to leave you alone with him?"

"Go," she said. "Have the boat prepared to sail. I'll send him down to you."

With a bow to her and a glower at Darion, Sebathiel was gone. As soon as the door closed behind him, Darion took Selene's shoulders in his hands.

"I'm sorry for all of this." His gaze was earnest with remorse. "I never would've betrayed you, and I hate that you're hurting like this. You have to believe me."

"Believe you," she murmured. "I've believed every word you've said to me these past several days, Darion. All your pretty lies." She inhaled a jagged breath. "I told myself you were too good to be true. I told myself not to be fooled by your kindness, your courage . . . your tenderness with me."

How deeply had she feared she was falling too fast, getting swept up in the spell he'd woven around her? He'd made her feel safe and alive, protected, cherished . . . loved.

Even now, her foolish heart was desperate to believe him.

"You said all the things you thought I wanted to hear, Darion. You acted as if what we had was real—all the while you had a plan in place to stab me in the back at the first opportunity."

His solemn gaze flashed with amber sparks. "I never gave that damned box a second thought after I took it. I never would've considered taking it had I known what the crystal truly meant to you. Your life, Selene."

She drew back from him. "Do not ever make the mistake of thinking me weak or in need of pity."

"I don't," he insisted. "You are the strongest, most extraordinary woman I'll ever know. I've meant every word I've said to you, Selene. I'm amazed by you, and I hate like hell that I've hurt you. Don't you understand? I've been falling in love with you from the start."

"No." She shook her head in denial, in fear of how deeply she wanted to believe him. It was too late for that, no matter how much it pained her to push him away. "How dare you say that to me now?"

"Because it's true. All my life, the only thing that mattered to me was my family and the Order. Then I came here. I met you." He reached out to her but she pulled away, putting needed distance between them. "Everything I thought I knew about you was wrong, Selene. And I've never been more glad to be proven wrong."

She exhaled sharply. "You made me believe I could trust you, even that day in my garden . . . right before you fucked me then stole that box as soon as my back was turned."

He released a harsh curse. "It wasn't like that. Not for me. You were the one who shut me out, just like you're trying to do now."

"How convenient for you then," she replied, scoffing. "It must have been an enormous burden lifted off your sterling sense of honor as you plotted to take the crystal, not only from me but from my people."

"I came here with a duty to uphold," he said tersely. "But that all changed once I got to know you."

Selene held firm to her rage. She had to. Tonight made one thing clear to her. She was not simply a woman who could give her heart freely, foolishly, to a man who could break it. She was a queen with a responsibility to her people.

"You had your duty to uphold," she said. "And I have mine for my people, however fewer remain as of tonight. I still have to protect them, and our crystal."

"You can't do that alone, Selene. I swear to you the Order had nothing to do with what happened to the colony. You told me yourself only two crystals can breach the veil. Selene, it had to be the Ancient. He found the colony."

In her heart, she knew he was right. Still, it staggered her to have her worst fear confirmed by Darion's grim logic. "How could he have found it?"

"He must've siphoned the information from the colony search party he slaughtered in the Deadlands."

She didn't want to picture the brutality of that attack. "He killed Taebris's team too."

Darion nodded. "And that means it won't be long before he comes for the realm."

Although the dread of that possibility had been clinging to her before he said it, hearing Darion put it into words sent a river of ice through her veins. She turned away from him to quickly slip into her gown.

"I have to prepare my people," she murmured.

"Let me help," Darion said, drawing her attention back to him. "I'll go to D.C. and I'll bring the Order's crystal to you."

Hope blossomed in her breast, but what if he didn't mean it? Or what if he did, but the Order refused to give up their crystal? She couldn't pin her hopes—her people's survival—on promises Darion might not be able to keep.

Either way, it wasn't enough. If her enemy had the colony's crystal in addition to the pair already in his possession, two would not defend her against him for long. She would need an army—one far greater in number than her legion, though skilled as they were.

The battle for the realm was likely already lost even before it began.

But she intended to fight to her last breath to save it.

"Unfortunately, I don't have the luxury of waiting to see if you or your brethren will make good on your offer," she replied. "It's too late, anyway. I have to put my defenses in place for whatever is coming. The boat will be ready for your departure by now."

His eyes snapped with amber fire. "I'm not going to leave you to fight this on your own."

"Every battle I've faced has been on my own. This is nothing new."

"Damn it, Selene." He reached out and took hold of her wrist.

She drove him back with a sudden flash of her light. It was pure reflex, only a desperate attempt to defend herself against the heartache that was only getting sharper the longer he remained in the room with her.

Darion stared at her, radiating a fearless determination. "You mean more to me than any fucking crystal. What the hell can I do to prove that to you?"

"You can go, Darion."

He scoffed. "That's it, then? That's really what you want?"

What she wanted didn't matter now. Not anymore.

"I have duties waiting for me," she said tonelessly. "And yours wait for you where you belong."

He didn't argue or try to stop her as she walked away, despite that she could feel his big body vibrating with frustration and anger. Exiting the bedroom where they'd spent the past many hours making love, she went to the door of her royal suites and summoned her guards.

"Yurec, escort Darion down to the dock. When you return, assemble my full legion in the throne room. I will be down shortly to address them."

"Yes, Your Grace."

She couldn't look at Darion as Yurec and his comrades collected him. Her heart ached for him, and he wasn't even gone yet.

It wasn't until the thick door had closed and the footsteps retreated down the stairwell than she gave herself over to the sorrow that heaved out of her in great, racking sobs.

# CHAPTER 41

They dumped him in Greece, back at the same small port where he'd originally departed for the Atlantean realm.

That night felt like a lifetime ago. Now, Darion stepped off the sailboat onto the dock and it seemed like he was entering a colorless, empty world after the vivid days—and nights—he'd spent with Selene.

If it had been up to him, he'd still be there with her. The only reason he'd allowed Selene's soldiers to take him away was because he knew he wouldn't be gone for long. He loved her, and there was no way in hell he was going to let her face this fight alone. Even if he had to defy the Order and every last one of his brethren to make good on his word to her.

He just didn't know how he'd be able to defy time itself.

The clock was running against him.

If the Ancient knew where the realm was located, he would waste no time launching a fresh assault. Which meant there was likely but a few hours before the realm would come under attack by him and his three crystals. An attack they could not hope to win.

The realm's crystal would give the Ancient his fourth, and then nothing would stop him.

Selene's warning about the power of multiple crystals played through Darion's mind with cold clarity. With all five crystals the Ancient could turn the world dark forever, and he would sit on a throne of his own making. A king with limitless power.

A god.

Darion could not let that happen.

The Ancient had to be stopped, no matter what it might take.

And whether Selene wanted Darion's help or not, she was damn well going to get it.

Hoofing from the sleepy dock into the adjacent port town, Darion walked up to a human male who had just staggered out of a pub alone. The soft blue glow of the man's phone lit up his face as he started to make a call.

Darion moved on him in less than a second.

A touch to the greasy forehead put the human into a trance while Darion wedged his shoulder under the deadweight bulk and walked the man into a nearby alley. While the drunk slumped unaware against the wall of a building, Darion called Order headquarters in D.C.

"It's me," he said when Gideon answered.

"Thank fuck. We were starting to fear the worst, Dare."

"I'm fine."

"Where the hell are you?"

"Just outside Athens. Gideon, we've got a problem. The Ancient's got another crystal."

"Yeah, we know. Jenna saw the whole bloody thing as it was happening. His raid on the Atlantean colony. The slaughter by all those fucking Rogues—"

"Hold up." Darion's heart seized, not only at the confirmation of his dread about the Ancient at the colony, but the even more disturbing detail. "What Rogues?"

"Ah, shit. That's right . . . you don't know. A few nights ago our daywalker teams took out Opus's inner circle, just like we planned. That's the good news."

Damned good news, but Darion couldn't appreciate it when his blood was running cold in his veins. "What's this got to do with Rogues and the Ancient attacking the colony?"

"One of our Opus targets in Prague was already dead when our teams deployed. It was pretty clear the Ancient got to him before we could. The guy had a storeroom full of Red Dragon. Most of it had been removed. We didn't know why until Jenna's vision. Darion, the Ancient's got an army of Rogues behind him. They wiped out the entire colony in a matter of minutes."

*Holy hell.*

"He'll be heading for Selene next," Darion said, dread strangling him. "He's got three crystals, Gideon. She can't stand against that kind of power. Not for long."

Gideon was silent for a moment. "That's not just concern for a crystal I hear in your voice, is it?"

Darion swore. "I have to warn her what's coming. Damn it, I need to be there with her right fucking now."

"Then you'd better get your ass to Rome ASAP."

"Why?"

"Because that's where everyone's going to be landing in about an hour from now. As soon as we learned what Jenna saw, and realized the Ancient would be moving on Selene's crystal next, we mobilized. We can't let him get another crystal, but equally important, none of us were going to leave you out there without backup."

Darion let out a breath. "The D.C. unit's on the way as we speak?"

"Not just D.C.," Gideon said. "The Order as a whole. Every team we've got in every corner of the world. Plus Zael and our other Atlantean friends. We've all got your back, Dare."

He could hardly believe what he was hearing, although he supposed it shouldn't surprise him. The Order was a brotherhood, a family. His family.

Still, the relief and gratitude that poured through him was deeper than he could ever hope to put into words. Yet it didn't fully erase his worry.

"It's not my back I'm concerned about, Gideon. It's Selene's."

"I had a feeling you might say that. If the Atlantean queen means that much to you, then that makes her the Order's priority too."

With thankfulness for his friends and family bolstering him, he couldn't help but think about his parents. They hadn't left his mind for a minute since he'd been gone, and now he was almost terrified to ask.

"Gideon . . . about my father . . ."

The sigh on the other end of the line wasn't reassuring. "He's not good, Dare. Lucan hasn't fed all this time. He's refusing your mother's blood out of fear of injuring her, and he also knows that drinking from her will only worsen his thirst."

The hopelessness carved him open inside. "Isn't there anything that can be done for him?"

"I'm sorry, Darion. We're keeping Lucan as comfortable as we can. Your mother too."

Darion couldn't recall ever hearing Gideon speak with such careful moderation in his voice. He hated sensing defeat in the usually optimistic, innovative warrior. Gideon had never met a problem he couldn't solve.

But not this time.

Darion refused to believe it. He refused to accept that his formidable father, the Order's indomitable founder and leader, could possibly be beaten by an insidious disease. There had to be a way to save him.

Damn it, he wasn't about to give up on that hope.

"You'd better get moving," Gideon said. "I'll alert the teams that you'll be waiting for them in Rome."

Darion nodded, corralling his thoughts around the fight he personally still had to face. Not only the battle against the Ancient and his army of Rogues, but the battle to prove himself to the woman he loved.

"I'm on my way," he told Gideon, ending the call.

Erasing the evidence from the phone, he then woke the human from his trance and disappeared into the darkness.

# CHAPTER 42

The sound of Gabrielle talking with Gideon pulled Lucan toward consciousness. The sedation doses he'd been demanding were becoming harder to shake off as the hours and days dragged on and his Bloodlust continued to own him.

He had been vaguely aware of recent commotion in the command center. A lot of boots thumping in the corridor outside. The jangle of weapons and tactical gear as teams of warriors rolled out on yet another patrol.

He hated like hell that he was grounded inside the UV bars of the Order's holding tank while his brethren went out to the streets to fight.

Give or take a few more days, this cell would be his tomb.

What he hated even more was the note of distress in his Breedmate's voice as she spoke with Gideon in hushed tones in the opened-door room adjacent to the cell.

He could feel the edges of her concern through his waning sedation.

She glanced over her shoulder at him, instantly aware that he was watching, listening.

"All right, Gideon. Thank you for letting me know."

She came back in and sat on the edge of the narrow cot. Even though Lucan didn't say anything—could only wait while the tranqs were slowly wearing off—Gabrielle studied him through the glowing bars.

"I know you can hear me," she said quietly. "I know you can still feel me, Lucan."

He wanted to tell her he would always feel her, even long after he was dust. His mouth was a fucking desert, his tongue too sluggish to form all the tender words he yearned to say to her.

He stared at her through his bleary, amber-hot eyes from his seated position in the corner of the holding tank.

She moved to the floor in front of the cell. "Gideon had some news about Darion."

Lucan frowned, memories bombarding him. He recalled looking into the horrified face of his son when Darion had discovered him inside Oliver Keener's car that awful first night.

Disconnected visual images flashed through his broken mind: Darion on the ground beneath him as Lucan attacked in blind madness. Darion and several other Order members trying to subdue him outside the headquarters mansion in the rain.

Shame swamped him as he recalled bits and pieces of his Bloodlust-induced rage.

"I hurt him?" The question scraped out of his parched throat.

"No, Lucan." Gabrielle shook her head. "You didn't harm him. Our son is a strong man. He's a born leader, just like his father. I always knew he would be, and now Gideon just confirmed it for me."

Lucan lifted his head, confused. Gabrielle smiled at him, even though worry lingered in her beautiful face. Then she proceeded to tell him how their son had stepped in for him in his absence, how Darion had cleared the way for the Order to take out Opus Nostrum's inner circle. She told him about Jordana's abduction and how Darion had gone alone to the Atlantean realm on a risky mission that had ultimately secured her release, but had also landed their son in Selene's prison until just tonight.

"Lucan, there is more . . ." Not even Gabrielle's distressed gaze could prepare him for what he heard next. "The Ancient attacked the Atlantean colony. He has their crystal. He also has an army of Rogues he created using Red Dragon he stole from Opus Nostrum. Gideon and Darion believe he will be heading to attack Selene and her people very soon."

"No." Lucan pushed the words off his thick tongue. "The crystal. Can't let him get it."

He wasn't so far gone that he didn't comprehend the peril for the entire world if the Ancient were allowed to amass the power of so many crystals. He had to be stopped.

Gabrielle nodded, understanding his alarm. "The Order has gone to lend their support to Selene and the Atlanteans as we speak. Darion will be joining them. Lucan, there's something else you need to know. Darion and Selene . . . it sounds like our son has fallen in love."

He wasn't sure how the Queen of Atlantis had gone from one of the Order's most volatile adversaries to someone Darion was willing to risk his life for, but the how and why of it didn't matter.

All that did matter was that Darion and the warriors were going to need all the help they could get.

Lucan groaned as he pushed himself to his feet.

Gabrielle stared at him. "What are you doing?"

"I need . . . to be there." It took more strength than he had just to remain standing. He kept himself upright by sheer, bloody-minded will. "I have to go."

"You can't be serious." Gabrielle stood up, wrapping her hands around the glowing bars. "Lucan, you haven't fed for a week. You've only been awake between rounds of sedation, and when you are awake you're in agony."

He didn't need to ask her how she knew. He had been putting her through hell with him the whole time. He wanted that pain to end for her, but he needed to do this last thing for their son. For his Order brethren.

"My love . . . please," he grated out through his teeth and fangs. "To do this, I will need your help."

He looked at her hands, clenched around the bars of the cell. The pulse points at her wrists raced, her frantic heart beat filling his ears. His dry mouth watered at the thought of her sweet taste. One taste to give him a surge of strength that he could take into battle, however short-lived it might sustain him.

One last taste that he would savor long after he was dust.

Her soft brown eyes widened with understanding. "You want to drink from me? You've refused all this time because it will only make you worse in the long run."

He slowly shook his head. "There is no long run anymore. We both know it."

"No." Her face crumpled with her choked sob. "No, don't say that."

"It's the truth." His feet wanted to bring him closer, but there was a part of him that was too unhinged to be trusted. Even around her. Especially around her, because she was everything he wanted and craved, everything he had ever dreamed of. "I would trade anything to have more time with you, but I don't want to live my last hours in this cell."

She blinked at him through her tears. "Lucan, I love you so much."

It killed him that he couldn't comfort her, couldn't hold her like he longed to. "I will love you forever, my sweet Gabrielle." He looked at her for a long moment, reflecting on all the ways she had made him a better man, a stronger man. A man who had lived every day striving to be worthy of her love. "You have given me so much, Gabrielle. More than I've deserved. Will you help me do this last thing?"

She stared at him, wiping away the wetness that stained her cheeks. Her nod was faint at first, then more resolved as she pulled herself together. Always so strong for him. His rock, whether she realized it or not.

"Okay," she finally whispered. "But only one condition. I'm going with you."

# CHAPTER 43

The throne room was packed from one end to the other with anxious civilians.

Selene had summoned the entire population hours ago to come and shelter inside the protective walls of the palace compound while she and her legion awaited their enemy's arrival. The soldiers had taken up positions on the many tower battlements, as well as on the island's hills and shore.

For Selene, it wasn't a question of if the attack would come, but when.

She strode through the crowded throne room with Sebathiel, heading toward the open-air solar. She had forgone her royal gowns in favor of the light-colored tunic and pants of her legion, her long hair braided into a single rope that hung down her back.

In one of the pockets of her pants was the crystal. She reached inside and held the egg-sized power source in her hand, feeling the hum of energy vibrating in her palm. If anyone had designs on taking it, they would have to come through her first.

Today, Selene was General as much as Queen, and if the battle did not go her way, she was prepared to fight to her last breath to protect her people and her realm.

"The sun is starting to rise," Seb remarked as they continued out to the garden promontory that overlooked the quiet citadel and beach below. "Daylight is our best advantage if we'll be fighting the Ancient . . . or the Order. Neither of them can withstand the sun. If an attack is coming our way, it may not happen until night falls."

Selene didn't have the same confidence when it came to the number of hours they may have before whoever attacked the colony decided to make a move on the realm. With three crystals in his possession, the bearer would have little fear of anything—including the sun.

She was certain of one thing, though.

"It's not the Order who attacked the colony, Seb."

He glanced at her. "So, you believe Darion Thorne even after he proved himself a thief and a liar?"

Selene met his questioning frown. "He stole the box from my chambers, but he didn't lie about it. He could've easily denied taking it. He could have said you planted the box in the east tower in order to make him look guilty. He could have said Taebris did it. I wanted him to deny it so much, I think I would have believed anything he said in his own defense." She released a short sigh. "I don't suppose I want to know what you think that says about me."

Sebathiel studied her softly, no judgment in his eyes. A quiet realization washed over his handsome, if crestfallen, face. "I think what it says, Your Grace, is that you are a woman in love. Alas, with someone other than me."

She smiled at that, reaching out to touch her fingertips to his cheek. "You have been loyal to me for a very long time, and for that I will always be grateful. You have been my trusted confidant, my friend. But Darion . . ."

"I know," Seb said. "I could see it in your eyes whenever you looked at him. I also saw the same feeling in his eyes every time you were in the room."

"You did?"

Sebathiel gave a wry laugh. "That Breed male looks at you as though you are the most precious treasure he could ever possess. Not the crystal, Selene . . . you."

"Then why did you encourage me to send him away?"

He shrugged, looking contrite. "Jealousy, I suppose. Protectiveness over you. I didn't want to believe he was a good man. Finding that box in the east tower only seemed to confirm my misgivings about him. I'm only sorry you were hurt in the process."

She couldn't fault Sebathiel for alerting her to his discovery. He had only done it out of duty to her, and to the realm.

Just as Darion had taken the box out of his own duty to the Order.

Selene stared out at the calm sea and the muted colors of the coming dawn. She had let her pride and paranoia rule her when she had told Darion to go. Her fear of being hurt had made her too weak to fight for what she felt for him. She had let him believe she despised him when that was the furthest thing from the truth.

She loved him, and now he was gone.

The jolting blast of a battle horn sounded from atop one of the tall towers—a warning from one of the legion's lookouts.

She and Sebathiel went to the edge of the garden promontory and scanned the waters that surrounded the island.

"There," Seb said, pointing.

A cold knot formed in Selene's stomach when she saw it. Beyond the veil, a mass of dark storm clouds churned near the horizon, filling the sky.

No, not storm clouds at all.

A swirling, intensifying wall of darkness.

It roiled and expanded, moving swiftly, devouring all the light in its path.

The tranquil, turquoise waters turned from gently lapping waves to surging whitecaps on the other side of the veil. The protective perimeter surrounding the Atlantean island began to glimmer . . . to tremble.

Her worst fears were materializing before her eyes.

"Faith," Selene whispered, agape with dread and a terrible awe. She pulled out the crystal, saw its light pulsing and struggling in her hand. "Seb, the veil . . . it's not going to hold."

As soon as she said it, a huge shadow began to emerge from within the thickening darkness.

A large boat.

It cut through the high waves, heading for the veil. The prow rammed through, and the barrier shattered and fell away like particles of stardust swallowed up by the unnatural night.

Then she saw him.

Standing on the bow of that enormous boat, the Ancient held an open-lidded box before him—the source of all that roiling, expanding darkness. Dark power erupted in cold waves from the heart of what that box contained.

"He has the three crystals," Selene said, looking to find Sebathiel staring at the enemy's approach with equal horror.

Because as bad as it was, the savage otherworlder wasn't alone.

Countless other large figures stood on the deck of the boat with him. Breed males. Rogues. Their eyes glowed like fireballs, fangs glinting white, in their seething faces.

The boat powered for the island's shore.

The wall of darkness swept across the water and onto the land, then over the palace.

A signal went up from the Ancient and the army of vampires surged airborne on a bone-shaking roar. They vaulted as one in a great leap that carried them onto the beach where the legion's first line of defense stood to meet them.

"Fuck," Seb hissed beside her, drawing the sword he wore sheathed at his side.

Selene tried to raise her light to fry the charging horde, but the power of the Ancient's three crystals was too strong. His darkness blocked her light, consuming it even before it could take hold.

She tried repeatedly to raise it, but it was no use. The darkness only deepened, lengthened . . . engulfing the whole of the island.

The beach was a chaos of violence and bloodshed and death. The Rogues swarmed. Atlantean soldiers fought . . . and fell.

Selene summoned her own power, throwing streams of light from her fingers at the melee. She managed to ash a few marauders, but it wouldn't be enough. There were too many to stop.

The light of her Atlantean soldiers' lives went out one after another as the vampires overtook the front line.

Selene could hardly contain her terror, her sorrow. She clung to her rage and determination, firing more light into the battle below.

"I'm going down there," Sebathiel said. He turned to face her, his expression grave. "You can't stay out here, Your Grace. You need to get inside the palace and stay there."

"No." She shook her head. "I'm not going anywhere when I can fight."

"It's not safe here for you, Selene."

"It's not safe for anyone now," she replied.

On a scowl, he pivoted then rushed away with sword in hand. She heard him rally the civilian men from the throne room, shouting to them that every able hand that could wield a weapon was going to be needed.

After a few moments, she saw him exit the palace with a group of men and head toward the skirmish along with more soldiers who'd been posted on the hills.

Down below on the beach, the sand was dark with blood and the dead.

Selene glowered at the Ancient as he calmly oversaw the violence he'd brought to her shores. She kept hurling streams of light into the fray, striking down as many enemy combatants as she could.

She didn't know how long her men could hold the Rogues back. The onslaught continued, leaving more dead Atlanteans on the ground and bringing the fight closer and closer to the palace compound.

Inside the throne room, civilians grew anxious, fearful. Children were crying as mothers tried to comfort them with reassurances that everything would be all right.

Selene prayed they were right.

In her heart, as the combat waged on and the darkness swelled, she wasn't sure how long she and her brave army of soldiers could hope to stand against such immense power and evil. Each pulse of light she summoned forth cost more and more of her strength. She would give it all to prevent the realm from suffering the same fate as the colony.

The crystal would renew her, but she feared it wouldn't be enough to stop the Ancient and his dark power.

Her pulse hammered in her ears as she kept up the fight from her perch on the promontory.

The rhythmic sound grew and grew, until she realized it wasn't only her heartbeat she was hearing . . . it was the low thump of helicopter blades high overhead.

# CHAPTER 44

W hat had started out appearing to be a strange, black storm in the middle of the Mediterranean Sea had grown into a vast, swirling darkness. The helicopter in the lead carrying Darion and a number of his Order comrades flew into the center of it, following his directions to the Atlanteans' island realm.

They flew in one of several military-grade helicopters currently en route to help Selene and her people fight the Ancient and his Rogue army. As Gideon had relayed to Darion, all of the Order had deployed to Rome where that city's commander, Lazaro Archer, and Andreas Reichen of Berlin had arranged for transportation to the realm.

Darion and his fellow warriors were suited for combat with UV-protective gear at the ready. As it turned out, they weren't going to need it.

The darkness they flew into was a thick curtain that consumed the morning sun's rays. Like a black vortex, the churning cloud completely engulfed Selene's island and surrounding waters, plunging the whole area into a night-like terrain.

As they approached from overhead, Darion peered down from where he stood in the open side of the helicopter. The carnage he spotted on the beach and the hill leading up to the palace compound took his breath away.

Slain Atlantean soldiers and male civilians outnumbered dead Rogues by more than ten to one. Blood painted the sand on the beach and the grassy plain below the palace stronghold.

The fighting was brutal, and ongoing.

Selene's legion had managed to hold their line on the hill below the towers, but from the looks of it they didn't have long before the horde of Rogues broke through and made a run for the bigger prize.

As the battle raged, streams of bright white light shot from one of the gardens that jutted out from the palace towers. Selene stood there, using her power to help her soldiers as best she could. One of her volleys hit a Rogue in mid-leap, ashing the big male before he could come down on Sebathiel, fighting in the middle of the chaos.

Darion couldn't hide his awed expression as he watched her in action. He had guessed she could have blasted his ass into next week if she'd wanted to, but seeing her turn all that firepower on the mob of invading Rogues gave him an all-new appreciation for just how incredible Selene truly was—both as a woman and the queen of her realm.

"That's your female?" Tegan asked from beside Darion.

He nodded, although he wasn't sure he could claim Selene as his now. His heart argued differently. And as he watched her blast another Rogue to dust, he couldn't deny his sense of pride—and possessiveness.

He also knew what all of that expended light meant to her wellbeing. No matter what it was costing her physically, Selene would keep up her fight until she had nothing left. Even if it killed her in the end.

Darion refused to consider the possibility. He itched to be on the ground where he could help keep her safe from the danger pushing ever closer to where she stood.

Nikolai's teeth and fangs flashed white from where he stood. He put his hands on the pair of semiautomatics holstered on his weapons belt, both of them loaded with Rogue-killing titanium rounds. "Let's light this shit up."

Darion nodded. "Come around and take us lower," he shouted to Trygg, the Rome warrior seated behind the helicopter's controls.

The aircraft swooped, giving him a better look at the battlefield and at the large boat moored offshore where the Ancient stood on the deck wielding the dark power of his three crystals.

He tilted his head skyward to look at the incoming threat, then sent a black squall high into the air. The helicopter tipped and swayed, but Trygg steadied the craft.

As soon as they were in a decent position over the beach, Darion gave the signal to evacuate. He, along with Tegan, Niko, Dante, Rio, Kade, and Brock all jumped from the opening with guns blazing.

Darion cut down several Rogues as soon as his boots hit the sand. With a gun in one hand and a long titanium blade in the other, he hacked his way through the clusters of combatants to join up with the Atlanteans.

The rest of his Order team did likewise, while the low thumping of still more arriving helicopters of warriors sounded in the distance.

As Darion fought, he spotted the Ancient readjusting his position on the bow of the boat. Another rolling squall began to form in front of him, a turning black ball of lethal energy. He turned it loose not on the skirmish on the beach and hills, but on the palace tower.

"Holy hell." Darion watched the pulse of dark energy smash into the stone column high above Selene's position in the garden.

The top of the tower exploded. Huge blocks of rubble began to fall.

Darion stowed his weapons, his feet already in motion.

Flashing with every ounce of speed at his command, he ran and leapt from the base of the hill to the ledge of the promontory—sweeping Selene out of the way of the tumbling stones as the top of the tower crashed to the ground.

His arms were wrapped around her, and damn if he could find the will to let go.

She stared up at him in surprise. "I told you not to come back."

He smiled. "Yeah, you did."

"Then why are you here?"

"Because there's nowhere else I want to be." He stroked the line of her beautiful face and the small furrow between her platinum brows. "You're never going to fight another battle alone, Selene. And you can't win this one without me."

A small sob caught in the back of her throat, but her gaze was tender on him. "You are easily the most arrogant man I've ever met."

He grinned. "Are you complaining?"

She shook her head. "Not in the least."

There was so much he wanted to tell her in that moment. Starting with how amazing she was to him. How much he loved her, and never wanted to leave her side again. How stupid he was to fuck things up with her.

More than anything, he wanted to kiss her and never let her go.

But there was a war raging below the palace, and overhead the dark sky had begun to crowd with helicopters arriving full of Order warriors ready to join the fight.

"I hope you don't mind," Darion said as the rumble grew nearly deafening. "I brought some friends along with me."

# CHAPTER 45

S he couldn't believe what she was seeing.

Not just Darion holding fast to her, staring into her eyes as if there were only the two of them in the world, but also the dark sky swarming with a battalion of helicopters coming to the aid of her and her people.

Darion had brought reinforcements—dozens of them.

As Selene watched in astonishment, Order warriors in full combat gear dropped from overhead, some rappelling down on cables, others leaping to the ground to battle side-by-side with Atlanteans.

Another combat-ready warrior leapt out from the circling aircraft, landing with catlike stealth on the garden promontory. Not an Order warrior, even though he was dressed like one.

Zael swiped off the black helmet that covered his golden hair and strode toward Selene and Darion. He pulled something out of a zippered pocket in his black combat vest. The object glowed from within his closed hand.

A crystal.

"Jordana and Phaedra and a few other Order women are on their way inside from one of the tower roofs where they've been let off," he said, nodding at Darion. Zael held the crystal out to Selene. "We all felt this will do the best good here with you, Your Grace."

Selene shook her head, incredulous as Zael put the crystal in her hand.

"It's yours," Darion said. "Not just for today, but forever. It belongs to you."

She couldn't speak. All her words of gratitude and affection clogged in her throat as she stared into Darion's handsome, earnest face.

She hadn't dared trust him when he said he would return with the Order and their crystal. She hadn't dared believe him when he'd said he cared about her, that he loved her.

Yet here he was.

Darion had come back. He had made good on all his promises, despite the fact that she didn't deserve them. Not the way she'd rejected him, shut him out with cold words she hadn't truly meant.

"Thank you," she whispered. Feeble words for all she was feeling. "I'm sorry I doubted you, Darion. I'm sorry for so many things. Can you ever forgive me?"

He smiled, reaching out to cup her cheek in his strong hand. "I think I can be persuaded, but we'll have to negotiate those terms later. Right now, we've got a war to win."

She returned his smile, drawing courage from his confidence—and strength from the pair of crystals now glowing with combined power in her hands.

Selene gathered that strength and power together, letting it build. Then she sent the bolt of pure white light across the battlefield and harbor, driving it into the side of the enemy's boat.

The vessel's hull exploded, leaving a gaping hole. The boat listed to the side and back again, taking on water fast.

The Ancient retaliated with a punishing blast of his own. The bomb of dark energy spun toward the palace. Selene threw her light into its path, blocking what would have been a catastrophic strike.

He sent another, then another, and still more.

She deflected them all.

The volley went back and forth, both of them neutralizing each other's strikes but failing to gain any ground. Selene couldn't hope for much more. With her two crystals against his three, it was impossible for her to overpower him.

To her alarm, she realized that down below the garden promontory the fallen tower had become a hill of rubble at the base of the palace. Rogues began rushing for it, a few of them breaking through the battle lines in a race to breach the palace walls.

Darion and Zael shot them from above with titanium rounds that ashed the Rogues in seconds.

"Fuck," Darion cursed, pointing to a skirmish on the ground near the base of the rubble.

Selene's heart clenched. Sebathiel was outnumbered by Rogues, battling hard with his long sword.

Without hesitation, Darion vaulted over the garden's ledge and sped toward the fight. He shot three Rogues one after the other, then tossed his weapon to Seb to finish the rest.

Selene watched in a mix of admiration and bone-deep fear as Darion ran straight for the center of the worst fighting.

Across the beach and sloping terrain, the Order was a wave of death on the Rogues. Titanium blades and bullets took down countless attackers. The Atlantean legion was right at their sides, taking Rogue heads and forming a phalanx to guard the backs and sides of their Breed comrades.

As brutal as the scene was, Selene had never seen anything so miraculous.

Atlanteans and the Breed united as one.

As allies.

As friends.

As brothers.

Selene did her best to cover them all, keeping the Ancient occupied with fighting her light while her soldiers and Darion's teammates took on the army of Rogues.

It wasn't easy for her. Each time she used her power, she felt some of her inner light fade. The crystals rejuvenated her, but she couldn't be certain how long she could last.

The Ancient sent another massive ball of darkness hurtling for the palace. It ripped across the distance, coming directly at the garden where she stood.

She prepared to block it—but at the same time, a sudden canopy of light went up over her like a dome.

The darkness collided with the glittering shield instead, disintegrating on impact.

She whirled around to find Phaedra and Jordana standing behind her. Phaedra's hands were uplifted, holding her own unique light.

"Hello," Jordana said, offering a small smile. "You remember Phaedra?"

"Of course, I do," Selene said. "My dear cousin Sindarah's daughter."

Jordana glanced from her friend to Selene. "We've come to help defend our people."

Selene nodded, emotion rising inside her like a warm wave. "Thank you. Both of you."

Jordana pivoted abruptly, just as a Rogue began to scrabble up onto the garden ledge. White energy pulsed from her palms, repelling the invader. He tumbled down on a roar.

The three women stood together under Phaedra's shield, Selene holding off the Ancient's dark assault, and Jordana using her unique power to protect the promontory from being breached.

But victory was not yet theirs.

Out on the disabled boat, the Ancient was far from beaten. He shouted a command, and the deck began to fill with even more Rogues from below. Scores of them, all fresh for the fight.

They poured over the sides and swarmed for the beach.

# CHAPTER 46

Lucan sat in the cargo hold of the transport helicopter he'd been loaded into in Rome.

His skull throbbed with hunger and madness, but after a brief feeding from Gabrielle's vein, his half-starved body was electric with feral strength and the craving for violence.

Her blood surged through his cells, giving him a jolt of power that allowed him to get a hold of his worst Rogue impulses, albeit temporarily.

Even so, he didn't trust himself around anyone he cared for, so while he was in the rear cargo area of the helicopter, Gabrielle was seated inside the locked cockpit with Andreas Reichen behind the aircraft's controls.

The German Order commander's voice crackled over the audio system. "About two minutes before we're in position."

Lucan's impatience was already more than he could control.

He pulled open the cargo hold door and stared out at the unnatural darkness cloaking the storm-tossed sea below. A large boat listed in the water up ahead. Beyond it lay an island crowned with a palace compound of gleaming stone towers, the top of one having crumbled to the ground.

The battle appeared to have been going on for long hours. A blood-stained white beach was littered with dead Rogues and Atlanteans, and the broad hill below the palace was currently under heavy siege, with dozens of Order warriors defending it alongside Atlantean soldiers.

Lucan spotted Darion in the thick of the fray.

Pride swelled in him as he stared down at his son leading the charge against a wave of Rogues. Darion's blade flashed as it swung, cutting down enemy combatants and coming to the defense of his comrades. The rest of the Order warriors fought with all they had too. They were a symphony of lethal skill and honor, and Lucan had never felt so proud of each and every one of his brethren.

If this was to be his last battle beside those fine warriors, he intended to make it count.

His gaze locked on the Ancient standing on the bow of the wrecked boat, now directly below the helicopter. The vessel was taking on water from a hole in its hull. It wouldn't be long before it started to sink.

He took one last look over his shoulder where Gabrielle watched him from the cockpit. Her beautiful face was tormented, gaze tender with both confidence and sorrow as he prepared to join the fight.

"I love you," she mouthed to him.

*I will love you forever.* He didn't have the words, but she didn't need to hear them. She felt them through their blood bond. He could see it in her eyes.

He turned back to the target of his fury.

Then he launched himself out the open door.

He came down hard atop the Ancient, taking the massive male to the deck with him. One taloned hand held onto the box containing the three crystals. The other swiped at Lucan, narrowly missing taking off his head as they both scrambled to their feet.

The Ancient's mouth peeled open in a snarl, fangs like daggers. A roiling black energy billowed up from the box and coalesced into a spinning ball of power. It flew at Lucan, driving him backward off his feet. His spine crashed against the deck. His lungs wheezed for breath, and he didn't want to think about how many bones he'd just broken.

Sheer will and rage brought him to his feet.

The Ancient hurled another ball of dark energy at him. Lucan dodged it, then leapt at his opponent in a flash of movement.

This time, the Ancient lost his grip on the box. It hit the deck, sending all three egg-sized crystals rolling across the tilted surface.

Overhead, the blanket of darkness filling the sky and all of the Atlantean island started to weaken. Sunlight struggled to pierce through the thick, shadowy fog.

If the darkness fell away, Lucan knew he would have little time to finish what he had to do before the sun's ultraviolet rays devoured him.

His son and his Order brethren too.

On a roar, he smashed his fist into the Ancient's hideous face. The Ancient shifted, flipping out from under Lucan and getting swiftly to his feet. Lucan stood, drawing one of the long blades strapped to his chest. He hadn't bothered with guns. Those weapons would do little good against the powerful otherworlder.

The only sure way to end the bastard was to take his head.

Lucan, being Rogue, could be reduced to ash with just a nick from a titanium bullet or blade. Or the sharp edge of a titanium box.

The Ancient seemed to know Lucan's vulnerability. He lunged for the box.

Lucan swung his blade, not at the Ancient's head, but at the talon-tipped hand right before it had a chance to close around the box. The Ancient roared, staring dumbfounded at the bleeding stump at the end of his arm.

He charged before Lucan had a chance to swing his blade again.

The full force and massive weight of the otherworlder's body collided into him. Lucan twisted in mid-air, refusing to let the Ancient take him down again. As he spun out of the way he felt a searing pain slash across his back, but it was no match for his fury.

He landed on his feet, crouched and ready to end the son of a bitch.

The Ancient faced off in front of him. Blood pulsed from his severed wrist, and from the tips of the talons on his surviving hand. He stared at Lucan, his chuckle an unearthly sound.

Lucan felt wet warmth soaking his black combat shirt and the backs of his thighs. He didn't have to look down to know that most of the blood pooling on the deck was his.

He lifted his blade, noting the thin ray of sunlight that kissed the edge of is as the heavy, dark mist continued to dissipate all around them.

"Come on, you fucker. Let's do this," he growled.

Time was running out from all directions.

# CHAPTER 47

D arion shot his last titanium round into the skull of a Rogue as it charged at Sebathiel and Yurec. The two Atlanteans were fighting beside him, part of the larger group of Order warriors and Selene's legion soldiers who were holding the hill below the palace.

Ashes from the scores of smoked Rogues swirled in the gloomy darkness. Their numbers had seemed endless, but finally Darion and his comrades from both armies were gaining the advantage.

Yet there was still the head of the snake that needed to be dealt with before this could really be over.

Darion chanced a look toward the palace where Selene still held her post with Phaedra and Jordana. She pointed upward, a look of worry on her face. He tilted his head and saw sunlight pressing down on the curtain of darkness the Ancient had constructed with the crystals.

And now that he was looking, truly looking, he realized the unnatural night they had been fighting under was fading fast. It was burning off, soon to be full daylight overhead.

*Holy hell.*

Darion whistled to catch the attention of the warriors near him. Kade and Rio caught his signal, both of them glancing up at the threat of the sun.

The same ultraviolet light that would finish off the invading Rogues would also take out Darion and every Breed member who wasn't a daywalker.

Why was the darkness lifting?

He glanced back up at Selene, but she was gone now. Jordana had disappeared too.

Out in the harbor, the disabled boat was nearly on its side. The Ancient was no longer standing at the bow with his box of crystals.

No, he was on the deck, poised for battle in front of Lucan with murder blazing in his eyes.

Then he pounced.

*Fuck.* Darion sped into motion, flashing past the skirmishes still taking place on the hill and the beach below. He took a running leap off the sand, soaring over the water and landing on the boat deck in a crouch.

The Ancient and Lucan were locked in a brutal hold, their boots slipping in the shocking amount of blood that soaked the deck. The Ancient had already lost a hand in the fight, but the disadvantage didn't seem to be slowing him down.

Darion had his long blade in hand, but there was no way to get to the Ancient's neck until he could get him away from Lucan.

Sheathing the weapon for now, Darion stalked forward and grabbed two fistfuls of the Ancient's shirt. He yanked the huge male backward and threw him off. The Ancient's boots skidded on the blood-soaked decking, but he didn't go down.

He bled not only from the amputation of his hand, but from a catastrophic cut to his shoulder and chest. Lucan held a blade in his hand, slick with the Ancient's blood. The wounds he'd delivered were severe, but not enough to take the bastard down for good.

Darion drew his weapon. "This ends here. You end here."

Before he could strike, Lucan charged forward in a turbulent blur. He swung his own sword at the Ancient's neck, but the otherworlder grabbed the blade in mid-strike and held on. Blood oozed from between his fingers, running down his wrist and arm.

Darion didn't waste a second of the opportunity he'd just been given by his father.

He spun, cleaving his blade through the back of the Ancient's thick neck in a clean blow. The head tumbled to the deck as the edge of Darion's blade sparked against the broad side of his father's sword.

They had done it together.

Darion stared into his father's fiery amber gaze—the same gaze he had seen in the faces of the countless other Rogues he'd slain over the course of the past several hours.

He didn't want to accept it.

He refused to accept it.

"Come on," he said, nodding to Lucan. "Let's get out of here."

Lucan hesitated, his expression pained both emotionally and physically. He took a step—then staggered.

"Dad?" Darion threw down his weapon so he could catch his father before his big body hit the deck. "Ah, shit. You're injured."

His hand came away from Lucan's back coated in blood.

"Darion." Selene was on the deck with him now too, apparently having teleported the distance.

As the Ancient's curtain of darkness dissolved away and sunlight began to blaze down over the boat and battlefield, she retrieved the three errant crystals and conjured a softer cloak to shield everyone from the searing rays.

Soothing shade unfurled over the island, hers to command.

She stepped to Darion's side and knelt next to him, heedless of the blood that continued to spill onto the deck around them. His father's blood.

She glanced at Lucan's back, then met Darion's gaze with gentle, sympathetic eyes. "We need to get him to the palace."

He nodded woodenly. Lifting Lucan's weight onto his shoulder, Darion carried him to the edge of the deck and leapt back to the beach with him. Selene reappeared at his side, using the crystals to clear a path for them up the hill to the palace compound.

Gabrielle was waiting for them just inside. Her face communicated everything Darion didn't want to acknowledge: Lucan wasn't going to survive this.

Between the ravages on his body from Bloodlust and the grievous wounds from his fight with the Ancient, he likely had only minutes left.

Gabrielle took his slack hand in her grasp, pressing his bruised and bloodied knuckles to her lips. "Oh, no . . . Lucan, no."

She held on as Darion carried him into a quiet chamber at Selene's direction and carefully laid him down on a soft rug. Beneath Lucan's torn, blood-soaked combat shirt, his skin was pale. His *glyphs* were nearly colorless. His chest was barely moving, his breaths infrequent and shallow.

With his mother weeping at his father's side, Darion slowly stood up, his own heart grieving for both of them.

And for himself.

He couldn't imagine what the rest of his life would look like without his father there as his example of what it meant to be a male of strength and honor. He couldn't fathom what the Order would look like without Lucan at its helm. Most of all, he couldn't bear the idea of losing Lucan as his father and his friend.

As for what his mother was feeling, Darion hoped he'd never know. Yet he had some inkling of it as he glanced at Selene standing beside him. She had only been his for a short while, but the thought of life without her was an emptiness he refused to consider.

Her blue eyes held him with solemnity . . . and tender devotion. "Darion, do you trust me?"

Uncertain why she was asking, he nodded.

Then she pulled one of the five crystals from her pocket, holding it in her palm.

"You can heal him?" Hope surged. "Can you restore him the same way you're able to draw life from the crystal?"

"No," she said, slowly shaking her head. "It will require something more than that. Something that cannot be undone."

Gabrielle looked up now too. "Do whatever you can . . . please."

Darion nodded. "Anything. I trust you, Selene."

The crystal in her palm began to glow. She knelt down on the other side of Lucan, across from Gabrielle.

Darion eased down next to Selene. "Can I do anything?"

"Remove his shirt for me."

Using his dagger, he opened the ruined black combat shirt from neck to hem. Then Selene carefully placed the glowing crystal on Lucan's bare chest.

Darion watched in wonder and no small amount of apprehension as the glow intensified. None but an Atlantean could touch the crystals without harm. Yet the one resting on his father's chest did no such thing.

Selene removed the others from her pockets, laying them next to her on the rug. One by one, she placed three more on Lucan's chest. The four formed a glowing circle around his heart.

"And now the last," she said, looking at Darion.

With the fifth crystal glowing like a small sun in her hands, she gently lowered it to the center of the four. Her hands remained after she placed it, hovering over the last crystal while its glow continued to build.

The four surrounding it burned brighter now too, until the combined light of them was too tremendous to behold. Darion brought his arm up to shield his eyes, but he couldn't tear his gaze away from the miracle of what he was witnessing.

A miracle created by the extraordinary woman he loved.

Selene withdrew her hands from the center of all that light. It burned for another moment, then extinguished in a stunning flash.

When the light was gone, only four crystals remained.

The one in the center had vanished.

But no, that wasn't quite right, Darion realized.

It still glowed, but now it did so from inside his father's chest. The wounds that had nearly destroyed him had vanished.

Lucan inhaled a sudden gasp of breath.

He opened his eyes. The molten amber of his Bloodlust was gone. His irises had returned to their normal steely gray hue, except for the outer ring. It glittered with pure, silvery light.

That same iridescence rode the edges of his *glyphs*, which now flooded with healthy color.

His gaze sought out Gabrielle. *"My love."*

She let out a ragged, joyful sob as she threw her arms around his neck.

# CHAPTER 48

Selene collected the four crystals as Lucan and Gabrielle's joyful reunion sent them scattering. She slipped them back into her pockets, watching the couple embrace and kiss as though they had been away from each other for an eternity. Their love was so pure, she couldn't help but share their unabashed joy.

A glance at Darion told her that he, too, was swept up in his parents' obvious love for each other. His gaze lit on Selene with a tender warmth and awe that was worth a hundred crystals.

Lucan still had Gabrielle locked in his embrace as he turned a solemn look at Selene.

"Thank you seems like a damned inadequate thing to say, but . . . thank you. Both of you," he said, glancing at Darion with pride and gratitude beaming in his silver-ringed eyes.

He let go of Gabrielle and took his son into a fierce hug.

To Selene's utter shock, Gabrielle did the same to her before taking her turn embracing Darion.

Lucan was staring at Selene as she watched Darion and his mother exchanging tender, private words. "How can I ever repay you for what you've done for me?"

She shook her head. "I couldn't have done anything at all, if not for Darion. The rest of the Order as well, including you. I'd say we're more than even."

Lucan glanced down at the *dermaglyphs* on his muscled arm. The skin markings were lit with the same luminescence as his irises. He touched the center of his chest where the glow from the crystal was no longer visible. "I feel different somehow . . . changed."

Darion and Gabrielle rejoined them, she taking shelter under her mate's arm, while Darion stepped beside Selene.

"You are changed," Selene said. "You're as indestructible as the crystal that now lives inside you. You're immortal, Lucan. Not even the sun's rays will harm you now."

Gabrielle inhaled a breath, looking up at him in amazement. "Lucan."

Selene had more good news for them. "Because of the blood bond you share with him, Gabrielle, the crystal will protect you too."

"How did you know it would work?" Darion asked, his deep voice quiet with wonder. "No one but an Atlantean can touch the crystals, so how could you be sure?"

"Because of something you said to me. You reminded me that Atlantean blood runs in the veins of all the Breed. That we are connected. I wasn't certain the crystal would help Lucan . . . but I had enough hope to try."

Darion pulled her close and kissed her.

At that same moment, other Order members entered the room. They packed inside, upwards of a dozen concerned Breed warriors who greeted Lucan with open awe.

A huge, tawny-haired male with green eyes was first into the chamber. He stared at Lucan for a long moment, then grabbed him into a tight hug. Both big males had raw emotion in their eyes as they parted.

More warriors followed suit, all of them gritty from the battle they'd fought alongside Selene's men. A dozen deep voices rose to a happy din as each of Lucan's comrades expressed their shock and relief at seeing him on his feet, whole and hale.

Selene and Darion took the opportunity to slip out of the room while the reunion continued.

Everywhere she looked the palace was full of new friends. Order warriors and their mates, Atlantean soldiers and civilians, all of them conversing and getting acquainted in the aftermath of their shared ordeal.

Outside the palace, the fighting had ended. The Rogue army lay dead on the beach and the hill below, and someone had lit the disabled boat on fire in the harbor. Selene let go of the shadows she had been holding over the land. The sunlight would turn the dead Rogues to ashes, and her people would collect their fallen for proper goodbyes.

Selene and Darion headed up the stairs to her private quarters. As soon as she had placed the four crystals in their chamber for safekeeping, Darion drew her into his arms.

His mouth crushed against hers, his warmth and strength like a balm after all they had endured. She didn't realize how much she needed to feel his embrace until she was melting into it, savoring the feel of his lips on hers.

"God, I've needed this," he rasped between kisses. "I've needed you, Selene."

"I know. I never want to let go." All the ugliness and pain of the battle washed away now that he was holding her. "Darion, I was never so scared as I was watching you in the middle of all that bloodshed and death."

He drew back, staring fiercely into her eyes. "I was never more amazed watching you." He stroked her cheek. "And what you just did for my father . . . you are incredible."

"I did it for you, Darion. I didn't want you to know loss like I have. I didn't want to you feel that kind of hurt."

He released a low curse. "I don't ever want you to feel those things again, either."

He kissed her again, softly now, his mouth tender as it brushed hers. When he opened his eyes, he stared at her with a question in his gaze.

"You gave up a crystal for me, for my father. Why, after wanting all five for the realm for so long . . ."

She shook her head. "What I've wanted was lasting peace and safety for my people. I wanted their future secured. And you've given me that, Darion. All our enemies are dead, the crystals are finally in Atlantean hands once more, and we have a new alliance—a kinship—with the Breed."

"I didn't do that," he said, humble when he had every right to boast.

"You did," she corrected. "You stood with me. You led the fight on the ground. I watched you step in and step up time and again, defending your own men and mine. You were there for me. I never should've doubted you."

"I'll always be here for you," he said, gathering her close. "You are the only woman for me, Selene. I knew that even before you told me to go."

Her breath escaped on a small sigh. "I love you, Darion. I was too afraid to admit it or to say it out loud to you, so instead I pushed you away."

He smoothed his thumb over her lips. "You asked me if I could ever forgive you. I'm the one in need of forgiveness. I'm sorry for misjudging you. You are the most caring, most courageous and selfless woman I'll ever know. Seeing you fighting for your home and your people only fortified what I already knew about you. You're incredible, extraordinary." A smile tugged at one corner of his perfect mouth. "You're also the hottest thing I've ever seen."

She laughed, staring at him besotted as he lifted her hand to his lips.

He uncurled her fingers and all the lightheartedness left his face. Blue veins stood out against the paleness of her wrist and arm. She knew that wielding the light for so long during the battle had taken a toll, but she hadn't stopped to think about the fatigue that clung to her.

Darion looked at her with stark fear in his eyes. "This is worse than the last time I saw it."

She gently extricated herself from his loose grasp. "I'll be all right. The crystals will restore me."

"Yes, but for how long? You used a crystal to give my father immortality. Can't you give one to yourself now too?"

"No. There was only one chance to use a crystal for that kind of healing . . . and it required all five. Four to make the circle, and one to give life."

He briefly closed his eyes before pinning her in a tormented stare. "That's what you meant—that it could not be undone."

"What is immortality if I have to live it alone?"

"You're not alone, Selene. You never will be again as long as I'm breathing."

"Your world is waiting for you," she reminded him. "The Order, your family, your future. It's not here on this island. I would never ask you to give all of that up for me."

He stroked her face. "I'm looking at my future. It's wherever you are."

His strong hand curled around the back of her neck. He drew her against him, kissing her sweetly yet possessively. Her body responded instantly to his touch, to his lips moving over hers.

Her heart responded to him even more intensely. Love swelled within her, filling her so completely she could hardly contain it.

She sighed against his mouth. "The only future I want is with you too."

He drew back slightly and she could only stare into the handsome face of the man she adored with every particle of her being. He was transformed now, his eyes filled with amber sparks, his fangs razor-sharp behind the lush curve of his lips. All that power and unearthly need stirring to her touch, her kiss.

Her veins drummed with longing and desire for him. She had never seen anything as fiercely beautiful as

Darion's face when he was looking at her with such unbridled hunger . . . and love.

He cradled her face in his palms, holding her still as he took her mouth in another bone-melting kiss. His lips moved down onto her throat, then farther still, to the sensitive hollow at the base of her neck.

He lifted his head on a groan, his molten gaze tortured. "You're mine, Selene. Your body knows it. Your heart knows it. Your blood knows it too. I want it all. I'm not the kind of man to settle for anything less."

She arched a brow. "So arrogant."

He smiled, fangs gleaming. "So I've heard. And I didn't hear you say no."

"Never." She kissed him hard and deep, catching his lush lower lip between her teeth.

The sound he made was primal and raw. It set her veins on fire.

Darion swept her off her feet and into his arms, carrying her into the bedroom. He laid her down then covered her with his body, his mouth claiming hers in a bone-meltingly hot kiss. When he moved down to the side of her neck every tendon in her body went taut with anticipation . . . and need.

"Yes."

Her whispered plea brought his head up on a growl. "This can't be undone, either." A warning, voiced in a low rasp that vibrated with the thinnest control.

"Nothing less than all of me," she said, holding his feral gaze. "Just as I won't be satisfied with anything less than all of you."

He swore harshly, then kissed her until she was reeling with desire, drowning in his passion. His mouth left hers and drifted to just below her ear. She heard his rough breath, felt the heat of it gusting against her tender skin.

Then she felt the shocking pierce of his fangs in her throat.

She gasped at the pleasure and pain of it. He took the first drink and every nerve ending in her body seemed to coalesce at the place where his mouth was fastened to her neck. It was bliss. It was staggeringly powerful and possessive. Like a storm sweeping her away, yet grounding her at the same time.

That was how Darion's love made her feel too. Lost in a tempest of new and unfamiliar emotions, yet safe and protected in the shelter of his strong arms.

As he drank from her vein, a new yearning stirred within her—a hunger she had never felt before. Hunger for him—for the untamed, darkest nature of him.

That hunger coiled within her like a living thing she could hardly contain.

"Oh, God . . . Darion."

Her fingers sank into his muscled shoulders and she arched beneath him on a raw moan.

# CHAPTER 49

If he lived for an eternity, he would never know anything as erotic as Selene's unabashed pleasure while he was drinking from her vein.

The first hot rush of her blood over his tongue was electric. She tasted like sunlight and stardust, a quicksilver flood of power and light that made every cell in his body ignite. Desire punched through him as he drank, possessiveness in every fiber of his being. And reverence, because he was holding the most precious treasure in his arms—his fierce, beautiful, extraordinary Selene.

His woman.

His mate.

His queen.

She belonged to him. He could feel the depth of that truth in her blood now, in his unbreakable bond to her.

Her light engulfed him, swamped him, infusing his body, heart, and soul.

Her hunger for him was a powerful force too. Not only the intensity of her arousal, but the darker thirst that he could feel pounding through her veins.

*Mine.* The declaration was hers, sent to him through the bond like a demand, a promise, a vow.

He loved hearing her moans and sighs, all her little sounds of pleasure while he drank from her. He loved how she clung to him, writhed for him. He simply loved . . . *her.*

With a sweep of his tongue he licked the twin punctures closed then rose onto his knees between her spread legs.

Selene was breathing hard, her bright blue eyes luminous with arousal.

"Mine." She said it out loud now, a sexy rasp to her voice. Her gaze rooted on his mouth, on his fangs. "I want all of you, Darion. Your body. Your blood. Your bond."

A wordless growl boiled out of his throat as she stroked his thighs. He was already hard as steel for her, his blood running molten in his veins.

With gazes locked, he brought his wrist to his mouth and bit down. He lowered his arm to her and she took it hungrily, not a moment's hesitation. That was Selene. There was no fear or uncertainty in his bold mate. She was a woman who knew what she wanted, and he would gladly spend his lifetime making sure he left none of her cravings unsatisfied.

He watched her emotions play over her face as she drank from him. He savored the intensity of her pleasure . . . and her need.

He noticed how the tangles of blue veins in her arms were fading as she fed from him. Her skin was losing its paleness, no longer the translucent, milky shade but returning to its normal healthy color.

She was healing.

His blood was restoring her before his eyes.

He wanted to point out the miracle he was witnessing, but his body had other ideas.

Her soft mouth sucking at him with such greed and enjoyment ratcheted his arousal to the breaking point. He groaned, dropping his head back as he struggled for control.

"Fuck," he grated out tightly. She was driving him wild with desire. Reaching down with his free hand, he caressed her soft cheek. "I have to be inside you."

Reluctantly, he drew his wrist away from her mouth and quickly sealed the wounds with his tongue. Her lips were ruby-red and slick with his blood. When she licked them clean with her gaze rooted on his, it was almost more than he could take.

They undressed each other with urgent hands, desperate to ease the fire raging inside them for each other. Darion brought her to an explosive climax, then followed her over the cliff with his own staggering release.

Afterward, they made love again, this time with unhurried reverence. The rest of the world would wait. This moment between them was too sacred to rush.

They explored every inch of each other's bodies with their hands, and lips, and tongues. They moved together, skin on skin, soul to soul. Their bond was a living thing between them, making every emotion overlap and entwine. When they finally gave in to their release, they came in unison, both rocked by the intensity of their connection.

Darion could have stayed inside her forever.

He would have, if not for the din of the busy palace below.

They showered and dressed, Selene in a pale aquamarine-colored gown, her long blonde hair in loose waves down her back, and Darion in a linen tunic and pants Selene had summoned for him from one of her attendants.

They walked downstairs hand-in-hand to join the rest of their friends and family that filled most of the chambers of the palace's main floor.

Lucan and Gabrielle met them outside the open doors of the packed throne room. They, too, had their hands linked, as if they couldn't bear to let go of each other for any reason. Warm smiles broke over both their faces as they greeted Darion and Selene.

Lucan rested a hand on Darion's shoulder. "There you two are. People were starting to talk."

"Let them," Darion said, giving Selene a wry smirk. "My mate and I had other pressing matters that couldn't be delayed."

Gabrielle arched her brows at Lucan. "Evidently, the apple doesn't fall far from the tree."

He grinned, unrepentant. "We all have reasons to celebrate today," he said, turning his luminous gaze to Selene and Darion. "First among them being the two of you. Congratulations on your blood bond. I don't suppose anyone has to ask if you're mated."

Gabrielle beamed at Darion. "Your joy is written all over both of your faces. We couldn't be happier for you."

"Thank you," Selene said, smiling up at him. "Your son is a good man."

"A fine leader as well," Lucan said, his silver-ringed eyes solemn. "We all owe you a debt, Darion. The entire world owes you a debt, son. Thanks to you, there are no more wars left to fight. Opus is gone, the Ancient is dead, and the now the Breed and the Atlanteans are forged in a friendship that will never break. I'm damned proud of you, son."

The praise coming from someone Darion admired and respected as deeply as his father humbled him. He hadn't done anything with the goal of winning accolades or changing the world. And despite what his father had said—despite what Selene had said when she, too, had credited him with more than he deserved—there was only one reason he was standing there now.

One reason he had fought with all he had.

He was looking at that reason right now. He brought Selene's hand to his lips and pressed a kiss to her palm. "I'd do it all over again just to share my life with you. Our life. Our future. Our family, if you're willing."

"Our family?" She smiled, her sparkling eyes soft on him. "You want a child with me?"

He caressed her cheek. "Nothing would please me more."

She took hold of his face and kissed him, her elation wrapping around him through their bond. "I love you, Darion Thorne."

He smiled. "I love you, too, my beautiful Selene."

They embraced for a moment, then linked hands to enter the throne room with Darion's parents following behind them.

The huge chamber was a hive of conversation and camaraderie. The battle had cost too many Atlantean lives, but it was over. Those dead would be honored soon, but this moment was for celebration. And for fellowship between new friends.

Everywhere Darion looked, he found Order warriors and their mates chatting with Atlantean civilians and soldiers. He spotted Sebathiel holding court with Mira and Kellan, the Chase twins and their mates, and several daywalkers.

Seb nodded at Darion, a silent acknowledgment of the truce forged between them as well, the kinship earned together on the battlefield. Darion nodded back, then let his gaze travel elsewhere in the room, noting Zael and Brynne chatting with a group of Atlanteans alongside Mathias Rowan and his pregnant Breedmate, Nova.

There were countless other fast friendships forming all over the crowded room.

Leaning toward Selene, he said, "If this is any indication, I think the palace will need to be expanded to accommodate future gatherings."

She laughed. "I'm sure that can be arranged. I suppose we might need a nursery eventually too?"

He smirked, arching a brow. "We'll need one sooner than that, if I have anything to say about it."

As they stepped farther inside the throne room, a cheer went up from everyone gathered.

A deep Atlantean voice boomed over the rest of the ruckus. "Glory to our Queen!"

The chant was picked up by others, until every Atlantean in the room shouted in her honor. Selene's eyes stayed rooted on Darion.

"And to my King," she said, devotion radiating from her loving gaze.

Darion lowered his head and kissed her, while all around them cheers and applause from the Atlanteans and Breed alike rose to fill the palace to its rafters.

# EPILOGUE

Lucan and Gabrielle were the last to depart the following day.

After saying goodbye to their incredible son and his equally extraordinary mate, they stood with arms wrapped around each other at the stern of a large schooner as it headed away from the island. An Atlantean soldier stood at the wheel to take them to the mainland. Above their heads, huge white sails billowed under a clear blue sky as the distance spread between the boat and the shore with its hilltop palace and gleaming towers.

Atop the tallest of those battlements stood Darion and Selene. She radiated in her diaphanous gown and golden coronet, but nothing shone as brightly as the loving gaze she held on Darion, her dark-haired mate at her side.

The Atlantean realm's new hero and king.

The sun glinted off Darion's simple crown as he held up his hand in farewell. With Selene's pure, royal blood to sustain him, daylight would never harm him. Not even time could separate Darion from his mate. He and

Selene would have forever to love each other, the greatest prize of all.

And often the hardest won.

"Look how happy they are together," Gabrielle said, her head resting against Lucan's chest. "That's what I've wanted the most for our son—to find someone who fulfills him and challenges him. Someone who loves him with all her heart."

Lucan dropped a kiss onto her soft hair. "What I've wanted most for him is to find a woman like his mother."

She smiled up at him. "Headstrong and stubborn?"

He grunted, nodding. "As well as kind-hearted, honest and wise, and infinitely patient when he's being an arrogant, insufferable ass."

Gabrielle slowly turned in his embrace so she was facing him. Her expression was serious despite his attempt at humor. "I would stand with you through anything."

"And you have," he said, tilting her head up for his kiss. "Thank God, you have. You didn't give up on me, even when it would've been easier, better for you, if you had."

She held him tighter, her tender brown eyes reaching into his soul. "Living without you will never be the easier or better thing for me. I can bear anything but that. We've been through all the storms life can send our way now." She glanced up at the sun-filled, blue sky above their heads before her solemn gaze returned to him. "We've weathered the worst and emerged on the other side . . . together."

He nodded, so filled with gratitude and renewed appreciation for his life that he could hardly find his breath to speak. He could only draw Gabrielle close and kiss her while he marveled that he was standing there with her safe in his arms. No more Bloodlust. No more pain for either of them, not ever again.

He was more than alive, thanks to Selene's astonishing gift.

He was immortal.

Indestructible.

And through their blood bond, so was Gabrielle.

"I'm not sure what this crystal makes me now," he said, touching the center of his chest where the power of it vibrated against his fingertips. "Am I still Breed? Am I Atlantean? Something in between?"

"Does it matter?" Gabrielle stroked his cheek. "Most importantly, you're still my mate."

He growled in happy agreement and kissed her again, unable to keep himself from touching her, from needing to feel her lips on his.

She tipped her head back, looking at him in question. "What will you do now that there are no more enemies left for you and the Order to fight?"

It was such a new reality, he hadn't actually paused to consider it. He shrugged. "I suppose we'll start by cleaning up all the wreckage Opus and the Rogues left in the cities. We'll have to work on regaining the trust of the human population too. God knows, after the havoc of the past weeks, they've got plenty of cause to mistrust all of the Breed again. There is corruption to be dealt with inside JUSTIS and the GNC as well."

"Those are all important things," Gabrielle agreed.

He nodded, still thinking aloud. "There will always be a need for peacekeepers, and the Order has trained for that for centuries."

Gabrielle tilted her head. "Okay, so after you've handled all of that, then what?"

He grinned. "I'm also looking forward to chasing you around our bedroom for a while."

She laughed, pressing her soft curves against his hardness. "I like the sound of that plan very much." She traced her finger along one of his silver-edged *glyphs*. "Do you suppose all of these new changes in you would pass down to a baby?"

He stared at her. "I have no idea."

"Hmm," she hummed, then kissed him. "Would you like to find out?"

There was a time when a question like that would make him think about all the reasons why bringing a baby into the world was a terrible idea.

The specter of war always looming on the horizon.

Enemies eager to make him suffer by hurting those he loved.

Myriad dangers on top of the endless risks of his work with the Order.

Now, he couldn't think of a single reason to object.

He smiled at his beautiful, amazing Breedmate. "I think we should go below deck to the cabin and discuss this intriguing idea of yours in explicit detail."

She beamed at him. "I was hoping you'd say that."

They kissed under the sunlight, then linked hands and walked together to start the next chapter of a future filled with new friends and family, a shining and eternal sense of hope, and enough love to last a thousand lifetimes.

# FROM THE AUTHOR

*Dear Reader,*

It would be unthinkable for me to close this book, the final one in the Midnight Breed series, without taking a moment to thank you for coming along on this journey.

When Lucan and the Order first appeared in my imagination nearly twenty years ago now, I never dreamed what their stories and this series would end up meaning to me. More than that, I never imagined how much the series would mean to someone else. So many of you have shared your personal stories with me about how my books have comforted you in difficult times, or inspired you, or simply brought you a little joy and excitement now and then. Having the added pleasure of meeting some of you in person at book signings and conventions are happy memories I'll keep with me always.

I've loved all of our interactions, and to say I'm honored is an understatement. Your enjoyment of my stories has been the most rewarding part of this journey for me.

Writing the books and spending time in the Midnight Breed world has been a privilege—one I never would've had if not for you. Whether you've been reading my books from the start or if you came to them somewhere along the way, please know that I am grateful you chose to spend some of your time with the characters and worlds I've created.

I hope you enjoyed this final novel in the series, and I hope you turned the last page with a smile in your heart.

Thank you for loving my characters, and for giving me so many years of great memories through your kindness, your friendship, and your support.

With love,

*Lara Adrian*

# ABOUT THE AUTHOR

**LARA ADRIAN** is a *New York Times* and #1 international best-selling author, with nearly 4 million books in print and digital worldwide and translations licensed to more than 20 countries. Her books have regularly appeared in the top spots of all the major bestseller lists including the *New York Times*, USA Today, Publishers Weekly, Wall Street Journal, Amazon.com, Barnes & Noble, etc. Reviewers have called Lara's books "addictively readable" (Chicago Tribune), "strikingly original" (Booklist), "extraordinary" (Fresh Fiction), and "one of the consistently best" (Romance Novel News).

Visit the author's website at
**www.LaraAdrian.com**.

# Thirsty for more Midnight Breed?

## Read the complete series!

Go behind the scenes of the
Midnight Breed series with the ultimate
insider's guide!

**The Midnight Breed Series Companion**

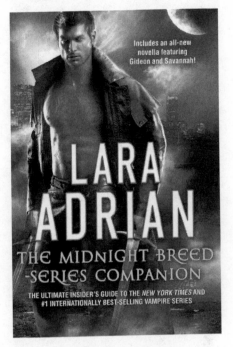

**Available Now**

Look for it in eBook and Paperback at
major retailers.

Revisit classic moments, characters, and events in the series while exercising your memory and concentration skills with this fun new book!

## Midnight Breed Series Word Search

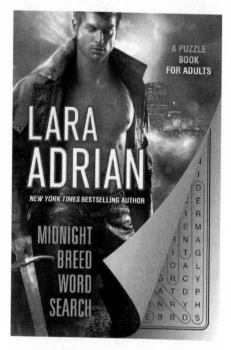

You'll find 60 puzzles, each with 24 series related words to find. Search for character names, story world lore, and other fun series trivia. Also included with each puzzle is an accompanying quote from the books, hand-selected by author Lara Adrian!

## Available Now

Look for it in Paperback at major retailers

# The Hunters are here!

Thrilling standalone vampire romances from Lara Adrian set in the Midnight Breed story universe.

## AVAILABLE NOW

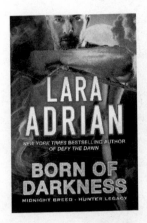

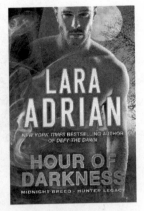

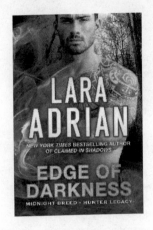

**If you enjoy sizzling contemporary romance, don't miss this hot series from Lara Adrian!**

## For 100 Days

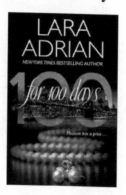

### The 100 Series: Book 1

*"I wish I could give this more than 5 stars! Lara Adrian not only dips her toe into this genre with flare, she will take it over . . . I have found my new addiction, this series."* —The Sub Club Books

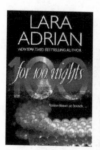 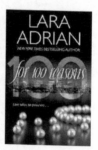

**All available now in ebook, trade paperback and unabridged audiobook.**

Gabriel Noble barely survived the war that took his leg, but now the stoic Baine International security specialist's honor is put to the test bodyguarding beautiful Evelyn Beckham.

## A 100 Series Standalone Romance

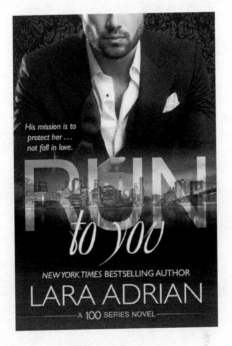

## Available Now

eBook * Paperback * Audiobook

"Lara Adrian has managed once again to give us a story with heat, high emotion, and angst that touches our heart. I absolutely loved it."
—*Reading Diva*

# Award-winning medieval romances from Lara Adrian!

## Dragon Chalice Series
### (Paranormal Medieval Romance)

*"Brilliant . . . bewitching medieval paranormal series."* –Booklist

## Warrior Trilogy
### (Medieval Romance)

 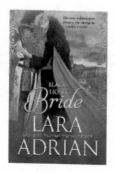 

*"The romance is pure gold."* –All About Romance

# Never miss a new book from Lara Adrian!

Sign up for Lara's VIP Reader List at
**www.LaraAdrian.com**

Be the first to get notified of new releases,
plus be eligible for special VIPs-only exclusive content
and giveaways that you won't find
anywhere else.

## *Sign up today!*

## Connect with Lara online at:

www.LaraAdrian.com

www.facebook.com/LaraAdrianBooks

www.instagram.com/laraadrianbooks

www.pinterest.com/LaraAdrian

www.goodreads.com/lara_adrian